RAINING FIRE

ALSO BY RAJAN KHANNA

Falling Sky

Rising Tide

RAINING FIRE

RAJAN KHANNA

an imprint of Prometheus Books
Amherst, NY

Published 2017 by Pyr®, an imprint of Prometheus Books

Cover illustration © Chris McGrath
Cover design by Nicole Sommer-Lecht
Cover design © Prometheus Books

Inquiries should be addressed to
Pyr
59 John Glenn Drive
Amherst, New York 14228
VOICE: 716–691–0133
FAX: 716–691–0137
WWW.PYRSF.COM

21 20 19 18 17   5 4 3 2 1

Library of Congress Cataloging-in-Publication Data

Names: Khanna, Rajan, 1974- author.
Title: Raining fire / by Rajan Khanna.
Description: Amherst, NY : Pyr, an imprint of Prometheus Books, 2017.
Identifiers: LCCN 2017009894 (print) | LCCN 2017013208 (ebook) |
    ISBN 9781633882744 (ebook) | ISBN 9781633882737 (paperback)
Subjects: | GSAFD: Science fiction. | Fantasy fiction.
Classification: LCC PS3611.H359 (ebook) | LCC PS3611.H359 R35 2017 (print) |
    DDC 813/.6—dc23
LC record available at https://lccn.loc.gov/2017009894

Printed in the United States of America

For those who fight for equality, who stand up for those in need,
who don't tolerate injustice.
For those who resist.

CHAPTER ONE

Hungover.

Hungover and running.

Hungover and running and trying not to vomit.

I race across the ground with Claudia in front of me. She holds her bow; I trail with my father's revolver. I beg my head to stop pounding, a development that only started when I began to pump my legs.

This was a bad idea.

The ground is dangerous. But so is facing the day sober. I was promised alcohol at the end of this. If it wasn't for that, I would have told Claudia to fuck off.

(In fact I might have told her to fuck off.)

Now I'm running toward a warehouse that keeps blurring in and out of focus. Claudia and I move together. By now we know each other well enough to coordinate without words, which is good because I'm a little sick of talking to Claudia. She must be a little sick of talking to me, too, since these days I mostly get sour looks. When she does talk to me, it's mostly to tell me to put down the bottle.

I tend to ignore her.

I cover her, she covers me, and we move, quickly now, up to the warehouse. Metal stairs climb up the side of the building, but they don't reach the ground. Too easy for Ferals to get up that way. But we stop quickly at the bottom. Me beneath them. Claudia runs forward and leaps, and I boost her up. I grunt as I heft her weight, but her boots sail over my head and I hear a slap as her hands come down around the bottom stair. Sucking in air, she pulls herself up and hooks her legs around the bars. Then she pulls out a harness, with a series of clips and straps and, most importantly, ropes, and secures it to the stairs and drops it down to me.

I climb the ropes, thinking as I do that I have let myself get out of shape. The dots of perspiration on my forehead are now rivers of sweat. My arms shake as I pull myself up, but I reach the stairs as Claudia nears the top, and I heft myself up to them. The trick now is to go slow so that we don't make too much of a racket. No telling who or what is in the warehouse.

Claudia moves to the door on the roof of the warehouse, the one we saw before approaching. It's locked, of course, but that's nothing to Claudia. I can get past locks—it's a skill most foragers need to learn—but Claudia excels at it. The only person I saw better at it was Mal. Using her tools, she has it open in a snap and then we're moving inside, slowly, cautiously, down some more metal stairs and onto a kind of walkway that looks down at the warehouse. Needless to say, we move as quietly as we can. It helps that we're not carrying heavy weapons. And that we're moving slowly. And that there's noise beneath us.

I catch sight of a bunch of rectangular structures and a few moving people beneath us. No one seems to be looking up, and there's no alarm. Good. Let's hope that continues.

A moment later I realize that the rectangular structures are cages. My skin prickles. Ferals? Are they Cabal? Or just crazy?

Then I make out what's in the cages. People. But they're still. Unmoving. Huddled into the corners or stretched out on the ground. I don't see any of them raving or pacing, don't hear any growls or cries or screams of challenge.

Humans, then? Prisoners?

As I watch, a man moves toward one of the cages. At least I think it's a man. He's large. Wearing dark clothing and a hood of some sort. He unlocks the cage door as a companion comes into view. This one holds a rifle. The hooded man pulls a man out of the cage. Rifle Man makes sure the gun is trained on him. Hood inspects the man, holding out each of his arms and opening his mouth, then instructs him to drop his pants.

It hits me what I'm seeing. Where we are. Who all of these people are.

Slaves. And where there are slaves . . .

A moment later, I realize that I've descended down the stairway and I'm halfway across the walkway. My revolver points forward, gripped tightly in my gloved right hand.

Slavers.

I'm vaguely aware of Claudia behind me, trying to catch my attention. She's waving to me, hissing my name, but it falls away, pushed back by this haze that clings to me.

I start counting the slavers below. Anyone that isn't in a cage. I get to six and then lose track. *Too many, then*, the voice in my head says, but my legs keep moving.

Two at the bottom of the ramp, near the first cage where the bodies are still. Dead? Or just sleeping?

Another one roams between the cages, keeping an eye on the slaves.

Two more stand over a table, looking at some papers. *They can read*, I note, but it's a fleeting thought, quickly lost in this persistent pressure behind my eyes.

I walk toward the first two. They look up as they notice movement, but my gun is already trained on them.

I fire. Once. Twice. A bullet tears out half of the first slaver's neck and he goes down, clutching at the wound with a hand that quickly turns red. The second bullet hits the other square in the face, turning it into bloody pulp. By now the noise is echoing throughout the room and the other slavers are preparing their weapons, getting ready to fire at the intruder in their midst.

At me.

I find I don't care.

I round the stairs, and the fluid haze that I've been walking through, that misty bubble, suddenly bursts and everything is cold and sharp and real. I see shapes raising weapons and by instinct I duck down behind a table, tipping it to the ground for cover. I catch a glimpse of straps dangling from its surface. Then gunfire erupts all around me. Shots whizz and fly and strike everywhere. The floor. The table. The walls. The cells.

The cells.

I think about the slaves inside of them. They're the slavers' livelihood, but maybe not valuable enough that they care about the cross fire.

I lean out from behind the table and hear a bullet rip the air so close to my head that I almost turn around and run.

But I don't.

A dark shape moves toward me, leaping over the table, and slams into me, crushing me down onto the floor.

I gasp as I lose my breath, and then grunt as the slaver punches me in the face. Then again. As he pulls the arm back for a third time, I slap one hand against the ground and bring the other one, the one holding the revolver, into the side of his face. He tilts and I shift him off, slamming the revolver barrel into his head again. Then again. The coldness that I've been feeling starts to fade, boiled off by a burning rage inside of me.

I'm vaguely aware of the blood that splatters the slaver's face, which is stippled across the side of my revolver, but I don't have time for that now.

I stand and shoot at the slavers across the room. Gunfire sparks and whines through the air.

I'm driven by one thing only—the urge to send all of these evil monsters to their deaths. The need to.

One of them, wearing a dark hood and a black scarf across the mouth, goes down with a cry.

There are still too many of them, though. And I'm pinned down where I am.

Then they start moving, taking shelter behind the cages, using the slaves' bodies as shields. Suddenly I can't shoot. I won't risk hitting one of those poor bastards.

The slavers have no such qualms. They reach through the bars and shoot at me, and I'm forced to take cover behind the table again. Bits and pieces of it crack and splinter with every gunshot. I take the time to reload the revolver.

Two more of the slavers come out from behind their human shields and make a beeline for me, one on either side, trying to flank me. I get off a shot at one, and miss, then the other pins me down. I switch targets to that one, and the other covers him.

Fuck.

Closer now. Any second, they'll both round the table from opposite sides, and I'll be caught between them. *Trapped.* The word brings up dark feelings, thoughts. Those feelings fuel this fire burning inside of me. I count to three, then scramble for one side of the table, leaning out to shoot at the man (or woman—I can't tell) on that side. The first bullet takes him in the thigh, the second somewhere north of there. But I keep going, using the table's straps to help spin me around to the other side of the table. The man coming around behind me tears up the ground where I was just moments ago. I manage to spring up to my feet and then over the table, crashing into the man and taking us both down to the floor.

He's stunned for a moment, and I roll on top of him. Then I jam the barrel of the revolver up against his chin, tilt my head away, shield my face, and fire.

Brains and blood and bits of skull explode from the top of his head, the splatter flying free.

I have a moment of triumph. Behind my scarf, a dark, bitter smile takes over my face. Then the chorus of gunfire returns and the table begins to shatter.

I scramble to one side, toward more gunfire, as holes start appearing in the table's wooden surface. No escape, then. I close my eyes.

Then I hear a scream. I spare a look and see an arrow take a man down, neatly hitting him in the face and punching out the back of his head. Another arrow spears another's slaver's chest.

Claudia.

Part of me sings to see it like always.

The remaining slavers turn toward this new threat, and I leap over the table and run toward them, the revolver out in front of me.

Now Claudia and I are both sides of a cruel set of claws, coming together around them.

One of the slavers turns to Claudia, turns back to me, and I shoot him . . . somewhere. I shoot again. And again. Arrows and bullets fly through the air, and we are alongside the cages so the slaves aren't in our cross fire. When my revolver clicks empty, I pull my backup automatic and empty that at the slavers.

Then it's all done. Just Claudia and I stand, and everyone else is on the ground, either dead (slavers) or scared (slaves).

"Thanks," I say to Claudia.

Her face is tight, flat. "Ben—"

"We need to get these people out of here," I say. "All of them."

"Of course," she says. She sounds weary. So incredibly weary.

"We can put them in the cargo hold."

She bends down and starts searching the men. For keys, I realize. I lower myself and do the same. We find keys on a couple of the men and start trying the cage doors.

"We're not going to hurt you," I say. "We're here to get you out of here." Never mind that it's not true, never mind that we came here for completely different reasons. This is where we are now and this is what we're doing. All of the slaves look tired and scared, but I think I see something like hope in some of their eyes.

Those that are alive, at least. One of the cages holds three dead bodies, dead before we got here. Another holds a form huddled against the bars on one side. He doesn't seem shot but I move toward him.

"He's been like that for a couple of days," a woman says.

"Dead?" I ask, as I search for the key to unlock the door.

"Almost," the woman says. She looks a little dirty and underfed. "He . . . he started doing bad just after we got here. A lot worse each day. He's not going to make it."

"Sick?" I ask.

She shakes her head. No. If he was sick, he would be gone already. No slaver would risk all of his stock by letting disease spread.

"What then?"

"Wounded," the woman says.

I move toward the man. As I get nearer, the stench hits me. Old blood, but even more, the smell of infection. The man is shivering and pale. His skin is waxy, and perspiration covers his face and neck. His fingers flex, his eyes bulge. There's a bandage around his midsection that's stained red around the abdomen. He might be too far gone. He might be. But he might also recover if he gets the right treatment.

"He looks bad," Claudia says, coming up next to me.

"Yeah," I say.

"Maybe we should——"

"No," I say, my voice low. "We might be able to save him."

"Ben—"

"We have to drop these people somewhere, don't we? Maybe we can get someone to help him."

"Ben—"

"I'm not leaving him behind," I say.

She meets my eyes. "We don't have to let him suffer."

"Let me try," I say.

She inhales, then nods. "Okay."

"Start getting the others on the *Valkyrie*," I say. "I'll get one of them to help me with this one." She does, and I do, finding a man who doesn't seem too impaired from his captivity and getting him to help me carry the wounded man.

We get just outside the warehouse doors when he stops shivering. Stops everything.

"Damn it."

The man helping stares at me, asks me what to do with him.

"He deserves some kind of grave."

The man carrying the bottom half of the dead body gestures with his head to a field at the side of the warehouse. Curious, I gently lay down the body and go to look.

I almost wish I hadn't, when I get there. The field looks recently disturbed. Nearby, white bones stick out from the ground. Probably some kind of mass grave. Better to bury them than leave them to attract Ferals above ground. The bones look picked clean—by the weather or insects or predators or maybe just time.

I realize what I'm doing is futile. There's no way to get peace for the dead. Not here. Better to focus on the living. So, leaving the body, I grab my helper and return to the others.

Claudia is gathering up all of the slaves, getting ready to take them back to the *Valkyrie*. I guide my man over to the group. "I have an airship," Claudia says. "I'm going to get it, and then I'm going to take all of you out of here."

"What if we don't want to go?" one woman asks, scratching at her arm.

"I'm not going to force anyone," Claudia says. "But I can get you to a trading post. From there you can find your way back to wherever you came from. Or on to someplace else. If you want to go your own way, I won't stop you, but on foot you're asking for trouble."

"It's the best deal you're going to get," I say. "Might as well take it."

"I'm going to get the ship," Claudia says to me. I nod back.

Claudia's going to have to bring the ship to the ground to load all of these people, so I stay with them until they're ready to move outside.

As I'm looking around the place, grabbing as many weapons and as much ammo as I can from the slavers (a man has to drink, after all), I hear a groan. I quickly locate the source—one of the slavers isn't dead. As I bend over him, I pull another of the men's scarves off and stuff it in his mouth. Then I return to the slaves.

When the *Valkyrie* hits the ground, I meet Claudia at the loading ramp and help shepherd the former slaves on board. "Give me a minute," I say. "I just need to take care of something."

Claudia eyes me, skeptical.

"Just a few minutes," I say. "You can take the ship up. Just get ready to lower me a ladder."

"Don't take long," she says at last.

"I'll be quick," I say.

When I get back to the warehouse, I strip the leather straps from the table I was hiding behind. Then I pull one of the chairs that the slavers had been using. I set it up, right up against the bars of one of the cages. Then I find the slaver who's still alive, and I drag him over to the chair. I lift him up and drop him into it. He's weak, so it isn't hard to get his hands strapped to the bars of the cage. Then his feet to the chair. It helps that I kick him in the bullet wound in the side of his leg.

When I'm done, I step back, let him get a good look at me. "This is lucky," I say, pointing at the space between us. At the situation. I smile. "Not for you. For me." I lower my face to his. "See, I think dying easy is too good for the likes of you."

His eyes widen. He starts making noises from behind the scarf, desperate noises. I shouldn't remove the scarf—I know I shouldn't. A voice inside of me screams not to, but I do anyway, making sure I'm out of range of his spit and making sure that I touch only the farthest part of the scarf with my gloved hands.

"Please," he says. His voice is weak, full of air. "I can pay you. I can get you food. Ammo."

I lean my head to the side as if considering. "Try harder."

His lower lip and chin start to tremble, sweat flecks his mouth. "I . . . what do you want? Tell me. I can help you. I can—"

"Save your breath," I say. "You're going to need it." I move to the large warehouse doors and pull them back. The ones on the other side are already open from getting the slaves out. Then I open the doors to what used to be the loading dock.

"What are you doing?" the man asks.

"Giving the Ferals a way in."

"What?" His voice is high, almost a scream.

I turn back to him. "Soon, Ferals are going to come, attracted to the noise or the smell or whatever gets them going. They're going to find a lot of meat. And you." I point at him. "Are going to be some of that meat."

"No," he says. "No, no, no. . . ."

"Just remember," I say. "Remember when they're gnawing on your face, when they're ripping off your eyelids with their teeth, when four or five of them start biting into your arms and legs and . . ." I wiggle my finger at him. "Your cock. When that happens, remember that this is because you're a slaver. Because you spent your time abducting people who were doing their best just to survive and get by. Because you took them from whatever life they were able to make for themselves. So you could barter them like possessions. Like an old blanket or a can of beans." I'm spitting now, my whole body rigid, a cold like the grave inside of me.

I stand over him. I think of something my father used to say. "All we have in the Sick, all we truly have, are our lives. And the choices that we make with them." It's like he's speaking through me. "You took that away from these people. Now," I turn and start walking away from him, "see what that's like."

"Please," he says at my back. "Please don't do this. Please don't leave me. Please don't, please . . ."

I leave him like that, tied up, dangling out in the open, a tasty enticement for any Feral that happens to come by. As I'm heading back to the *Valkyrie*, I remember what we are really here for. The job that Claudia was hired for. We were trying to recover a religious relic that a bunch of Jesus-worshippers were desperate for. It was a hand. The remains of one, at least. Finger bones. Belonged to a holy man from back in the Clean. Not much more than a pile of bones. But to them, these religious types, it was blessed, by God. Some even say that it had the power to raise the dead.

What a load of rat shit.

With that in mind, I visit the mass grave, and, using the butt of a rifle, I dig a little into the dirt. It doesn't take long to find a skeletal arm. I follow it down to what's left of the hand. I pick up the bones, wrapping them in a handkerchief.

Some cleaning and some fixing up, and they'll look like holy relics. I mean, how different can hand bones be? And I know holy folk. They're always twisting what's in front of their eyes to match their belief.

I tuck the bones into a pocket, then I take the ladder up to the *Valkyrie* and join Claudia in the gondola.

"Did you take care of what you needed to?" Claudia asks me over her shoulder.

I nod. I certainly did.

Then I go back to the compartment I've been using as a bunk, and I slug back what's left of my alcohol supply.

When I throw up, I tell myself it's because of that.

At some point, I think to pull out my father's revolver and clean it. There's dried blood splattered across the barrel, and a sticky, gummy mess at the end. Blowback from when I shot the one slaver in the head. I see my father's face, hear his voice like he's right beside me. "What the hell is that?" That's what he would say. "I had the revolver since before you were born. And this is how you treat it? I taught you to take care of your weapons, Ben. To clean them, to keep them well-maintained. And blood? Jesus, Ben. You know how stupid and dangerous that is? You don't deserve that weapon."

Fuck you, Dad. You're not here anyway.

I start a fire. Just a small one, mind you. In a small metal bowl, using some old paper and some gas. I hold the barrel in the fire, hear the sizzle as blood and skin and hair and for all I know brains burn off into the air. I'll use some alcohol, then some oil, to get it completely clean. But right now fire is the only way I know to burn out the Bug. I hold it in the fire for a while until the metal gets nice and hot and I'm even forced to put it down with my gloves on. Then I douse it in alcohol, wipe it down with a cloth, then the fire again, then alcohol again. Only then do I reach for some oil and start oiling it up. It takes a while.

I know this revolver as well as my hand, better, since my hands are always covered in gloves. My father had it for as long as I can remember. For most of my life he wouldn't let me touch it, not even to clean it. "Always clean your own weapons," he would say. "You can't rely on anyone else to do it right. You have to do it yourself."

I remember the first time I touched it. In the dark, huddled down behind the wreck of a car, raiders firing at us. The air smelled of cactus and gunpowder. Dad fired it, then pulled a backup, slid the revolver to me. "Reload!"

My whole body was shaking with fear because we were outnumbered. But I still felt a thrill as I picked up the revolver. It seemed so huge back then. I reloaded it and passed it back, and Dad handed me the backup and together we filled the night with bullets.

The revolver is much more tarnished now. Scratched, too. The words "Smith & Wesson" are barely visible on the barrel. The grip's been replaced twice that I know of, first rubber, now wood. It bears a lot of scars. It's seen a lot of action. It's done a lot of damage.

Claudia appears in the doorway, arms crossed, eyes like cold steel. The jagged scar that comes down over her eye almost shines in the light of the cabin. For a moment I'm back in that apartment building, bending over her, sewing the gash up with my gloves on, blood everywhere. A mark on her that will always say, "Ben was here."

"What the motherfucking shit was that?" she says. I flick my eyes up to her, to the face almost as familiar to me as the revolver. The strong cheekbones, the strong nose, the shock of white in her dark hair. Everything about her seems to radiate strength and competence.

I rub at the barrel of the revolver, not meeting her eyes. "What do you mean?"

She jerks her thumb at the window. "What happened back there. Your rampage."

Now I meet her eyes. It's hard to not look away. "They were slavers, Claudia. They deserved what they got. And worse."

"They're filth. They deserve to die. That's not the point. You ran at them, without any plan, without telling me what you were doing. You could have gotten us both killed."

I shrug one shoulder. "It worked out, didn't it?"

Claudia gets this disbelieving look on her face and shakes her head. "I don't know why it took me so long to see it." She shakes her head again. "You've given up."

"I've given up on this conversation making sense."

"You've spent so long focusing on survival that you just don't know how to do it. You're hoping someone else will do it for you."

"Do what, Claudia?"

She levels her eyes at me again. "End it. Kill yourself."

"That's ridiculous."

"Is it?"

Anger grips my stomach, my spine, and I stand up out of the chair and take a step forward. "Yes," I say, clenching my jaw. "Because I'm not done here. Not yet. Not until Tess pays."

Claudia nods slowly. "And then what?"

The anger and the steel drain out of me at the thought, and I sag backward. "I'll figure that out when the time comes. We're not there yet."

"*We,*" she says. "You keep throwing that word around."

"Claudia—"

"Spare me." Her smile is humorless. Bitter. "I've been trying to help you, Ben. Help you break out of whatever this is that you've fallen into. Because we have a past, and because you were always special to me. But I don't know that I can do it anymore."

I should feel something at that—sorrow, loss, grief, recrimination, guilt. Take your pick. But I don't.

"I'll get you to Tess, I promised you that. But after . . ." She shakes her head and lowers it, running a hand through her long dark hair.

"Fair enough," I hear myself saying.

After she leaves, I look around for a bottle that's not empty.

I hold a small wooden box in my hands. I don't remember reaching for it, but I keep it close to my sleeping mat. It's never far away when I'm on the *Valkyrie,* though I don't bring it out in front of Claudia. I open the lid and pull out the burnt and battered notebook. I hold it for a moment, just feeling the weight of it. It's solid. Real. Then I pull off my gloves and run my fingers over it. It's rough now, not nearly as smooth as it might have once been. But I try to feel each wrinkle and crease. Which ones did she make, I wonder?

Not much survived the attack that killed Miranda. The house was completely demolished. The wood burned quickly from the explosions. Most of what was found inside was melted metal—the remains of tools or instruments or weapons. But miracle of miracles, three notebooks survived. They were partially burned. And pages were blackened or later damaged by water—two were missing whole sections. But there were still pages with Miranda's words all over them. Legible pages. Or, with her handwriting, *mostly* legible. But even now, as I touch them, as I flip open the cover and run my fingers over the words, I am amazed by what I have here. These are Miranda's thoughts. Her hopes. Her fears. Her opinions on all kinds of things. Still here. Still accessible to me.

I've read them all. Many times. But I never get tired of them.

I've tried to consume them, to let those words inhabit my mind in such a way that I don't always know the line between her thoughts and mine. Which she would have thought insane since we always saw the world so differently.

From the moment I met Miranda, she was always jotting something down in a notebook. Often it was just notes on Feral movements. Or notes about blood. Or notes about the Bug. But as I got to know her better, I realized that she also wrote down personal things. From the beginning, I wondered what that would look like. I know how to write. I write directions or notes or messages, but I never wrote in a journal. Never saw the need to write down my thoughts in any permanent way. I guess that's one reason I am the way I am.

I wonder what purpose it served for her, a woman of science, of fact, of observation. Maybe it helped her to organize her thoughts. Maybe it purged the feelings that she was having—she could write them down and then move on. Or maybe it was just to talk to someone. We never discussed it. But she did it, wrote in her journals, all the time.

It wasn't until . . . until she was gone that I looked inside one of them. Say what you will about me, I respected her privacy.

Only she's not here anymore to need privacy. So I open the cover for the thousandth time and start reading.

CHAPTER TWO

. . . easier to fight when we only had one enemy, Maenad—a single virus that upended the world. But now . . .

Now I fight a war on two fronts.

No pressure or anything, Miranda.

I'm not fighting alone, at least. Not now that I have the others back. If there's any hope for a cure, it's because of them. Because they're good scientists, good people, and I'm so happy to have them back. More than they'll ever know.

They all look to me. To lead them. To show them the path that we're heading down. I suppose I fought for that, all these years. Back at the commune, after my mother died, everyone was ready to overlook me. They certainly didn't take me seriously, not back then. I was just Ilaria's little girl. No matter that I was already doing lab work and theory as well as anyone there. No—better. Sergei was the only one who ever recognized that.

So of course I spent all that time proving myself. Showing everyone there that I could do the science, yes. But also more than that. Showing everyone there that I could lead. That I could point the way.

So now, when everyone looks to me, they expect me to point the way. But they don't realize how much I lean on them. How much of the weight they bear. How they lift me up, on their shoulders, so that I can see the terrain.

Sometimes I feel so lost. They don't know that, how

truly in the dark I feel so much of the time. <u>I can't let them
know.</u> Even drowning in doubt and fear, I need them to believe
that I know which way leads to the light. I won't have all of
us wandering in despair and darkness.

<u>I won't.</u>

I just get weary, from keeping it all hidden. I choose to,
I know, and I deserve the consequences. But here, and only
here, I can at least admit how tiring it is. I get so weary of
the charade, so tired that I just want to take off this mask
of hope and fall into something resembling relaxation. Or maybe
truth.

That's the part that Ben doesn't understand. He thinks I'm
all about truth. The science—the <u>science</u> is all about truth.
Always. Searching for it even if we can't find it at first. But
everything else? Being a leader? That's as much truth as it is
fabrication. Tamoanchan's leaders, like Lewis, they understand
that. The irony is that Ben is good at lying. Most of the time,
at least. It's just that the well that he usually pulls from
is Fear. The one I reach for is Hope.

You really must be tired, Miranda. You're waxing philosoph-
ical. No one has time for that.

Maybe I should go find Ben. We may approach all of this
differently, but one thing that has been true from the beginning, despite all the fighting and all the tension, is that he
doesn't expect anything of me.

(I expect batshit craziness, he would probably say.)

But he doesn't expect me to lead. He doesn't expect me to
know it all. He just expects me to be human. It seems like
he's always trying to remind me of that. Most of the time it
does drive me batshit crazy. But right now . . .

<u>Right now I just might need it.</u>

CHAPTER THREE

I t's always worse after I read the journals, like I opened a door and the memories just come walking through.

This time it's Miranda, on the *Cherub* before we blew it up, back before the Valhallans took Apple Pi. I'm flying her back from collecting blood samples, but at the moment that's forgotten. A Prince record spins on the phonograph. Miranda dances through the gondola, liquid and light. And I just drink her in.

Then another night, on Tamoanchan, music in the air again, and Miranda drinks from a bottle of wine. Her tongue licks the excess from her lips and she smiles. She holds the bottle out to me, and as I reach for it, our hands touch.

Then that moment aboard the *Cherub* right before we threw ourselves into the ocean, when we kissed and despite all the danger, all the fear, everything else just stopped for a moment. We were the spindle, standing still, while the world revolved around us.

It ended too soon. It all ended too soon.

I put the journal away before my tears blur the ink.

CHAPTER FOUR

S hale Station isn't much as far as trading posts go, but it is safe, and it's been stable for at least a few years. Not big enough to attract unwanted attention. Not small enough to fade away. That's where Claudia set up the meet to drop off the hand bones, and it seems as good a place as any to drop off the slaves we freed. Some of them might be able to get word back to loved ones through the use of the message station there, or find work on a passing ship. Or barter what meager things they were able to take for some clean clothes or lodging or whatever. I feel bad. I truly do. I wish I could do more for them. But there's no safe place I can take them, and Claudia can't feed all those extra mouths.

For a moment I think about Tamoanchan. Alone and on the sea. I think about how at one point I could have sent all of these people there, given them a chance at a decent life once they got past the quarantine. But now that would require a time machine. There's no going back.

The thought brings a sour taste to my mouth, and so of course I start thinking about drowning that taste with another. Shale's got booze and food and most human necessities. But first I need to take a piss, so I head to the outhouses. A thin, young man hovers outside one, eyeing me as I walk up. "I'll get you off," he says, not meeting my eyes. "We can use your gloves." I wince as I recognize him, one of the people we rescued from the slavers.

"No thanks," I say, pushing past him into the dark stink of the outhouse, the kind of smell that seems to get inside of you and never leave. When I exit, I feel like I need a bath, though I'm not sure that's from the outhouse.

So when I lean up against the stall of the hooch seller, it's a relief. "What you got?" I ask.

The woman operating the stall, all gray hair and missing teeth, holds up a dusty glass jar and swirls the liquid inside. "This here's a premium beverage. Distilled from potatoes."

I grip the bottom of the jar and eye it. It's cloudy, but transparent enough. You can't be too picky about these things. Not without making your own, and even I know that that would probably kill me.

I nod at the woman.

"What you got?" she asks, tonguing one of the gaps in her teeth.

I reach into the pocket of my long coat, feel the hard lump of one of the ammo clips I took from the slavers. I pull it out and place it on the stall.

Her eyes widen a bit. "Big spender."

"I'll take five," I say, holding up my fingers.

Her eyes narrow as she continues to tongue her gums. "Four."

I shrug. I'm not looking to bargain right now. "Fine." I put one jar into each pocket and then carry the other two in my hands. Think better of it, put them down, screw off the top of one lid, and smell what's inside. The fumes make my nostrils burn.

"Hey," the woman says, her face full of exaggerated insult. "That's quality stuff."

"I'll be the judge of that," I say. I tip some back into my mouth. It carves a fiery trail down my throat and into my body. I cough a little—it's definitely harsh, and there's the barest hint of a gasoline taste, but really when it comes down to it, I'm not too picky. And I can definitely say that I've had worse.

"My compliments," I say, giving a mock bow. Then I pick up the open jar and the closed one, and walk away, making sure to take a few more sips just to be sure.

The jar is about one third of the way reduced when I see Claudia. Contrary to my recent experience, she almost looks happy. Excited, even. She waves something in the air. Some scrap of paper or something.

I move toward her, shifting the unopened jar under one arm and gripping the other jar, keeping one hand clear to push aside the people in my way.

She heads straight for me, still waving what now appears to be cardboard. "Ben," she says.

"Is that the payment?" I ask. "For the hand?"

"No," she says. "Though I did get that. They were . . . very pleased."

I point at the cardboard. "What is that?"

Claudia holds it up. "He wants to meet."

It takes a moment for the words to sink in. I feel everything just stop. My breath is loud in my ears. *He wants to meet.*

The jar slips out from under my arm and crashes to the ground, breaking with the sound of shattered glass, strong alcohol fumes wafting into the air.

He wants to meet.

I got you, you bitch.

Imagine a world of dull and gray. Always rain. Always this fuzz, this haze, this blurriness to everything. Sounds are muted. Colors drained. Nothing tastes good. Not the grilled rat you ate a few days ago, not the jugs of rotgut you pour into yourself. It's all just . . . gray.

Then, suddenly, color. Light. That cardboard that Claudia was holding was like a miniature sun. It's not a way back to the way the world was before. There is no back. But it's a way to something better than the gray. A warm place, hot even. Sticky. Red. A world of emotion.

Yes, that emotion happens to be red and raw. Anger, rage. Revenge. But I'll take what I can get.

Hold on, now, Ben, the voice in my head says. *You have to be smart about this.* And it's right. Play the game if you want to win. Payment comes at the end of the job.

"Set it up," I'd said to Claudia. She'd said my name, and I saw the depth of the questions, the concern, the warnings in her eyes.

"Set it up," I'd repeated. My voice had sounded strange in my ears, as if it bubbled up from a great depth and lost some of its volume along the way. There was a relentless hammering inside of me: my heart, my blood. Pressing out against my temples. It started two days ago, with the cardboard message, and it's pounding away now that I'm here.

The man standing in front of me, on the other end of this abandoned hallway, is tall and thin, with dark-brown skin and dreadlocks that he keeps short. Rufus is second in command to a woman who calls herself Lord Tess. Tess is a knowledge broker, a keeper and trader of secrets—and an amoral cunt. Rufus is the heir apparent to the kingdom, only the old bitch doesn't want to die.

I seek to help him with that.

"How go things in the knowledge business?" I ask. There's no warmth to my voice, and he knows it, but some talking is necessary.

"The business is the same as always," he says, his face serious. There's a slight echo when we speak, because of the emptiness of the hallway.

"You sell anyone out lately?"

His face stays blank, but he looks away. He knows what Tess did to me. To all of us. How she traded away the location of the island I used to live on. How she worked with the enemy, helped spread the infection that led to Sergei dying. How she is directly responsible for . . . for . . .

I can't think of her. Not right now. Because I need Rufus. Alive. And to think of her now will make that difficult.

"What made you come?" I ask.

He shrugs. "I'm getting impatient," he says.

Meaning he's waiting to be the one in charge, and Tess, old as she is, has her anchor firmly lodged in the ground.

"Good," I say.

"What are you offering?"

I let out something that's part laugh, part grunt and show him my teeth. "You know what I'm offering. You can't advance until Tess moves on, and the old relic won't die on her own."

He crosses his arms. "Betrayal isn't good for business."

I shrug. "So leak that I went crazy and killed her. Or say that I was acting alone. I don't care, as long as you get me to her. That's the deal—you get me in, and I take care of your problem for you."

"It's a tall order," he says. "You know how many guards she has?"

"I also know that you're on the inside. Find a way. That's your job."

"What reassurances do I—?"

"None." I bite the word. "None at all. Except that you know what she did. What she set up. The information that she leaked to us. The information that she sold to them." I inhale. "What it cost us."

He holds his hands out, palms up. "And you don't blame me for any of that?"

It's a good question—he's worked for Tess for years. But I know who runs things. We both do.

"I give you my word," I say. "Whatever that's worth. I only want to see *her* dead." *Preferably with my hands around her wrinkled throat.*

"I'll need help," he says.

"What kind of help?"

He holds up a hand placatingly. Then with the other he waves behind him. Someone moves forward. My hand moves to my revolver. I know Rufus didn't come alone, but I don't know who this is. I'm aware of Claudia, at the end of my peripheral vision, moving forward as well, her bow in her hands.

The woman has brown skin and dark hair pulled back behind her head, a sharp nose, full lips. Then I realize I know her. Sarah. I rescued her from a naval base. At her request. Seems like that was decades ago. She looks different. More relaxed. She looks more confident, too, both in the way that she walks and because of the automatic pistol strapped to her waist.

"What are you doing here?" I ask, my hand still resting on the butt of the revolver. If it comes down to it, I wonder if I can beat her to the draw. She grew up at a naval base. And she's younger. Healthier.

Rufus holds out a hand, and she grabs it. Oh. It's like that.

"Hello, Ben," she says. When I don't respond, she says, "Rufus asked me to come. We're . . ."

"I get it," I say.

She meets my eyes. She seems . . . I don't know. Her back is straight, shoulders back. There's poise there. Certainly a shift from when she left the only place she ever knew. "I run Tess's guards now."

I raise my eyebrows. "Really."

She shrugs. "I have the training."

"All those big men and women with the scars and the guns. You're in charge of them."

She shrugs again. "What can I say? I'm good."

I nod. She must be, to lead that gang of cutthroats and killers. "Doesn't that mean that you'd want to keep me out?"

She's still holding Rufus's hand, and she gives it a squeeze. She looks at him. Adoringly. It's almost sweet, but gives me a sour taste. "I want the best for Rufus," she says. "That's all. Tess gave me a chance, and I'm grateful for that, but this way Rufus can run the show and I can help guard him instead."

I think back to my adventure in the naval base, and leaving Sarah with Tess afterward. I had assumed that she would have moved on, found passage somewhere else. Anywhere else. It's hard to imagine her sticking around, but if Rufus had caught her eye . . .

You've stayed in places for a lot less.

It's true, but it makes me think of . . . her . . . and so I push the thought away.

"So, what can you do for me?" I ask.

Sarah takes a deep breath. "I don't want to risk my people, but they listen to me. They don't ask a lot of questions. I can arrange for there to be a . . . gap in the security. I'll time it so that when you arrive, Tess won't have any guards."

"None?"

"Well, not any guarding her. I'm good, but I'm not that good. I can't take away all of them. The exterior will need to be manned. The stairs as well."

"Then how am I getting in?"

"An old utility corridor," Rufus says. "It enters from the back of the building. We had it barricaded and closed off years ago, but we can arrange to leave it open. No one will think to look. You come in that way, and we leave you a path straight to Tess."

I nod. "Then all I have to do is take care of her and . . . what? You live happily ever after?"

"Something like that," Rufus says.

"But you have to get in, do it, and then leave," Sarah says. "If any of the guards find you, I can't promise your safety. I have to keep this tight. I can't let anyone know about this. Not even after she's found."

"What you do afterward is none of my concern. All I care about is Tess. Ending her. I'll leave the way I came in and . . ."

"And?" Sarah asks.

I meet her eyes, my jaw set. "And you'll never see me again."

It's her turn to nod, a strange look on her face. "I am more than okay with that."

I stifle my reaction. It's not surprising, I guess. Things didn't go so well when we left the base. And where I go, calamity tends to follow.

"So we have a plan?" I ask.

Rufus looks at Sarah, then back to me. "Yes," he says.

"Yes," Sarah says.

Yes, I think.

CHAPTER FIVE

FROM THE JOURNAL OF MIRANDA MEHRA

Dear subconscious,
   I wish you would stay "sub."
   Instead you send me a dream—of Ben and Claudia. And now I can't stop thinking about it.
   It's stupid, I know. I feel like a teenager again, worrying if Kurt Nagata liked me. Worse still, it was almost exactly like what actually happened. I was back on Gastown. I went to find Claudia on the _Valkyrie_, and Ben opened the door, naked.
   He wasn't naked in real life. Though he was close to it. And I was pretty sure he had fucked Claudia, or at least spent the night in bed with her (which always felt somehow worse).
   But in the dream he was naked. How I remembered him from the night _we_ fucked. In the dream, he stood there, staring at me, like why was I there? Then Claudia came out, and he put his arm around her, and they both glared at me. At that point, it wasn't really the _Valkyrie_. But it was this place I remember on Gastown. But I clearly felt, in that moment, that I didn't belong. That I wasn't wanted. Then I woke up gasping.
   So why is this coming up now? That happened weeks ago. Claudia isn't even around anymore. She stayed behind to finish her job, get the information on Gastown's helium plant to whoever hired her in the first place.
   She's gone.
   But not forgotten. Is that what's worrying me?
   Claudia and Ben are of a kind, that much is obvious.

They move in the same way, they speak the same zep language. Watching them, you can see the way they fit, how they connect after all the time they spent together on the <u>Cherub</u>.

I come from a very different world. It might as well be a different planet.

Claudia is also tall, powerful, and dashing. The shock of white in her hair, the scar over her eye, the lopsided grin. She's deadly and attractive. Not my type, but I can see the appeal.

Still, Ben and I have been together, working together at least, since that moment I ran into him. He's raged against me and against the cause, but he keeps coming back. I think he believes that this is worth it. That what we're doing really has a shot.

So I think there's something drawing him here. Something more powerful than whatever drew him to Claudia.

But maybe what I'm really wondering is, can he live in my world? Will he ever be content to stay in one spot, on the ground? Will he be satisfied living in a world of scientists and experiments and discovery? Or will the lure of the sky and old connections win out?

Ben cares for Claudia, that much I know. They've known each other for years, were together for a large part of that. Claudia must have been Ben's first. There's not a lot of touching in his world, not a lot of room for sex, something that I grew up taking for granted. I had my first sexual encounter in my teens, and had a liberal sexual upbringing. It's hard for me to imagine growing up fearing sex, fearing intimacy, fearing an essential part of humanity.

I remember that time, that first time, all those years ago with Kurt Nagata. I remember that awkward, fumbling moment when it happened the first time, and then all the much-better times after it. I also remember feeling so much, believing so strongly that there was something special between Kurt and me. For Ben that first time happened when he was practically an adult. For someone like him, I think that kind of event would stay with him and would leave an indelible mark.

Do I have the time or the interest in attaching myself to someone who might be attached elsewhere?

I don't know.

So, for now, I wait, and I watch and I do what I always do—I try to figure it out. Based on my observations, on my data.

There's this persistent voice inside of me, this annoying, nonscientific urge that keeps bubbling up and saying, _Miranda, just talk to him. Ask him how he feels. Go from there._

But I couldn't trust myself to believe what he might tell me. I couldn't properly gauge his response.

So I wait. And I watch.

And stay, for the time being, alone.

CHAPTER SIX

T he trick with getting to Tess is that she has a lot of protection. Rufus and Sarah are going to take care of the guards inside the library, but Tess has people on the upper floors, keeping watch on the outside and the entrance. They would easily spot the *Valkyrie*'s approach, so Claudia had to put me down well outside of their sight, and I'm going to have to make my way on foot while she gets to sit up in the sky.

No big deal.

Remember why you're here, Ben.

I'm alone, on Old San Francisco's streets, without any backup. Things are likely to be safer the closer I get to the library, but there's a lot of ground between me and it. A lot of ground that's probably crawling with Ferals pissed off about not getting into the library. And because we planned this for night, based on Sarah's recommendation, the dusk light is fleeting.

It should petrify me, but I'm more focused on the thought of making my entry. Of what I could do to Tess once I make it in. So many images flash through my mind—putting a gun to her head, using a knife, stabbing, slashing, beating her with a rusty pipe.

So many fucking images.

In all of them, she reaches her hand out to me. She pleads. She begs. She brings up our old friendship. The times we worked together. She tells me that she never meant for Miranda to die. She was just doing her job. And all of those words, all of her entreaty, just falls away, like water washing up against a wall. The wall is unmoved.

Dammit, Ben. Keep your head in the game.

I snap back to where I am. In the street. Alone. Outside. I try to keep my vision in that tricky zone in which you're focusing on where you're going, but you're also focusing on everything around you. I like to think of it as trying to see with all your senses. Using your hearing and your sense of smell and your peripheral vision to help fill in the picture of your environment. At least I hope that's what I'm doing.

Visions of a dead Tess keep trying to pull me away.

I fight like that for some time, trying to find that sweet spot, that groove, yet it never comes. It stays just out of reach. A fish flickering just beyond the lure.

Then I hear howls echoing through the streets. First one, then more. Not Feral howls, though. Not that strangled human shriek that I've come to know too well. This is something different, a low, animal keening that scares me all the same. Wild dogs. A pack of them.

Dogs are scary, no doubt about it. Even scrawny, underfed dogs have sharp teeth and jaws like steel. Still, a dog or two will die to guns just fine. Or at least they'll run off. But a pack of dogs is terrifying. A gun is only so good against a pack. You can take one or two out, and the others will overrun you, pinning you down, one or two holding you while the rest tear you apart. And they know it. My father always used to say that dogs could sense fear, and I defy anyone to face off a pack without being afraid.

I scan around me, looking for some way to get off the ground. Dogs can climb, but not like a Feral. Not up a ladder or over a tall wall. I need to get off the ground, where they have the advantage.

Howls again. This time closer. Or at least I think they are. It's hard to tell with the echoes in the streets.

A collapsed building leans nearby, one side of it fallen down into the street. From an attack, or from an earthquake, or just from old and worn-down materials. In this area, it's hard to tell. I move toward it, keeping my pace steady and even. That was another thing my father taught me—not to run from dogs. It just attracts their attention and gets their blood up.

It's hard, though, not to make a mad sprint-scramble up the rubble alongside the remains of the building.

A chorus of growling and snapping sounds joins the howls, and I can't help myself from moving a little faster, scrabbling up the crumbling wood and drywall, my nose filled with the smell of long-dusty materials and mold.

I spare one look back and see dark shapes moving toward me. The pack, bolting down the street now that they've got my scent.

I'm almost to the second floor, but the wreckage I just crawled up is easily accessible to the dogs, and the floor up above me has stairs leading up. Dogs can climb stairs.

Fuck.

I grab for the edge of the floor and yank myself up, turning back for a moment, my revolver out. I fire two shots at the dogs, which are a lot closer and a lot bigger than I expected. If I'm lucky, the shots will scare them off. Or I'll hit one, and that will do the trick. I fire once, and the shot disappears into the quickly growing dark. Then two more shots. On the second one, I hear a yelp and one of the shapes spins off. At least I think it does. But the rest of them keep coming. I turn and head for the stairs, pounding up them, hoping for a door or something to close behind me.

Instead, I end up in hallway, with more stairs going up and closed doors around me. I keep moving to the stairs. No way to tell if any of these doors are open and unlocked, and I can't spare the time. I can hear more growling and snapping, and some yelping and whining behind me. *Fuck fuck fuck.* I race up the stairs, my legs burning, my arms shaking, my heart beating hard in my chest.

Up and up and up. Higher is always better. As far away from the ground as possible. Always up. Always.

I slam through a door with a push-bar on it, and then I'm on the roof. Nowhere to go. I turn back to the door and try to slam it shut, but the hinges are bent, or the door's just swollen, and it hangs open no matter what I do. I can hear the sound of the dogs echoing through the stairwell, their claws on the stairs, their breathing, their animal grunting.

I don't have enough bullets for all of them, and I can't hold the door against them if they all work together. So I move to the edge of the roof. There's another building, slightly shorter, but it's not close. I might be able to jump it, but I'm not sure of my chances. And, judging from the condition of this building, who knows what shape that one is in.

The door slams open, and I see three dark shapes bound toward me, lips skinned back from yellow fangs, growls vibrating through me. And the door slams again and again and again.

I snarl back at them, and then, pulling on all of my fear and my hate and my visions of killing Tess, I pump my legs across the roof, running at an angle to the other building. As I hit the edge, I leap, putting all of my hope into my boots and my legs and the stability of the edge of the roof and—

My footing holds and I leave the roof, and for a moment I am in the air and gravity doesn't have complete hold of me. I am hurtling through space, free of the ground, free of everything, beyond reach of the dogs behind me. For a moment, I fly, and something in me sings.

It lasts only a microsecond, and then gravity snatches me up again. I feel every gram of my weight as I start to be pulled down toward the ground. The dirty, dangerous ground. And the other edge of the roof seems oh so far away. I'm moving fast. Heavy and fast. I reach out my arms and hands, the gloves worn, and I wonder if they still have enough grip. And then—

SLAM. My arms come down over the edge of the other building, but my body follows my feet, and my chest crashes hard into the wall. My hands start to lose their grip, and I scramble to keep hold.

My fingers catch, and I dig my boots into the wall, hoping for a firm hold. Everything's pounding and I'm completely tense, and then the wall that I'm hanging from breaks away and I start to slip down. I'm slamming my boots against the wall, and they catch against glass, and I'm half falling, half swinging into and through a window. *WHAM.* I land hard on my back against the floor.

For a moment, I just lie there. My chest hurts where I hit the wall, and my head and my back and everything feels tired. I suck in air and will everything to slow down. To stop. Through the window, I can hear the dogs yelping, growling, barking their anger at the night.

Fuck you, dogs. Not tonight.

I have better things to do.

✳︎　　✳︎　　✳︎

The area around the back of the San Francisco Public Library is covered with wreckage. Deliberately.

Covered.

In the thankfully bright moonlight I spot what looks like old, broken furniture, swollen by many rains. Metal sheets. Old cars. Chunks of masonry and torn-up asphalt. In front of all that stands a series of spikes and spears to really keep the Ferals away. Looking at it, it's obvious that I'm not getting in.

Except Rufus and Sarah were supposed to have left an opening for me. I tried to get them to tell me exactly how to find it, but they told me I would know it when I saw it. Sarah insisted on that. They weren't sure how much time they'd have, how they would create a path, but that they would leave a sign I would clearly recognize.

It makes me uneasy. If they didn't actually complete my entrance, or if it somehow collapsed or got blocked, or if I can't figure out where it is . . . well, then I'm possibly going to end up as Feral chow. If I'm lucky, Ferals already know to keep away from this place.

Then again, I'm rarely lucky.

So I'm here, roaming this barricade, my hand around the handle of my revolver, listening for the sounds of, well, anything above the dripping and the wind and the creaking of old metal and the flapping of cloth.

Then I see it. A picture on a piece of metal, probably an old sign or decorative art. A picture of a plump baby, curly hair, innocent smile. A pair of white, fluffy wings sprouting from its back.

A cherub.

Smartasses.

Grumbling to myself about how I'm still taking shit for what I named my old ship (and, God, how I miss her), I push aside the sign, and behind it is a cramped but passable-looking path through the obstacles. I make sure to carefully replace the sign behind me. Rufus and Sarah are doing me a favor. Themselves, too, to be honest, but I don't want to risk a stray Feral finding its way in.

It's an uncomfortable shimmy-crouch-crawl past table legs and large chunks of rubble sprouting rebar. I take care. I'm in a hurry, but there's no use risking open wounds. So it's inch and sweat and think about what's about to come.

It's a . . . strange feeling. To be so close. I waited months to get here. Months during which I wondered if it would ever happen. Months during which I couldn't figure out how to get into Tess's heavily guarded sanctum. Knowing that I needed to, because that's the only thing that can put to rest this swirling storm inside of me. The thought of never being able to do this, of never getting here, was almost too much to bear at times.

Now I can practically taste it.

I finally get to the end of the makeshift tunnel and rise to a crouch. In front of me is a door. My hand trembles as I reach out to it. It's supposed to be unlocked. The space beyond it is supposed to be clear. We went over this again and again. The timing. The placement. Making sure Sarah would clear the way. If this is locked, everything's fucked.

I look up at the sky. Judging by the moon and the stars, I'm right on time. Or near enough. My gloved left hand curls around the door handle. My right hand grips the revolver where it's strapped to my leg.

I pull both.

The metal scrapes against the frame, but the door slides free. Beyond . . . darkness.

I instinctively pull back from the opening. If anyone's inside, I'm not going to give them an easy target.

Nothing.

Still gripping the door handle, I swivel around the entrance, the revolver out and pointed in front of me. Still nothing.

I crouch down to the ground. I need light, and Rufus had agreed to leave something for me just inside the door. I grope about in the darkness until my hand falls on something hard. I pull it to me, and in the moonlight coming in from the still-open door I can make out the shape of a lantern. I find the knob on its side and turn. A moment later, it flares to life, fed by the propane tank beneath it. It's portable, about the size of my two fists stacked on top of one another. A valuable find. I'd get good barter for one of these. My wonder turns to bitterness. Tess probably has a ton of valuables stocked up in the place as a result of her dealings.

But all I really want, all I really care about, is making her pay. With my newfound light in hand, I close the door behind me. No need to invite in any unwanted guests.

Being able to see my surroundings also means that anyone in the place can see me. The path to Tess is supposed to be clear, but if anyone happens along or stumbles across me by accident . . .

Even with that prospect at the forefront of my mind, I slide the revolver back into its holster. The lantern leaves me only one hand free, and I don't want that hand tangled up in a gun. Not at the moment, at least. I rigged the holster to allow me to draw quickly, and right now I have to depend on that to work as planned. And, like I said, the way is supposed to be clear. With my free hand, I pull from my pocket the folded piece of paper that Rufus gave me. It's a map of the library (a simple one), and Rufus marked the route I should take. If I deviate from it, I'm likely to run into some of the guards, and that would be bad for everyone. Me being me, I memorized the map, but it doesn't hurt to refresh my memory.

Now that I can see my way, I can make out that I'm in a kind of service entrance that opens up into a larger area. Probably where they brought in deliveries of, well, books, I guess. Bring in the boxes, sort them, and lug them up to the shelves. There are plenty of boxes and crates filling the space, too. Full of what, I wonder? A quick look finds them carrying supplies. One crate contains nothing but boxes of salt. Another one holds bottles of water. One on the other side of the room is filled with car batteries. All in all, it's a fortune in barter. I'd always thought that Tess had all the guards because of the books, and her information. But there's value here, too. Lots of it. I see something that looks like bottles of beer in the lantern light.

As I'm leaving the room, I see one box full of cables. I pause for a moment, then pull on one, untangling it from its fellows. I wrap it around my chest, over one shoulder, and loop it through the handle of the lantern. It's a quick, crude job, but when I'm done, the lantern is hanging in front of my chest. This way my hands will be free, at least.

I move out of the storage area into another hallway. Other rooms sit off of it, rooms containing more supplies, probably. All of it is unlit. Why waste the energy? Simply send someone down with a lantern when you need something.

I move slowly but confidently up the hallway. So far, so good. I listen as hard as I can, though, for any doors or approaching footsteps. I might not dim the lantern in time, but I could certainly take cover.

At the end of the hallway, I take a staircase up, then up again until I reach the main floor of the library.

From here, it only gets more dangerous. Before, I was hidden in closed-off back areas. Now I'm out in the main, open area of the library. Where Tess and her guards and her people can see me.

Once more I hesitate before passing through the door leading out. I pull out the revolver with my right hand. Then I open the door and step back. Again, nothing. When I look through the threshold, still nothing.

I move into the library proper. Rufus told me that at night, when they don't have visitors, they often turn off the lights to conserve energy. Instead they rely on fire, in barrels, and in the lanterns like the one strapped to my chest.

Those fires help in keeping the visibility low. If anyone saw me now, they would probably take me for someone who belonged here, and that would buy me some much-needed time.

I move. It won't be long now. Tess has a large study/office where she spends most of her time, a private space she can retreat to when not meeting with people. But Rufus said that in the evenings she often likes to sit in her chair, in the audience chamber, reading and drinking hot water and warming herself beneath a blanket. If you ask me, it probably has something to do with the library, being surrounded by all those books. All that knowledge. That probably gives Tess a thrill, even now.

So that's where I head. Rufus and Sarah assured me that Tess often likes to be left alone while she reads. At night guards are moved to the periphery of the library, or take up position outside. Disturbing Tess's reading, according to Sarah, means a shit detail.

I have to admit, the audience chamber is pretty impressive—open, with the high ceiling, and surrounded by stacks of books situated off in lateral wings.

And there she is. Exactly where they said she would be.

Lord Tess sits on her chair, her throne, reading a book by lantern light. She's old, the oldest person I know, and even in the dim illumination I can see the wrinkles and crags in her face. She usually wears a pair of thick, dark glasses, but the ones she has on right now are clear. Her short, gray hair still has a good deal of black in it. She's wearing thick, soft clothes, no gloves, and no face covering, and a thick, woolen blanket over her legs.

From where she sits, I'm guessing I look like just another of her guards. So I move in a meandering path, trying to get closer without alerting her. When she realizes who I am, and that I'm here for her, I want it to be far too late.

My breath is loud in my ears. I move closer, trying to seem like I belong there, like this is nothing more than routine, even while my body and mind scream for me to run to her and press my gun to her head.

I move one foot, then another. One, two. One, two. But my eyes never leave her. Her eyes are focused on whatever she's reading. The only movement she makes is to turn the pages with her arthritic hands.

One step. Then another. Closer and closer.

Then I'm there, near enough that she looks up. My long coat is already pulled back around the revolver, ready for me to draw it.

She looks up, squinting behind her large glasses. Then her eyes widen. "Benjamin," she says.

I feel a smile, full of bitter hatred, twist my face. I draw the revolver. Slowly. Casually. Like I have all the time in the world. I intend to savor this. I lower my scarf so that she can see my face. "Yes," I say. "It's me. I'm here to—"

"I know," she says, dropping her head. "I know." One wrinkled hand grips the arm of her chair, and her shoulders begin to shake, her head starts to tremble. Then she raises her head again.

A sound I can't process breaks the silence, and Tess stares at me with watery eyes and a red face. The meaning of the sound hits me a moment later.

Tess is laughing.

Light flares all around me. In front of me. Above me. Behind me. I blink against the sudden brightness, and yet even through the spots I can see the people. Hear them. Smell them. Lots of people. On all sides. I catch a glimpse of weapons. Big ones.

I raise the revolver, urgent now, but Tess isn't there anymore, whisked away by someone, hiding behind the lights. Then gunshots rip into the floor around me.

"Put the pistol down, Benjamin," Tess says, her voice echoing around the room. "There are over a dozen guns trained on you. They will tear you to shreds without hesitation."

I blink my eyes, still full of spots from the lights that illuminate me, and no one else. I try to make sense of what's happening but keep coming up short.

"Benjamin . . ."

I force myself to place my revolver on the ground. I don't want to. I want to shoot her. But I'm a defenseless target. I won't let myself die without taking her with me. Not if I can help it.

You might not be able to help it.

My eyes start to adjust to the onslaught of light and Tess reappears, stepping forward into the brightness. A moment later, she's joined by two people. Rufus and Sarah. My stomach twists and suddenly I feel like I'm going to throw up.

They played me.

"Oh, Benjamin, Benjamin," Tess says, shaking her head. "You did everything as I expected." She clasps her arthritic hands together. "I thought that maybe you would surprise me, but . . ." Her face falls. "You didn't."

I don't say anything. I look around instead, now that my eyes have adjusted. Guards stand at the ready, everywhere I look. Most of them carry assault rifles. Two large, metal barrels stand in the space, lit with fires. Above me, spotlights point down at me. More guards, little more than shadows, stand on the stairways leading up.

"I really didn't want it to come to this," Tess says. "All of this—" she waves her hand around, "—all of it—is just business."

My jaw clenches so hard that it sends shooting pains up the sides of my face and into my head. "She's dead," I spit. "Because of you."

"See?" she says. "That is why this has to happen. I can let things be, but you . . . you can't. You've always been too emotional. And now you're letting that emotion guide you. Run you." She shakes her head again. "There was a time when I thought you understood, understood that in this world, you have to make hard choices. Sometimes you just have to survive to live another day. But what do you do beyond that? Sometimes you have to make choices to live another year. Another ten years. And beyond that. . . . So many people—they think small. Food to last the week. Gas to last a month." Her hand curls into a fist. "I built this business, this . . . empire to last forever. You tried to appeal to Rufus, to get him to turn on me, but the truth is, he knows I won't be here for too much longer. But when I'm dead, he will take over. Because this, all of this—" she waves her hand around again, "—is more important than me. Or him. Or you. All of this will outlive all of us. It has to."

Her mouth forms a thin line, and she shakes her head, as if in regret. "But it will outlive you more. I can't have you out there, plotting to kill me. It's . . . inefficient." She walks up to me and places that wrinkled, liver-spotted hand on my shoulder. "So you have to go."

I consider grabbing her. Throttling her, or trying to break her neck. If they tried to shoot at me they might possibly hit her. Possibly. But these are trained guards. Crack shots. And they surround me. It's far more likely, given her confidence, that they would take me down and she would live.

She smiles at me and pats my cheek. I flinch at her touch. "Good-bye, Benjamin," she says.

Then she turns and walks away from me.

"Do it," she calls out into the room.

CHAPTER SEVEN

FROM THE JOURNAL OF MIRANDA MEHRA

I've been sitting here for a little while now, unsure of how to start this. I wanted to write "Fuck, fuck, fuck . . ." and just keep going, let it pour out of me and onto this page in hopes of, I don't know, purging this feeling of futility. I just don't know what else to do right now. And I can't let on to anyone how lost and close to hopeless I am.

Enigma, this new fucking virus that came out of nowhere, is winning. And I don't know where to go from here.

We've made some headway, yes. We're better off than where we started. But we still don't know enough. What it is. How to stop it. And while the Maenad virus transforms, Enigma kills. And keeps killing.

So I'm racing against the clock.

I think, in a way, that this virus has exposed my fucking weakness. Not that Maenad is any more forgiving, but I've been thinking about the infected, about Ferals, as still in play. I've always thought, in the back of my mind, that when we find the cure, which we will, that we can save those who are infected. If someone like Ben were infected, by Maenad, then I would try to contain him. Then I would continue to work on my cure, hoping that one day I could reverse the virus's effects and regain a person who's dear to me.

But Enigma doesn't leave any open doors. This is a new kind of test for me. One that I don't know I'm up for.

I mean . . .

I know I can crack it. Or I don't know, maybe I can't. No. ~~I can.~~ Given enough time, enough materials, enough resources. But time is the one thing that we don't have. So I have to spend every moment fighting this. Which is what I've been doing. Only now, with so little sleep, delirious and frantic, what if I make a mistake? What if I miss a breakthrough?

What if I let more people die?

I've been working on Maenad for all my life. We're closer to a cure, but it's taken years. Decades.

We don't have years. If this thing continues, we likely all die.

~~I think~~ I'm just very fucking angry. That Enigma came along to pull me away from my work on Maenad. The real enemy. The real target. The one that I was pointed at the moment I could think for myself.

How can I not hit that target?

It's what I was meant to do, isn't it?

Of course, the irony is, if I do ever do it, find the cure, what will I do afterward?

I haven't ever really thought about it much. I think I avoided it because I didn't want to tempt myself, think of scenarios that are too fucking far away.

But now, right now, I need to know that there's something else. That there is a life on the other side of all of this. And not fucking well-traveling the world, giving the cure to any Ferals I find. Maybe that's what I should do, but fuck that right now. There's this part of me, and it grows louder every day, that says on the day I cure Maenad, I will have done my part. I will have given enough. Let others take that cure and carry it forward. Let others do the work of spreading it around the world.

What I keep coming back to, my hidden secret shame, is this burgeoning belief that I deserve a life. For myself. Owing no one. A life, if I want to, of reading and growing plants and maybe even making liquor or wine or, for Ben, beer. This dark, shameful voice which talks to me of getting fat and old and not caring about the whole world. Not even caring too much about those around me, but just me, and maybe one special person.

Ben always says I deserve that. That I work so hard, that I do so much to keep the flame lit. He's the one always telling me to take time for myself. To take a break. To forgive myself. Most of the time when he says that, it makes me furious. Because in those moments I feel like I can't take that time. That him telling me to do so is ridiculous, because this work needs to be done. This work is important.

But I wonder now, as I'm writing all of this, if what really makes me furious is that he speaks with my own voice, that repressed voice, and that's the part I resent. It's easier to hate him for it than to hate myself.

Plants. I keep coming back to those. Growing things. A garden. Crops. Fruit. That's something I would love to do. Help feed the world. Help just make living things grow. Put more life back into the world. Why couldn't I do that? Why couldn't I just live out the rest of my life making green things grow?

When I imagine all of this, I see a picture. Me in a place much like the one I'm in now, a home, somewhere near green things, surrounded by people dear to me. And I picture . . . someone with me. I picture someone by my side, hand in mine, there to help support me, to listen to my dreams and fears. Someone who will help prop me up when things seem too hard. Someone who will help keep everyone away when I'm just too tired or when I've had enough. Someone to hold me in the night and in the morning and most of the times in between. But someone who keeps my own fire lit, and who stokes it, even. Someone who complements me. Who knows me. Who sees me for who I am.

I see myself with that someone, I see us together, after the cure, after the worst of the hardships, after all the loss and the pain. And I see us just . . . living.

. . .

Speak of the devil. I think that's him at the door now. I better put this away . . .

am rigid, muscles taut, dripping with regret for not trying to kill Tess when she was close, for not ending it when I could. Now I'm surrounded, and they're going to shoot me.

I'm sorry, Miranda.

Then, above me, a light blinks out, with the sound of tinkling glass. Then another, and I hear a familiar voice yell, "Ben! Run!"

Claudia.

She was supposed to stay with the ship, keep it ready for when I was done. That she's here means she didn't trust my plan. But I can't complain.

Saving Ben's Ass: The Claudia Nero Story.

The fires are still lit behind me, but I grab for the revolver, still on the ground, and run as the assault rifles open up. The guards surround me, but I'm out of the spotlights and they can't see one another clearly. At least, I hope they can't. I move for the nearest barrel, keeping low. I slam into it, tipping it over, almost falling myself, and spill the burning detritus onto the ground. And onto the guard who was standing next to it. He screams and falls back, slapping at himself, and I run for the nearest hallway and entrance into the book stacks.

Behind me, guards run for the barrel and the spilling fire, to contain it. A few less of them to worry about at least.

Gunfire staccatos behind me. As I round one series of shelves, grateful for the darkness, everything that just happened starts to sink into my adrenaline-soaked brain. Tess played me. I thought I had finally gotten her, that I had lined everything up, and all the while she was just sitting back, waiting for me to walk into her trap.

I'd be seething if I wasn't running for my life.

Claudia's still behind me. Probably shooting guards down with her arrows. After all of this, after everything, she's still risking her life for mine.

I have no idea why.

Weapons rattle nearby, and footsteps pound around the bookshelves. I'm at a disadvantage here. They know this ground better than I do. Even now, they may be heading me off, sending people to cut off my avenues of escape. I need something to even the playing field.

I stop in the darkness, hoping I can remain hidden. I stay very still, try not to give any hint of a target. I don't make any noise, except for my incessant breathing, which can't be helped. I turn my lantern off.

I think back to the barrel that I knocked over and the resulting commotion as people tried to deal with it. They're afraid of burning the books. This is Tess's true wealth—all the knowledge contained here. Even more than that, this is what she loves.

I reach for the lantern against my chest. Like an external heart. I stoke the fire again, burning whatever little fuel tank is in this thing, and I tear off the protective top, until the element is exposed. I press it to one of the books next to me. They're a little damp, a little moldy—any kind of reliable climate control died many years ago—but they're made of paper and so it doesn't take long for them to burn. I get one book going and then move on to the next.

The light attracts attention. A burst of gunfire tears through the books nearby.

I wait until the next burst stops, then, around the corner of the bookshelf I'm hiding behind, I toss one of the burning books so that it slides right up against the next shelf over, the one where the guard is probably hiding. By now, flames are eagerly licking up the book and, as it connects with the shelf, those flames start reaching higher, to the books there, and one of them takes light.

Bullets send bits of paper and books fluttering all around me. I drop down and crawl away. During a pause in the shooting, I reach for another book, light it, then toss it again over to the next shelf.

The flames reach up, find other books, and wreath the shelf in fire.

I shimmy over to the edge of the shelf, bend myself around, and raise the gun. Now that the shelf is starting to burn, I can make out a dark shape that I take for a guard. I squeeze off two shots at him. He goes down, even as the fire continues to spread.

I don't wait. I run for the next stack, light another book, and toss it away from me.

The fires are mostly at my back, but I'm hoping that Tess will be forced to choose between saving the books and sending the guards after me. If nothing else, it will thin their numbers.

As for anyone trying to head me off, I intend to keep this trick going, so as I reach the next shelf, I set another book burning, wedge it in the shelves where I think it can do the most damage, and then move to the next shelf, taking shelter behind it first.

A guard appears in front of me, but something about the fire slows him for a second. As he raises his rifle to me, I already have the revolver up and I'm firing. Once. Twice. He goes down in a bloody heap.

I quickly strip his rifle (taking care to avoid any blood) and move to the next shelf, ducking behind it, lighting whatever books I can find that will do the trick.

All the while, I'm running back through my head the map that Rufus gave me. The thing about that map is that it had to be mostly true. I've been here before, to the library, and I know some of the basic layout. If anything in that map had read false, it would have tipped me off. So they kept it real.

But a thing about foragers is that the layout of a place, especially a place we're going into blind, is very important. Hence me studying the map and memorizing as much of it as I could. Now, the library is a big place, and with the brain that I have, not all of the map was going to stick, but I made sure to mark the placement of the important stops and the paths in between them. Those included my entrance, where they told me Tess would be, and her private office.

It was only smart. Tess was likely to be in the audience chamber, reading (or so they told me); but if that went bad, or if she wasn't there, then she was almost certainly going to be in her office. And seeing as I wasn't planning on leaving until she was dead, I made sure to memorize both the location of the office and several ways to get there.

So even now, as I'm moving through the library, burning books behind me, I am mentally plotting a route to Tess. The moment that Claudia started firing and I went off into the darkness, they would have moved Tess to a safe location. Maybe it wasn't the office, but it seems the most likely place.

I move forward, ducking behind shelves, popping out to fire the gun, spreading the fire wherever I can.

After months of wanting this, Tess is so close I can practically smell it. *Time to make this happen, Ben.*

* * *

Run. Hide. Fire. Duck. Burn. Run again.

I do it. Moving up through the stacks. Up a ramp, then down the other side. Drop the rifle when it runs dry. Then to the stairs, back down to the ground level. Reload the pistol. I see guards moving everywhere. Some with weapons. Some with buckets of water. Some just running.

I keep on my path until I get close.

Up ahead of me is Tess's office, and above the low roar of the flames behind me I can hear voices inside. The voices are urgent, raised.

"—will not be hurried off into a ship from my home. My *empire.*" Tess.

"But the place is going up," says a voice I recognize as Rufus's. "We might not be able to contain the fire."

"Nonsense," Tess says. "We'll pull water up from the stores and put it out. I am not leaving all of this. Everything that I've accumulated. We'll stop it."

"You should at least get ready. Just in case." Sarah.

Grumbling, in Tess's low rumble. Then, "Thank you," from Sarah.

"Have all the men not chasing after Benjamin focus on the fire," Tess says. She sighs. "In the old days, this wouldn't be a problem. They had systems back then. Fire suppression. Chemical systems to help snuff the fire without damaging the books. I doubt even I could find someone to help re-create that."

"Tess . . ." Sarah says. Insistent.

I inch forward. Listening. Assessing. Sounds like it's just the three of them. But Tess is there. I am so close. That voice in my head starts nattering on about being outnumbered, and probably outgunned, but I beat it down. I am so close. I reload the revolver.

The door is partially open. I push inside.

Straight into Rufus, who holds an open bag in one hand, his other, grabbing for something that looks like a portable computer. His eyes widen. I wonder what my own face is doing—the same? Or are my eyes narrowing? Is my face stony or stretched into a grin? I can't tell. I'm inside this machine, inexorably moving, and I am so close to my goal.

Things slow down in the way that they sometimes do in moments like this. Rufus turns his head, his short dreadlocks swaying with the movement. The bag drops from his hand, falling slowly, like through oil, to the ground. I feel and see my own arm raising. Slowly. Ever so slowly. Feel my finger curl around the trigger of the revolver. I'm dimly aware of Tess and Sarah moving syrupy slow in the background.

I gave you a chance, Rufus. This is on you now.

Rufus is turning now. His head whips around in seeming slow motion, his torso following suit, a twist in his waist as his legs struggle to follow through. And that's when my arm reaches the horizontal. It's not a wide target, but my finger tightens and pulls against the trigger, and then the revolver is bucking in my hand.

Once. Twice.

His shoulder erupts in a bloody shower. Then his side, right near the ribs, and the impact adds some force to his spin, so he twirls against a bookcase that shudders as he slams into it. Then he droops to the ground, leaving bloody spray across the books.

A scream of horror breaks the slow bubble of time. My eyes snap to Sarah, her face twisted in anger and grief. I realize that it was real between them. I just killed someone she loved.

Join the fucking club.

Time goes from molasses slow to slipstream fast in a fraction of a heartbeat and Sarah is racing toward me, her face etched with rage, her limbs pumping. I aim the revolver, but she's on me before I can get a good bead and she slaps it away with one hand and kicks me in the chest with a boot that feels like it's made from metal. I lose my grip on the revolver, which clatters to the floor, and try to stay on my feet.

Punch, punch, kick, and throw is followed by pain, pain, blood, and more pain. Then I'm twirling through the air until I land hard on my back. Sarah's small, but she's trained to fight since she was a child, and I can't match her there.

Then I remember through the haze of pain that Tess is still there. Still needs to be dealt with. So I grab onto that like it's a bobbing raft in the ocean, and I climb aboard.

I'm trying to regain my feet when Sarah jumps atop me, pinning me down with her knees, and I see the cold gleaming of a knife in her hand. I just have time to get my own hands up to block the downward strike. I catch her wrist with my hands, but she's got a wiry strength and now gravity, that great fucking terror, is aiding her. My arms start to tremble. My legs are trapped.

What else do you have, Ben?

"Should have picked your boyfriends better," I say, through gritted teeth.

Her pressing intensifies.

"Rufus was second-rate." My arms feel like they're going to give out completely. "He died second-rate."

Then the knife slashes down and I push as hard as I can. It scrapes against my collarbone, carving the skin at the top, and I grit my teeth. But I feel Sarah unbalance as the blade hits the floor, and I twist her off.

She's on her feet in a second. It takes me a few more to stagger to mine. The pain in my shoulder is incredible. But Tess is still behind her, and that means I need to get Sarah out of the way. Sarah has other ideas and spins into me, kicking again, and I take the blow on the bleeding shoulder and almost black out from the pain.

I reach out with one hand, blindly grasping, flailing. I grab something—a book—and I throw it at Sarah. Then another. And another. I actually hear Tess protesting, but I ignore her and roll over, standing up again and throwing a few more books at her and a couple of hard things that I don't have time to actually identify.

Then, when Sarah is dodging my barrage, I run and dive. She susses out what I'm trying to do and is instantly after me. I land hard enough that it squeezes the air out of me, but my extended hand falls on the revolver, and I curl my fingers around the grip. Then a boot comes down hard. On my back. And my spine crunches.

The pain shoots through me, and my finger contracts on the trigger, sending a shot out. Down to three bullets now and I don't think I can move.

But you have to.

I plant my free hand and push, rolling to the other side as I see another boot coming down. I whip the other arm up and fire. Twice.

Sarah looks shocked as the first bullet takes her in one thigh, and then she drops. The second explodes her throat and one side of her face. What's left of her expression still looks surprised as she topples to the side.

I hear movement behind me. Tess.

With a supreme effort of will, I try to raise myself to my feet, even though my spine feels snapped in two and I can barely feel my legs or my body.

But amazingly, I stand. Amazingly, I can move.

Tess is shuffling away from me, a bag over her shoulder, her feet in oversized, cushioned slippers.

I raise the revolver. Only one shot left. Have to make it count.

"Stop," I say.

She keeps moving.

"Tess!" I want to shoot the gun to make her stop, but I can't. So instead I stalk after her, slapping back the pain, grab her shoulder, and turn her around. Her face is impassive. Her eyes stare at me from behind the large glasses. I jam the barrel of the gun up against her chin.

"An execution?" she asks.

"One I've been looking forward to for a long time."

"And what was my crime, Benjamin?"

"You know," I say.

She tuts at me. "If this is an execution, a justified killing, the tradition is to read out the list of crimes."

The pain of Sarah's kick is still swelling inside of me, and Tess's words are making a fuzz in my head. I jam the gun against her face, pressing hard just under her right eye.

"You know," I say again. "When we were here last . . . you gave us the location of the boffins. You deliberately fed it to us, so that they could infect the island with the new virus. Enigma. And you sold out the location of Tamoanchan to your Valhallan friends and their allies. And . . ." I feel the tears start to well up. And my voice is thick with the emotion of all of this. "And because of that, people died. *Miranda.* Died."

Tess just stares at me. I think about pulling the trigger. Then she sneezes. Or at least I think it's a sneeze. Soon I catch it for what it really is—laughter. Great, heaving, wheezing laughter.

Heat is starting to flood my face. "What are you laughing at?"

She doesn't reply. She's still shaking with it.

"Stop," I say, my voice low and dark. I cock back the hammer of the revolver.

Tess holds up her hands and manages to get herself under control. She sighs. "Sorry, Benjamin. It's just . . . your version of events is so typically . . . you."

"What do you mean?"

"Benjamin, what is it that I do? I'm an information broker. I trade information. Yes, I gave you the location of Miranda's scientists. Because she was looking for them. And because of me, you got them back. Did some other unsavory types take advantage of that? Yes. And apparently that caused a lot of problems for you. But that isn't my problem. I only provide the information. The location of Tamoanchan? Another piece of information. Which I already had. And, you should know, it wasn't really of any value once you let your spies escape."

"I don't want to hear your excuses."

"Excuses?" She shakes her head. "It's business. It's . . . survival. We do what we need to do to survive. For me, the only thing I've ever been good at is knowing things. Learning things. So I rely on that."

"There are lines," I say.

Tess holds up her hands. "Of course there are. But I think if you look closely enough, you'll find that we're standing about the same distance away from those lines."

The barrel of the revolver comes away from her face. "You were my friend," I say, my voice strained. My arm feels like cold stone, fixed, with the gun still pointing at her eye.

Her smile is humorless. "Maybe," she says. "But we both know that friendship has its limits. Friendship didn't stop you from leaving Malik behind, after all."

A flush of something bitter pushes up beneath the cold rage. My gun arm trembles.

"The difference, of course," she continues, "is that I didn't know what was going to happen to you. Or Miranda."

"Don't. Say. Her name."

"But you knew exactly what you were doing to Malik."

"I was trying to save you and Claudia."

"I know," she says. "Benjamin, I know. And I'm grateful for it. But it's just one example of the hard choices we sometimes have to make. In this world. . . . If it helps, I am sorry that you had to make that choice. I'm sorry that the world is like this. I'm sorry that Miranda—"

Blood flows back into me. I press the revolver against Tess's sternum. "Do *not* say her name." Tess presses her lips together. "Mal taught me something," I say. "Yes, we make hard choices. But he taught me that those actions have consequences. This is yours."

Tess shakes her head almost imperceptibly. "Think hard about that, Benjamin. Think very hard on what you just said. 'Actions have consequences.' What consequences have your actions brought? Malik. Your father. Sergei. Your friend, what was his name—Diego? Even Sarah over there. What consequences did they face from your actions?"

"Shut up, or I will shut you up."

The voice in my head is saying that she's stalling me. Hoping that one of her people will come to check on her and take me out. So the voice tells me that I need to take care of this now. Do it quick, easy, and get out. I put the barrel against her head.

"You're a coward, Benjamin," Tess says. "What did you do when your father Faded? You ran away. And since he's been gone, you've been fumbling around trying to stay alive, and you've fucked over all the people you come into contact with. You've fucked your friends, the people who care the most about you. I'm surprised Claudia can stand you anymore."

I go to pull back the hammer, but it's already back.

Something cold and wild comes into Tess's eyes. "And you ran from Miranda. Go ahead. Shoot me for saying it. But she was sick and you locked her away and . . . well, did she die because of me or because of you?"

"No," I say, shaking my head. "No."

"No? Remove yourself from the equation, Benjamin." She's raising her voice, practically yelling. "Where would she be—right now—if you hadn't been there?"

"I saved her," I say. "Without me she would have died."

"Maybe the first time," she says. "But would she have been infected? Would she have been bombed? You want to shoot me because you think it will assuage your guilt, blame someone else. But it's you, Benjamin. It's always been you."

Tears blur my eyes. A buzzing fills my head. My body. Everywhere. And I'm willing my finger to move and end this when the voice cuts in.

No. Not like that.

Right. That would be too easy.

I step back and lower the gun.

The barest hint of a smile curls Tess's lips.

My finger tightens around the trigger, and I raise my hand and shoot Tess in the stomach.

She crumples to the ground, her liver-spotted hands going to the bloody ruin of her midsection, and her face twists in pain as it sets in.

"That probably won't kill you," I say. "At least not right away. And maybe your men will come get you. But even if they do, that wound is probably going to be infected. And that certainly will kill you. But slowly." I shrug. "Of course, you know that. You know everything."

As I'm coming back to myself, I realize the smoke that's already seeping into the room. A dull roar fills the air, somewhere beyond us. "Or," I say, "if I'm lucky, you'll lie here, until this whole building, all your work, all your treasure, burns down around you, and you slowly roast on the ashes."

Tess opens her mouth, as if to say something. But nothing comes out.

"Good-bye, Tess," I say. "I hope you suffer."

Then I run for the exit.

It's only as I'm running out that I remember Claudia. I look back inside, but everything is smoke and the bright orange glow of the fire.

Did she get out? I didn't even see her.

I stand there for a moment. Unmoving. I couldn't find her if I wanted to. Not in there.

Tess's words come back to me. *You're a coward, Benjamin.*

Then lights hit me, from the direction of the street, and I see the *Valkyrie* descending to pick me up.

She's alive.

I exhale loudly, then move my aching body toward the ladder leading to the *Valkyrie.*

Pain jolts through me with each rung I climb, starting in my back and radiating everywhere. But eventually I make it inside, falling into the cargo bay, gripping the edges, and hanging my head from the opening as we pull away.

Beneath me, orange flames are already licking at the edges of the roof and smoke pours out of several of the upper windows. The San Francisco Public Library, and all the assembled knowledge it contains, is dying. And I'm the one who killed it.

Tess's other words come back to me. And the words of others. *Look at all the wreckage you've created, Ben.*

I push the words away. Now is not the time for that. Now is the time for celebration. Because Tess is dead.

I remember once reading something that said, "revenge is best served cold." I didn't know it at the time, but that's Feral shit. It's not served—you need to take it. And it's nothing but hot. Revenge is a fire, and once it starts burning, it will continue to burn and consume until you're able to put it out.

And what's left when you do? Ashes?

Shut up, voice, I think. It's a celebration. And what's a celebration without something to drink? So I dig up my next bottle (there are only two left) and I tip it back. It tastes bitter as it crests my lips, but I gulp it down and wipe my mouth with the back of my hand.

I drink, and I drink, like there's a bottomless hole inside of me. I don't go to find Claudia. She doesn't come to find me. I just drink until I'm fit to bursting, until it's all ready to come out of me. And as my eyelids flicker, and the darkness beckons, I think, at least in this one moment, I am full.

CHAPTER NINE

FROM THE JOURNAL OF MIRANDA MEHRA

Dear Ben,

~~If you're reading this, I'm dead . . .~~

No.

Dear Ben,

~~The odds of you finding this are slim, but I wanted to write some words to you in the event . . .~~

Fuck, Miranda.

Ben—

I miss you. I know it hasn't been that long since I saw you last, but with everything that's been going on . . .

Fuck. Fact is, you'll probably never see this. That this entry will find you, that it will navigate this world, that it will speak to you . . . it's too improbable. But I need to believe that it will. I need to fill each word with you. With thoughts of you. With feelings.

There are things I need to say to you, things you need to know in the event that I die. I know that despite your best intentions, you would go to your death without saying the things that I would guess need saying. I won't let that happen.

So much has changed in the past weeks. Since reaching Tamoanchan. Since Enigma. And we never had that chance to sit down and talk things through.

If you're reading this, it's probably far too late. Too much has happened. Too many enemies are at the door and—

Damn it. Speak of the devil. I hear them now.

✳ ✳ ✳

That I have this journal at all is a miracle. Yeah . . . that's a word that I've never been comfortable with—never liked to use, never liked to hear—but when the odds are so slim that such a thing would be possible at all . . . well, it captures the idea.

But I do have it, and I'm able to write in it, and I've been, at least so far, able to hide it away in this room so no one will find it. So yes, Ben, I'm going to be writing to you. Because even if you never see this, because even if a stranger is reading this, it needs to be expressed, it needs to be let out into the world. The things here must be known.

So . . .

Dear Ben,

I fucking miss you.

If you're reading this, then the world is a better place than I think it is.

Fuck. I should probably start at the beginning: back on Tamoanchan. Back in that room, barricaded in, so fatigued and weak that I could barely stay awake, even as the bombs were dropping.

I remember the door opening, being battered open, and shapes rushing into the room.

You would have been proud of me. Even as worn out as I was, I reached for the gun next to me, and, taking a moment, only a millisecond, to make sure it wasn't you, I shot at them. I swear to ~~God~~ Science that I hit one of them. I remember one going down. Dead. But there were more of them. Too many for me to recover and reload and fire. Then I felt a sharp pain, and that was it. I don't remember much about that moment, but I remember thinking, "This is the end." I knew death was coming for me, and I felt rage. And frustration. I wasn't done yet. There was still so much more to do.

Then . . . I woke up.

If I'm being honest, my first feeling was disappointment. I don't know why. I'm ashamed to even admit it, but it's true.

I later figured out that they had used a trang gun, like the ones I used to use on Ferals. That was the sharp pain. It must have been quick acting, or else I was weak from Enigma. I also recognized that I was aboard an airship, from the feeling of its motion, that sense of being up in the air. I thought to myself—no bullshit—that Ben should be here. Because he loves the air so much.

But you weren't there.

I was so angry with you for a while. A long while. Angry that you weren't there to stop them. Angry that you had left me all alone. Weak and vulnerable.

I _know_ that you were trying to help. Trying to defend the island. Trying to . . . not think about yourself.

No, that's not fair.

You didn't think about yourself. You faced the attackers. You put your life on the line without being asked to. But . . . part of me wondered, maybe still wonders, if you didn't partially do it because you couldn't face the thing that was killing me: Enigma. Them . . . them, you could shoot at. People you could kill. A disease . . .

You couldn't defeat a disease.

But then again, neither could I.

And that's one of the most fucked up things about all of this. These people, the Cabal, who had infected me in such an insidious way, were able to reverse it like . . . well, like that. Even as they ushered me off of the airship, to wherever I am (I'm still trying to figure that out), they just stuck a syringe into me and pushed the plunger and then . . . voilà. I was cured.

It filled me with rage. Such fiery rage. Because these

people, who tormented us, who killed Sergei, who literally poisoned the well of our community, the home that we'd found, could have reversed it in an instant.

Knowing that made me wonder. If Maya, the saboteur in our midst, if she had offered me the cure, when Sergei was sick, is there anything I wouldn't have done to save him? I don't know. I really don't.

But she didn't. And Sergei died. And now I know that he didn't have to.

So, yes, there's all this hatred and rage and bile leaking out of me all the time.

But, hey—I'm not dying of Enigma anymore.

Don't get too excited about that. There's a lot more . . .

They took me off the ship (cured me) and tossed me into what amounted to a cell. I thought, as I lay there, that I had ended up like you. Tossed into a cell. Because that seems to happen to you all the time.

Damn it, Ben, I miss you. I don't know where you are. If you're even alive. I don't know if Diego and Rosie are alive, or Clay and all the others . . . Crazy Osaka, James, Coral, everyone. I don't know if the island survived.

(And that's part of the whole mindfuck, because I'm not completely convinced that I'm not on the island now, but—)

I can't help thinking that I've been ignoring the real enemy. It's not that Maenad isn't the ultimate goal. It's the mountain we <u>have to</u> climb, but—these evil fucking bastards are using it. They're working with it. They're mutating it and who knows what else. And they're muddying our path. So I can't help thinking, in retrospect, that we should have focused on them first. Because maybe if we could have stopped them, if we could have, to sound like you, <u>taken them out</u>, then the path to curing Maenad would have been so much clearer.

But we didn't. And this is the world we live in now.

I wonder what else I might have done better. I think about it all now. When I have time to think. When I'm not wondering what they're going to do to me.

There they are. I better put this away again.

✳   ✳   ✳

They didn't leave me in my cell for very long. They left me long enough to use the makeshift toilet, to think about what was happening, the choices I'd made, and then they sent for me.

I should probably explain who "they" are, especially if it's someone other than you, Ben, reading this. We called them the Cabal. It seems silly, in retrospect. That seems like far too benign a word for an organization of such evil; but all I can say is that we didn't know back then. Back then, they seemed like a curious faction within the Valhallans, one more concerned with knowledge and science than strength. But the truth, it's been so much worse. I and my people grew up with science; we cultivated knowledge, but for one ultimate purpose: to cure this world of the Maenad virus, "the Bug" in your parlance, the destroyer of civilization. We wanted to heal the world. To patch up the wound that kept it bleeding for so long.

(When I talk like that, it's my dad coming through—he was always a little melodramatic. I think I picked it up from his writings).

The Cabal (though they have another name I will get to in a minute), they studied and they accumulated knowledge and they honed their skills for one purpose, too—only that purpose is abhorrent. Instead of fixing the world, they want to use science, Maenad, their skills, for personal power. And fuck anyone who stands in their way. I mean, we've seen the lengths that they'll go to. Each one more sick and twisted than the last.

I was horrified when I saw that they were trying to engineer Maenad. Then you, Ben, told me about the mutated Ferals that you saw. Then we had Enigma. Evil after evil after evil.

The rest of the world, what's left of it, has paid the price.

Now it's the Cabal who has me. Every moment since I realized that, I've been expecting anything. Everything. After all, I stole their data. I defeated Enigma. I killed Hector.

So let me say that I was surprised, and more than a little confused, when they pulled me from my cell and dragged me to get washed. It was oddly welcome, because I needed to bathe so badly, and because after all that time alone, after being so sick, it woke me up.

They scrubbed me down, then gave me a clean set of clothes. I thought, this protocol makes sense, it minimizes the chance of infection or contamination.

When I was dressed, in a loose pair of pants belted with rope, and a large, flowing tunic, they brought me to her.

My skin still prickled from the wash, and my hair was still wet when I met Blaze. She walked into the room, all confidence, tall and thin, her black skin practically shining in the lights that lit the place. Her hair was up, and her hands were behind her back. I tried to size her up, of course. She seemed sure of herself, attractive, well-cared for, healthy. I don't believe for a second that you can see intelligence inside of someone, but it seemed to radiate from her. That was probably the confidence, but her eyes were as assessing as mine were.

She walked forward until she was about a meter in front of me, and then she stopped. She inclined her head ever so slightly to one side. No more than fifteen degrees. Then she said, simply, " I am Blaze. Welcome to the Helix."

The name brought up connections. "After the double-helical structure of DNA," I said.

She nodded. "And the structure, a stairway leading up. Onward."

"Why am I here?" I asked.

Blaze nodded, her hair bobbing behind her. "A fair question," she said. "Especially after you caused us so much trouble."

I remained silent.

She nodded again, ever so slightly. "You're here because you're valuable. As much of a thorn as you've proved, your knowledge of 2602 is impressive."

"'2602'?"

"What we call it. 'The Bug.' I believe you call it 'Maenad.' Colorful."

I narrowed my eyes. "You brought me here for my scientific knowledge?"

Her eyes fixed on mine. "You know we value that."

"What makes you think that I would allow you to benefit from what I know, what I've spent my whole life working on?"

She held her hands out, palms up to the sky. "Helping to further scientific knowledge is its own goal."

"Not if you use it for your own personal gain."

She cocked her head to one side. "Do you think what we're doing is for ourselves?" A tiny scoff or sigh erupted out of her. "We're doing this for the world."

"The world?" I asked, my contempt and surprise bubbling out of me. "How?"

"What do you value?" Blaze asked. "Intelligence. Safety. Caring. Structure." She marked each of these on her fingers, as if counting. She shook her head slowly. "We crave the same things. Those are the things that we want from the new world. Someone needs to wipe away the chaos of the old world and create the new. Create order. You have to build the house before you can live in it. Sometimes that requires clearing away old debris."

"And allying with the Valhallans? What part does that play?"

She moved forward. She's taller than me, and she loomed over me. "An alliance of convenience." She showed her teeth. "When the old world collapsed, the Valhallans moved to fill the vacuum. They created structure on the ashes of chaos. They built Valhalla, and then they took Gastown. Who better to work with? They have the sheer manpower to help accomplish many of our goals. They provide housing and protection and, most of all, time. And one day . . ."

I narrowed my eyes at that. "One day?"

She smiled again. There was nothing human behind that smile. "We can talk about that later. For now I want you to get used to the idea of being here. Working here. We will provide a place for you to stay, food, water to bathe, and, if you are good, recreation."

"I'm sorry," I said. "You still haven't reached the part where you give me [and I think I shrugged here] one good reason to want to help you."

Her face went hard. No emotion at all. Blank. A cipher. Then she held up a finger. "One reason, then. Because if you do not help us, we will kill Ben."

✸　　✸　　✸

It took me a while to stop from shaking after that. To stop from feeling this crushing sense of desperation. Now you can see why I don't have much faith in this reaching you. How would it even get to you?

But I wanted to write it all down. It needs to be known.

So, yes, they threatened you. How could I not work for them after that? I know you would tell me that I shouldn't, that you aren't worth it. At least, I think that's what you would say. I know you've spent a lot of your life trying to stay alive, and maybe you'd want to buy some time until we figured something out, but you know what, Ben? You're not here. It's not your decision. And I couldn't live with myself if I let you die. If I let them kill you. So, I'm trying to figure it out. I'll work with them long enough to find my break. Our break. It hasn't come yet.

Otherwise, it's a pretty rote life. I have my little room, which they call a dormitory and I call a cell. Every morning, they wake me up, I wash and dress, and I go with some others to a lab where I study Maenad, or a Maenad variant. At first, it was just a huge debrief, they wanted everything I knew, and everything I could give them. I tried to hold some things back, but it was hard. They had already retrieved some of our notes back when Maya was on the island (and more about her in a minute), and they knew the direction of our research. They had me reconstruct the screening protocol we put together to see if someone was infected. Every time I tried to leave something out or obfuscate, they would ask me questions, sometimes probing, other times innocent, but they would always ferret out the inconsistencies, always get to what I was hiding or trying to falsify.

It would be impressive if they weren't so hateful.

I don't see Blaze much these days. Not after she welcomed me to the fold. She visits the lab, and sometimes she checks on my progress, but most of the time she's off being the evil leader of the Helix, plotting her plans and planning her schemes. No, I have a different handler now.

Maya.

That I didn't claw the bitch's eyes out when I first saw her still remains a wonder to me. I guess I was thinking about you, and how they might not be so inclined to keep you alive if I bashed one of their people's heads open with a electrophoresis machine. I can't imagine what Rosie saw in her. She still wears those ridiculous hoop earrings, still looks like I could break her in half with my bare hands. Every time I see her insipid smile, I think back to Sergei and how she and Hector brought the Enigma virus to the island and how Sergei died as a result. I also think about what I did to Hector. What I would have done to Maya had she not escaped.

Hector. That's an interesting thing. What bothers me most when I think about him is this feeling of absence, because I don't feel guilty or bad about him dying. I don't feel remorse for killing him. I think I should feel bad, and I don't. What does that say about me?

At least I'm not alone here. This "dormitory" that I'm in is in a long row of them. I have someone on either side of me. At night, when we're left alone, we talk some. The man to my left is named Dimitri. He's older than me, though I've never seen him in person. He told me a little about his past. I think you'd like him, he's a little rough around the edges. He comes from out east, used to travel a lot. He said he bought passage on airships by offering medical help. He hasn't told me yet where he learned those skills, though I've asked. It seems like a tender spot for him.

The woman on my right side (when you're facing the door) is named Carmen. She's closer to my age, and we have a lot in common. She grew up in, well, she says it wasn't a commune, but it sure sounds like one. They didn't all study science, but they studied something. She studied biology, disease. They weren't really hoping for anything on the scale of a cure, just protection really. They started studying Maenad to chart how it worked, what it did, how it was transmitted, how they could avoid infection. They gathered more information than most. She decided, get this, to travel, to teach people about what she knew. That, of course, brought her to the attention of the Helix and they . . ."recruited" her for their efforts.

Which is one of the interesting things. The Helix is already full of smart, learned individuals, people who flocked to the cause, willingly. But that's not enough for whatever they have planned. They have to draft in others, people like me and Carmen and Dimitri. They need us. What we know. What we can do.

Do you know what the greatest thing about that is, Ben? The greatest thing about that is it means we're valuable. So hang in there. Stay as safe as you can. Because I intend to use that to my advantage.

CHAPTER TEN

I spend a lot of time in my cabin, sitting with my back against the wall, knees drawn up against my chest. Two empty jars of hooch roll slightly on the floor next to me. A third is open between my legs. I can't get my head to clear. There's all these . . . thoughts swirling around inside. Feelings, probably, too. But I don't want them. I can't bear them. So I reach for the jar and slug back some booze and try to kill all those moving things. Try to drown them. Scour myself from the inside out.

I haven't made much progress.

But if I drink enough, I'll pass out and then, at least, I'll get a break. You have to have backup plans, after all.

With one hand, I absently twirl the revolver on the ground beside me. It helps a little. Moving. Touching something. Only a little. But it takes me outside my head.

I can fuzz out the thoughts, most of the time. But the worst are the faces. They're harder to avoid, and they're instantly recognizable. My father, Miranda, Mal, others. All of the names Tess brought up back at the library. All of the people I failed.

The first to come, oddly enough, was Sergei. Odd because it was Miranda trying to find a cure for him. I wasn't the one who infected him; I wasn't the one who could save him.

But you were *the one who brought back the traitors. And it's because of you that they infected Miranda and Sergei.*

That voice keeps bubbling up, and I keep trying to push it down, but it's somehow more buoyant than it used to be. Louder. More insistent.

And it's right. I was the one who hatched the plan to save the boffins from the prison camp. Another trap set up by the Cabal, baited by Tess and the information she leaked to Miranda and me. I was the one who fell for it, who went to rescue the boffins and brought back people I didn't know, people who brought a new virus with them. A virus that infected Miranda, that killed Sergei.

And Miranda . . .

When I think about her, it's like everything goes white for a moment. My feelings are too vast to even comprehend. Crushing, like a gigantic wave. And they make me, my thoughts, my sense of myself, so incredibly small by comparison.

Miranda was infected, yes, by the same disease that killed Sergei, but that's not what killed her. What killed Miranda was a bomb that fell on the house that she had been living in. Yes, the bomb came from an attack by raiders. And yes, they found out the location of the island from any number of places (Tess being one of those), but . . .

Thinking about the raiders makes my blood boil. Thinking about Tess brings up rage, too, even though she's dead.

I see the burning library. I smell the burning books.

I spin the revolver next to me. The barrel rotates several times before pointing back at me.

I take another drink from the jar. A long pull. Place the jar on the floor.

What killed Miranda was that she was trapped in the house when the bombs fell. She was dying, so maybe she wouldn't have been able to get out anyway, but I'll never know. To protect her from whatever was attacking us, I barricaded her in. So that nothing could get to her from the ground. But I didn't even stop to think that it might come from the sky. Me. A man who spent almost all of his life up in the air. I didn't see it coming.

That's bad enough. But what's the worst in all of this, the thing that keeps me up at night, the thing that cracks me into so many tiny pieces, is that I left her. I left her alone. While she was sick, dying, and about to face god knows what, I left her. I could have stayed with her. I could have held her hand in the darkness. I could have been there to defend her from whatever might have found her. I could have been there next to her when the bombs fell, so that she wouldn't have had to die alone. I could have died with her.

I *should* have died with her.

The truth is that I dream about that. I wish it. I crave it. Because now I have to live with this pain inside of me. All the time. And the regret. The guilt. If anyone should have died that day, it should have been me. But the universe doesn't run on justice or fairness. That much is obvious.

I reach for the revolver again. My left hand on that, my right hand on the jar.

"Ben, what are you doing?" Claudia's voice breaks me out of my introspection. I look up at her, then follow her gaze back to me. The jar is still on the ground, my right hand curled around it. It's the revolver that is halfway to my lips.

"Nothing," I say, putting the pistol down on the floor. "Just drinking."

"I think we need to talk," she says.

"About what?"

"About you," she says, incredulous.

I look at her, my face blank. "I'm fine," I say. "Everything's fine."

"Like hell it is," she says.

"What do you want me to say, Claudia?"

"I don't know," she says. "We just finished what you spent the last six months planning—you got your revenge. I thought that warranted some kind of response."

I look at her blankly some more. Trying to get a sense of what she wants, trying to find meaning through the swirling and whirling thoughts. Then it dawns on me. "You want this all to be done, don't you?" I say. "You think Tess is dead and now . . . Ben can move on. Put this all behind us. Be the way it used to be."

She crosses her arms and glares at me. "I *think* that you are pathetic. I'm standing here looking at you and all I see is a wretched excuse for a human being. I see ballast that I should dump at the next stop because it's weighing me down."

She shakes her head. "And I keep thinking that it's a good thing that your father isn't here. Frankly, he'd be disgusted."

It stings. But it conjures up a memory. One of the early days, after Claudia had joined us. She and Dad had worked out a deal—she would help us find places to forage and he'd provide transport and shelter on the *Cherub*. On one of those first trips, we upset a Feral nest. We stood there, three of us, back to back, Dad and me firing our guns until they went dry, Claudia taking out Feral after Feral with her bow and arrows. The breathless excitement of being alive, with good barter no less, at the end.

Already the hero worship for Claudia had started, already the crush and the attraction. So when she gave me a pat on the shoulder, as if to say, "good job," it was a mix of delight at her appreciation but also embarrassment and shame at the fact that she clearly thought of me as a kid.

That night, Claudia and Dad stayed up, drinking a bottle of wine, while I lay on my mat nearby. I couldn't sleep, though, too keyed up with that potent mix of adrenaline, fatigue, attraction, and shame.

Through slitted eyes I watched them, drinking, their faces flushed. Happy. Equals. I remember Claudia saying, "He's a good kid, isn't he?"

My father, looking at me, took a sip of the wine from the bottle's neck and wiped his mouth with the back of his glove. "Yes," he said, nodding his head. "He is." He took another pull on the bottle. Wiped his mouth again. "I'm hard on him, I know. But I'm not always going to be around. And when I'm not . . ." Another pull. "I want him to be able to take care of himself."

"Ben!" Claudia snaps. "Are you even listening to me?"

Suddenly I'm angry. I'm not even sure at whom, but there's a fire building inside of me, and Claudia is in front of me and I spit that fire right out. "Shut up! Just . . . shut up." I clench my hands into fists. "You have no fucking idea. Things will never be the way they used to be, Claudia. The world is changed. I'm changed. Nothing can be . . ." I feel something heavy and dark surging up inside of me, something to make me want to curl up in a ball, so I stomp down on it hard, the way that Sarah stomped down on my back. "It's all fucked."

"So what? You just . . . carry on the way you have been? Tell me, Ben, do you drink yourself to death? Or do you throw yourself into another room full of armed men? Or maybe you've figured out some other way to end it all."

"Claudia—"

"It's pathetic."

I glare at her.

"Do you remember after your father Faded?" she asks. My mind sends me snippets of sensations—the harsh fumes of alcohol, a spinning sense of being unmoored, the feeling of too much space in the *Cherub*. "It was a lot like this, but you got through it."

I remember that, remember pushing her away. Running hungry. What really brought me out of that was Miranda.

"I thought that getting your revenge on Tess would give you back the fire that you lost. Yet here we are, and you seem even worse than before."

"We burned down a library," I say through gritted teeth.

"There's that word again. 'We.' I don't remember lighting any fires."

I just stare at her.

She shrugs. "Besides, that's the Ben Gold way, isn't it? Get what you want and god help anyone or anything around you?"

"Fuck you, Claudia." It lands hard, hits me right in the space that Tess had bloodied.

"No, fuck you. You think your life has no value? Fine. Mine does. You used to know that."

She's right. She's saved me so many times, at the library and many times before. I should be begging her forgiveness. Instead, I say, "Leave me alone, Claudia."

She nods, her eyes cold. "I will. Next place I put down, you can go."

"Go where?"

"I don't care. Any place other than here."

"You're kicking me off?"

She bends down and lowers her face to mine. "I won't be dragged into your death wish." She straightens up again. "You're on your own."

She stalks out, her head hanging low, the tension visible in her shoulders. That sensitive part inside can feel the anger and the frustration in her, and it tells me to get up and apologize. Explain.

Instead my hand finds the jar. For a moment, I'm seized with the urge to slam it against the wall, but thankfully my better instincts kick in just in time. That would be a waste of booze, so I swallow it down instead. It's the only way I see myself sleeping, after all.

I dream of Miranda. Alive. That first time we met. So real that I can feel the gnawing of the hunger in my belly, the hollow feeling, like skin stretched over a skeletal frame. Around me only ashes and dust, and no food. Just the crumbling buildings of Old Monterey.

Then the howls. The screams. Loud and insistent. A Feral hunting pack that sends me running back to the *Cherub*.

Then that collision. Like a bolt from the Blue. Such a slight thing, Miranda was, but when she slammed into me, I felt it jar my bones, and we both went down in a tangle of limbs and guns.

I feel it in the dream. Laid low.

She stands up and brushes herself off. She looks like she did then, barely covered, skin peeking through—her neck and the top of her face, her arms. In real life I was horrified by the lack of protection, but now I can't help but smile. I see the smattering of freckles on her face. I want to reach out and touch her.

"Well?" she asks. "Are you going to get me out of here or what?"

It's not what she said. But I lead her to the *Cherub*'s ladder and help her up.

I follow and we're both on board, in the cargo hold, where I first kissed her (though that was later, too). I reach for her hand. "I've missed you."

She smiles, and nods. "Me, too."

"I thought I'd found my place," I say. "Now it's all wrong."

"You don't have anyone to protect you," she says. "From yourself."

She steps in and raises up her head and kisses me. Her lips are warm and I press myself into her and wrap my arms around her. I pull her close. I am filled with such a feeling of warmth and home, here on the *Cherub* with Miranda.

"Stay with me," I say. "Let's fly away. Somewhere. Anywhere."

She nods. "I just have a few friends to bring with me."

I nod, too. Suddenly I'm at the controls of the *Cherub*. Miranda comes up behind me. I turn, smiling, then stop when I see who's with her. Three Ferals stand next to her. I shrink back. "Get them off my ship," I say.

"Ben," she says. She moves forward and grabs my hand. It's warm. And I clutch at it. But my eyes don't leave the Ferals. "They deserve to be saved." She reaches into her bag and pulls out a handful of dried meat, offers it to me. "What do you say?"

I want them gone, and the fear rises up in me, but there's also that feeling of hunger. I stare at the food.

With her other hand, Miranda pulls one of the Ferals closer. "Besides," she says. "It's his home, too."

I look at the man whose hand she's holding. See the gray hair. The serious expression. Recognize my father.

I wake up in a haze, my mouth dry, my head spinning. Names are caught up in the swirl—Sergei, Malik, Miranda. Their faces, filled with accusing looks. I try to shake them, but they dog me. Then they're joined by another. The one from my dream. A lean face, graying hair, a couple of days' worth of beard, dark brown eyes that seem almost black. Something wolflike in his look. Eli Gold. My father. *No.*

I sit up, run a hand through the sweaty tangle of my hair. The ghostly memories remain. My father, turning to me with a smile as we pick through the bones of an old mansion. He holds out a book. *The Maltese Falcon.* By Dashiell Hammett. I look back at him, and he's still smiling. "I think you're going to like this."

Another time, a few years later, another foraging trip. A whoop as he returns to the *Cherub* with his bag of haul. "You know what I have, Ben?"

"What?" I asked.

He pulls out a square base with a circular pad on it. I shake my head at him. "It's a music player. Records." He grins and pulls out a round, black disc. "My father used to have one." For a moment he's lost in his own memories. Then he snaps back to me. "C'mon. Let's go hook it up."

"You can get that thing to work?" I ask.

"Yes," he says, his smile disappearing, and an assessing look coming over his face. "And soon, you will, too." And he did. That night, as the *Cherub* flew over the Rockies, he pulled out one of the records he had taken from the house, that same boyish smile on his face as he placed it on the player. "David Bowie," he said. "One of my favorites."

Then some voice from another world sang about changes, and my father leaned back in his chair, head tilted back, resting on one arm, one leg hitched up on the seat. He floated in that song like a ship in flight, buoyant and free.

That perfect image is washed away by another one, the *Cherub* ripping apart into fiery debris above me. My father's ship. That same chair. That same record player. All those songs and moments.

My father's ship.

My ship.

That transition happened slowly. I'd take the controls of the *Cherub* more often. I'd be the one covering him when we went down to the ground. His hands would shake sometimes when he was trying to navigate through a storm. He'd have trouble getting through doors. His aim wasn't what it used to be.

Dad was getting old.

You don't see it often in the Sick. Old people. You have to be very skilled or very lucky. Tess, one of the oldest people I ever knew, was both. Sergei was about my father's age, had lasted that long in a world that constantly tries to kill you. In Sergei's case it was through a general hardiness and strength of character. With my dad, it was because he was good at getting us through another day. He wasn't overly smart or an exceptional shot or even a master forager, though he was good at all of those things, but he put it all together and figured out how to get us through.

Dad was a thinking man. I'd seen other foragers buy information off of people in zep hangouts. Dad never had to.

I remember exactly how it happened. We'd found a bookstore, on the second floor of a shopping center. Dad thought it was worth checking out. Also we'd been running low on reading material and I think Dad had reread the same August Wilson play three times already. Many of the books were trashed by the time we got there, swollen and blurred by water getting in, or just deteriorated over time. But we found a few shelves of decent material. I got caught up piecing through the fiction section. I picked up *Frankenstein* and a copy of *Hamlet*, which I had read before but which I felt like revisiting.

After tucking them both carefully away, I found Dad in the magazine section. He often liked to find magazines or newspapers, something local. He had a few rolled up and tucked into his coat. He was also carrying a copy of *Death of a Salesman*. "That all you taking?" I asked.

He nodded. "This place is mostly cleared out. Not much to choose from. But I have enough to keep me occupied for a few days at least."

When we were back in the air, I set a leisurely course and then flipped open *Frankenstein*. Dad pored over his magazines. He was still doing that when I fell asleep. The next morning, while I ate some mushy fruit and some tough, salted meat, Dad slapped down a magazine in front of me, the cover bent back. "There," he said. "Our destination."

I pulled the magazine toward me. The picture captivated me immediately. A large structure on the top of a hill. Rounded domes. Minarets. Like a fantasy castle. Something from another age, before the Clean. It was . . . magnificent. I'd seen some grand churches and synagogues, but this was another beast. I stared at it, captivated.

"Where?" I asked.

He raised his eyebrows, an expression on his face that meant it wouldn't be that easy. I scanned the page and saw the location. "Utah?" I looked at the picture again. "But it had to have been cleared out by now."

Dad tapped the magazine article with one gloved finger.

No choice, then, but to read the article. The place was a Hindu temple. I didn't know much about what that meant, just that it was a religion from the Clean.

I'm sure someone, somewhere still practices it now. Religion is one of those things that clung on after the Sick pissed down on everyone. If anything, the Bug made it stronger wherever it held on. I always thought that was weird as a kid—the world was so fucked up, why would you think there was a god or gods running the show—but I guess people sometimes need to feel like there's something bigger than themselves in hard times. Besides, I'm a hypocrite anyway, because while I don't believe in God, I still have a healthy respect for Judaism and the Torah, so I get it in a way.

I think.

But this temple, it was out in the middle of nowhere. Or not quite nowhere, but it was surrounded by farmland. A couple of houses. A couple of roads.

The temple had become a target in the community. Some people didn't like those who worshipped there because of the way they looked or the religion they practiced, or something like that. The temple had experienced break-ins. Theft. People defacing the walls. So the community, the Hindus, took up a collection and with some donations from near and far they were able to install a state-of-the-art security system—high-tech, very hard to crack. I knew that was what Dad had seen. What set this place apart. The average forager doesn't have the skills to crack the kind of security that place had. Your average forager can barely access Clean tech beyond maybe getting it powered up again.

But I had Mal. Smiling, cocky, proud Mal. So many times we anchored the *Cherub* at a trading post or a zep rest spot and I would see him there, surrounded by a crowd of foragers or pirates, telling stories of his travels. My father told me to ignore him, but I couldn't. Mal was around my age, he was colorful and confident, and I just couldn't look away.

The first time I met him, he was holding court, talking about the daring heist that he pulled off—how he broke into a secure medical storage and got out with a crate full of supplies through a mob of Ferals. I was standing nearby, looking at some barter, listening in. I thought it was the biggest load of shit I'd heard in a while.

Eventually, I couldn't hold back. He was talking about holding off the Ferals single-handedly when I rounded the corner and spoke up. "What kind of weapon were you using?"

He turned to me, surprised at the interruption, and there was a quick moment of him sizing me up. Then, never taking his eyes off of me, he pulled loose the gun at his hip, a large automatic. "This beauty," he said.

"What's that?" I asked. "Twelve rounds?"

"Fifteen." He turned to face me more squarely.

"Well, then," I said. "Even with the position you claim to have had, you wouldn't have been able to take out all of those Ferals before having to reload."

He looked annoyed for a second, and then a smile stretched across his face. Which irked me. "Ah," he said. "You're assuming each Feral took one bullet."

I nodded. That was if he was a great shot. Usually it took more than that when facing a pack.

His smile widened. "I like to use one bullet for each *two* Ferals."

I almost called bullshit right there, but something in his eyes, some twinkle, some dare, some fuck-you-to-the-world made me like him instead.

So we went on like that. He would challenge me on how I got my barter out of the last forage. I'd challenge him on his tales of daring heroism. Then he started testing me.

At first it started with shooting, after I'd challenged him on some of his stories, which always seemed to feature trick shots and almost-magical gunplay. "I swear—the bullet went through the left eye of the first pirate and then through the right eye of the second." Or, "I shot him right in the heart."

"While running," I'd say. "Over your shoulder."

And he would get this serious look and say, "Benjamin, why would I lie to you?"

So, on a few occasions, we had someone set up a target. Or targets. And we would shoot at them. It quickly became apparent that I was at least as good as him with a pistol (if not better), so his stories moved on to other things. Most often locks.

Even the dumbest forager can break a couple of windows or batter a door down, but most of that brute work has already been done (and sometimes by Ferals). Any forager worth their haul can pick a mechanical lock. It's not too hard, and the tools are easy to come by. But electronic locks are another thing entirely.

That was Mal's specialty. It was why we tapped him for the police warehouse job. So soon his stories were all about locks. I thought it was just more boasting—until the Idaho job. Dad and I clued into it, arrived to find the electronic locks still working. We cut the power, but the locks wouldn't disengage.

Mal flew in a few weeks later and made off with the whole haul.

"How'd you do it?" I asked, as Mal passed around quality booze to all of his associates. "We cut the power. We still couldn't get in."

He smiled, his cheeks already flushed from the alcohol. "There was a separate power supply for the locks," he said. "Long-term batteries, still working. You cut the main power, but that didn't go to the locks."

"Teach me," I said.

He waved his head from side to side. "Bring me something next time. Something good. And maybe I will."

So I did. I brought him my best barter for weeks afterward, skimping on food and sometimes ammunition, hiding the whole transaction from my father.

In return, Mal showed me what he knew about locks. Of course, Mal being Mal, he didn't just teach me. He'd test me. He would give me a quick lesson and then make me race him with a practice try.

He always won.

But those moments spent trying to beat him wired that knowledge into me. I was never going to be as good as him, but I learned things my father never knew.

The memory brings up feelings of shame. This hot, dark feeling, like ink boiling in my soul. Because after spending all of this time around Mal, I started having thoughts. Thoughts of going off on my own, or at least with Mal, of leaving my father.

At least with Mal I was practically an equal.

Dad loved me, I knew that, but he would never see me that way. It didn't matter that he was getting older and slower, or that I was a better pilot than him by then. He would never see me as anything other than his son. His little boy.

It drove me crazy.

So, yeah, I was fantasizing about going off with Mal. Running our own ship. Letting Dad do his own thing. I'd keep in touch. See him in between jobs or journeys. But I felt more alive when I was with Mal or on my own.

It was almost sacrilege. But the truth is I felt it so strongly that I had to fight it. Had to push it down. Stomp on it. When my father would call me to come take the controls of the *Cherub*, I had to force myself to stand up and walk out to do it.

So by the time my father learned about the Hindu temple, I already knew about electronic locks. When I looked up at him over the magazine, he said, "Grab what you can. We go tomorrow."

CHAPTER ELEVEN

The temple complex spread across the hilltop like a strange series of growths, only instead of unsightly it was ornate, a pale jewel among its rough surroundings. Grass covered the hill, and a road, now overgrown, curved down to a larger road that passed a couple of nearby farms and disappeared off into the distance.

There, like a marvel, its surface faded with dirt and weather, but no less spectacular, stood the temple. It had two levels, the lower surrounded by a series of arches and pillars. A large staircase led up the main entrance to the second level, which was crowned with pointed domes. Several of the spires had crumbled or fallen away, and one or two of the domes were collapsed, but it was otherwise intact. Part of the reason for that were the large metal shutters that covered the windows on both levels. They weren't fooling around when they installed security here.

I was surprised that it hadn't been bombed out. Foragers sometimes resorted to brute force when subtlety was beyond them. It jeopardized the score, of course, but sometimes a partly broken haul is better than nothing. Later, I would see scorch marks where smaller explosives had been used, but they hadn't made a crack.

I wondered at that. Zeps would see this kind of place for sure, if they were looking. But if Dad was right, the security might very well hold.

Thing is, Dad was often right.

We dropped the *Cherub* right down to the ground and lowered the ramp. The hill had enough space, and with all the buildings around, the shape of the ship might not stick out to anyone in the air. Ships with bigger crews would have probably dropped a few people down, sent someone else off with the ship, accessible but not a sitting duck. But it was just Dad and me.

The first thing we did was check to see if it still had juice. Most systems didn't survive the Sick, but in the case of the Hindu temple, the power was still on, as a result of tenacious solar cells that were still drinking up sunlight. The lights were on, and the lock held firm.

"It's still intact," I said to Dad, the excitement sending a tingle through my fingers. Power to the locks meant that they shouldn't have been opened before. The trick, of course, was getting them open ourselves.

"Can you do it?" I don't actually remember if Dad asked that, or if he just gave me that look.

"I think so."

"Then . . ." He waved his hand. "Do your magic." There was the hint of disgust to his words. Dad preferred mechanical locks.

I pulled out the device from my pocket, careful not to damage it. It was the result of one of Mal's trials. We would race, assembling them from old, antique camera circuits and other bits of machinery. A portable EMP.

I held it out, then looked at Dad. I gave him a little nod, then fired it off.

The lock disengaged with a clank. Dad was ready—he grabbed the handle and pushed it open.

I covered him. He had his revolver, and I had the pistol I was using at the time, a big black beast that was a little heavier than I liked to carry but had some crazy stopping power. We stood by the open door and waited, listening for any sounds. You'd think it was clear, seeing as the locks had held all this time, but Ferals had a way of finding holes and collapses and working their way into warm, sheltered environments. They used to be people, after all. And people aren't equipped well enough for the elements.

The inside of the place smelled sour, and dusty. A hint of mold threaded through the still air. Dad's boots kicked up a carpet of dust on the floor, disturbing the eerie silence.

"Shut the door," Dad said. I did so, and when the power kicked back on and the lock clicked, I jumped a little. I hated being locked in again, but we had both been through things like this before. If there was an alarm system, and it went off because of the door being open, that could set off sirens, and *that* could attract Ferals or opportunists or whatever bad things were around.

It also meant there was a locked door at my back. From the inside, the windows looked like normal windows, but large metal shutters enclosed them. Keeping intruders out, but also us in. So, yeah, we were trapped.

"Dad . . ." I said.

He held up a hand. Always cautious. He was listening. He'd drilled it into me often enough when I was younger. "You need to use your senses. All of them. Not just your eyes. Your ears—to hear for their scrabbling, or their yammering. Your nose—to smell their stench." Back then, I would complain about how I could do that with the goggles and the scarf and the hat. But now . . .

Dad cocked his head, as if he heard something. But his revolver remained down, his posture still relaxed. Then I heard it. A low hum. Dad pointed. I looked in that direction, my gloved hand resting on the butt of my pistol. I saw a dim but definite glow there. Some kind of power or status light.

"The juice is still working," I said. "Everywhere."

"It's a good sign," he said. I could practically hear what he was thinking. If this place still had power, and it was untouched, there could be useful tech here. Intact computers were valuable to the right people. Later, when I hooked up with Miranda, I saw exactly why. Yet again, this could be the score that we were looking for. Just maybe.

In hindsight, I realize we thought that a lot. I suppose that's part of what kept us going, the hope that we would find something that would set us up—if not for good, then for a long while. That we could stop scrounging and scavenging for food and supplies and that we could, maybe for the first time in our lives, relax.

We were naive.

I don't push the voice away this time.

We were fucking naive. Thinking that there was some score, some hidden way out, a door into another life. But there is no other life. There's just the Sick. Shitting on you all the time.

The upstairs area was wrecked. By time, by the elements, coated in dust and mold, the bright colors faded to a muted gray. Here and there hints of what once were peeked through—a vibrant red echo, a bright blue ghost—but the Sick had pissed on this, too.

The thing I remember most was the image, still visible beneath the dust and grime, of a man, or what I took for a man, with an elephant's head. He had four arms arrayed around him, and a fat belly, the kind I had never seen on anyone aside from the leader of a fringe cult. It was unclear what the many hands held. One seemed to clutch a weapon. Another, a flower. It was the strangest and most beguiling sight I'd seen in a while.

Later, when I was foraging through a library, I had identified the figure. Ganesha. A Hindu god. God of beginnings, and the Remover of Obstacles.

For years afterward I thought on that, after everything. Whose obstacle was removed after all?

There was nothing to be found on the ground level, nothing valuable at least. It looked like a meeting hall. Crumbling chairs and hanging pictures and a small stage or dais at one side. So trying to find the basement occupied our attention.

The basement level was even more sprawling than the ground floor. What looked like offices lined the walls, containing, as expected, computers. Dusty but intact. Dad looked at me as he hovered over one, and pressed the switch that would turn it on.

A moment passed as we both held our breath, and then the screen flickered to life.

"What does it say?" I asked as my dad peered at the screen (I had begun suspecting that his eyesight was worsening).

"It's asking for a password," he said.

I thought back to something that Tess had once told me. "Try password."

"What?"

"The word 'password.'"

He shook his head but did it. "Fuck me, that worked."

I smiled.

He smiled back at me, youthful in that moment. "It works," he said. Then he clapped me on the shoulder. "This will earn some nice barter."

"And there are more."

"Get the bag."

We set about carefully disconnecting the computers, making sure to retain all of the cords and attached pieces. The plugs wouldn't work outside of this place, of course, but enterprising tinkers or boffins could hook them up to solar cells or batteries, or both, and get them running again. There was a tinker back on Gastown, before the Valhallans took it, who could wire and rewire computers any way you could want them. I never did—they didn't do much for me—but I know he did a brisk business.

I wrapped each piece in a bit of fabric to help protect them and carefully placed them in the bag until it was full. "We might need something else," I said.

"We'll look." His voice was exuberant, and he moved with more energy than I'd seen in a while.

We kept on going throughout the basement, rifling through the offices, removing any electronics that we could find, stacking things in old worn boxes, even in drawers that we removed to use as carrying devices. We amassed quite a stack of things, though we hadn't even begun to figure out how to get it all out. Carrying everything up one by one seemed to be the only option available to us, but if I knew Dad, he would try to come up with something better.

At the end of the floor, we saw a door, and behind that, another stairway leading down. There was even more to this place. I knew what I was thinking— that if these were the offices, where the people who ran the temple worked, then beneath would be the storage. The gear and maybe even the food and water. Like Tess's stash in the library. That's where it would have the most protection.

So Dad reached out to the door handle and opened it.

The Feral behind it barely gave him time to react.

It must have been waiting just at the top of the stairs, attracted by our noise, the footsteps above it. Was it just coincidence that it was right there when Dad opened the door? Or was it smart enough to know he was approaching? I'll never know. But that Feral sprang out of the door like it was fired.

It took Dad completely by surprise. It slammed into him, and he fell to the ground, with the Feral landing hard on top of him.

I had my pistol out in an instant. The moment I saw that thing, I reached for the gun and pulled it free of the holster.

Then I hesitated for a moment before I took the shot. It was only a moment, and it was what any good shooter would have done in the same instant. Make sure I wasn't going to hit my father by accident. Make sure I aimed the shot so as not to splatter Dad with a spray of blood. It was the smart thing to do. And yet . . .

I've spent a lot of time since then wondering if that was when it happened. If just a drop or two of that Feral's saliva fell onto my father, a tiny drop catching him in the eye or on his lips, which he later licked. Or maybe he just inhaled it. It would have only taken that moment.

Then the moment passed, and my finger closed on the trigger and two quick shots rang out from my pistol. That moment of assessment had worked, at least with regard to my aim. The two shots caught the Feral in the side, up near his back, sending him spinning off of Dad, the wounds not likely to cause too much spray, and in the other direction.

As my senses started to return in the wake of the adrenaline spike, I heard whooping, chattering—more Ferals, coming from below. I made a quick decision. I ran for my father, grabbed his arm, and hauled him to his feet, and half pushed, half pulled him toward the way out.

I was vaguely aware of him protesting, shouting at me, but I just shook my head. "There's no time!" I screamed. "More are coming! We have to get out of here."

He must have still been shaken from the attack, and having been through something similar, I can imagine what he felt like. Legs like limp rubber. A kind of sharp yet hollow feeling inside. A pressure inside the head. So he let me guide him out. I don't know, maybe he really wanted to get away in that moment and knew that's what I was trying to do. But I got him up to the ground floor and then to the door.

The locked door, I realized, as we barreled toward it. I threw Dad ahead of me, almost slamming him into the door as I fished in my pocket for the portable EMP.

I heard Dad yelling at me again.

"Ben!" It finally penetrated my panic. "It's open!"

Because of course it locked people out. Not in. Dad had his revolver out. I realized I was still holding my pistol. I nodded, taking up a covering position as he yanked open the door. I checked his exit path, then whirled around to cover his back when I saw the outside was clear.

Then it was a mad sprint back to the *Cherub*, and up into the Blue.

✳   ✳   ✳

"What the fucking hell were you thinking?" Dad yelled, his face puffy and red from anger, or maybe from the excitement of our exit, or both. His hands gripped his hips, something he did only when he was good and furious.

"I was trying to get you out. Get us both out. Who knows how many Ferals were down there?" I was trying to be reasonable, but I was still buzzing, too, from the adrenaline. I had just gotten him out. Alive. And I could feel the anger there, simmering down below. Starting to surge upward.

"We could have barricaded the door," he yelled. The tendons in his neck stood out like steel cables.

"That Feral was already through. It knocked you down, for fuck's sake."

"It was the only one out of the door, Ben. You should have moved to the door after you shot it. Shut that door. Put a desk or a bookcase against it."

I closed my eyes for a second and willed the heat to stop flooding through me. I passed a hand through the tangle of my hair. "There could have been another one just behind."

His eyes narrowed, then, and he got that mean look that he sometimes got. It seemed to be more frequent in those days. "There *could* have been anything. There *was* a huge haul down there. There *was* a shitload of good barter. And you know where it is now?"

I couldn't bring myself to say "still there."

"Exactly where *you* left it," he said.

I shook my head. "You raised me to be safe. Not to take unnecessary risks."

A bitter smile crossed his face. "Sometimes the risks are worth it." He threw his hands up in the air. "Do you just want to continue the way we have? Getting by on scraps and the occasional mediocre find? That haul was worth it."

I gritted my teeth and looked at the floor.

"Dammit, Ben, you could have at least closed the door. Now the place might be crawling with Ferals."

"We got out."

He nodded and the bitter smile returned. "We did. But now we're going to have to go back."

"What?"

He nodded again. "That's right. We'll wait a little while. Let them figure out that there's nothing there for them to eat, and then we go back in and grab the bags and boxes."

"The place could be swarming with them."

He met my eyes, his expression cold. "We're going back. We'll just have to make sure we're armed and ready in case there are other Ferals."

"I don't think that's a good idea," I said, my voice low and dark.

"I don't care what you think, Ben. We're going."

And that was that.

I went back to my room on the *Cherub*. I told myself that maybe after a couple of hours he would cool down and reconsider. It wasn't that I didn't feel the pull of that haul down there. It wasn't that I didn't see how it could set us up for a long while. I remember being hungry at the time and cognizant of our rapidly dwindling food stores. But something about that place, and the Ferals there, spooked me. We'd been in places before where things got crazy, where everything fell to shit, but usually it was a surprise, and usually we ran like hell. This time, we were going back into the shit.

I didn't get it at the time, or for a long time afterward. But I think now, being older, possibly wiser, but certainly wearier, I get it. Dad was getting old. He was definitely feeling his age. Those scraps he mentioned—we'd both been living like that for a while. But of course it had been a lot longer for him. He had always been hoping for his score. For the find that would set him up for a good long time. Looking for a rest. He'd spent his life trying to stay alive, then trying to keep my mother alive, then me. I didn't really understand that until Miranda. Until I had someone else I was worried about, someone I needed to protect. So it was the need to feel safe, for him and me, but also the thought of not having to hustle. Not having to run away or go down to the ground to pick at the carcass. Finally being able to fucking relax.

I get it now.

He'd found his score. Maybe not the one of his dreams. It was a little more practical. And it would require a little more work finding the right barterers, but this was the closest he was probably going to get. I think he was thinking of his time, which I'm sure felt like it was pissing away. Where's the fun in enjoying a rest if you're old and falling to shit? No, I see it now—his way out of the life.

So, in retrospect, I'm not surprised, though I was at the time, that he came to me two days later. "We go now," he said. He tossed me a spare automatic pistol and a box of ammunition. "Make sure you're fully loaded." I noted the second pistol in his own belt.

I thought about fighting him. I still had that terrible feeling. But there was something in his eyes, something in the way he stood, that frightened me. Like an obsession. This score was all that mattered in that moment.

So I loaded both pistols, made sure they were working, and together we went back down to the ground.

We did it the same way we had done it last time. Kept the *Cherub* close. Kept each other covered. Crossed the ground to the temple as quickly as possible. The portable EMP still had some juice in it, so we used it again and opened the door. This time inside was more nerve-racking. I pulled the door open and Dad swiveled around with the revolver out. He wore another gun strapped to his leg, within reach of his off hand. We were both wrapped to the gills, too. I mean, we usually were, but we'd taken extra time to minimize the visible skin. I had my goggles on. Dad wore the swimming mask that he liked, with all of its careful modifications so he could breathe well, so it wouldn't fog up. Scarves wrapped around our faces. Knit caps covered the tops of our heads. We had shirts and jackets. Pants tucked down tightly into boots. Form-fitting gloves on our hands. We weren't taking any chances this time. It's ironic.

We moved again through the main hall. Again I saw the picture of Ganesha. One of his hands was empty, held out, palm forward. It almost seemed to be saying stop.

But there was no stopping Dad. He moved confidently toward the end of the hall, toward where we found the stairs, and then . . . he paused.

"What's the matter?" I asked, my gun up. It's difficult, talking with the scarves and the masks and the ear covers. You almost have to yell to be heard, but then of course anyone or anything around can also hear you.

"Dad?"

He shook his head for a moment. Like a dog might.

"Dad?"

Still facing away from me, he pushed the swimming mask up over his forehead and pulled the scarf down. I heard a cough.

I moved forward. "What's wrong?"

He coughed again as he turned toward me. He finally faced me, skin pale, perspiration all over his face. Sweat freckled his upper lip, and dripped down over his eyes. He shook his head slightly. "I don't know," he said. "I feel . . . sick . . . all of a sudden."

He wiped his face with the back of his sleeve.

Then he doubled over, dropping to the floor, bent. The revolver spilled from his hand and thumped on the ground. I bent down to him, picked up the revolver, tucking it into my belt for the moment, and helped pull him back to his feet.

"Are you going to throw up?" I thought back to what we had eaten over the last day or two. Not much, that's for sure. It was easily possible that our meager stores had turned and gone bad. "We need to pull out," I said. "You can't do this in your condition."

"I can," he said, forcing himself straight. "I don't . . ." His face twisted. In confusion.

"Dad?"

"Need," he said.

"Need what? Dad, let me get you out of here."

He looked up at me, utterly confused now, and I was suddenly very scared. More than I was for all of the run-ins with Ferals, more than for all the times we ran out of food, more than for every time we almost lost the *Cherub*. I was more scared than I'd ever been in my life.

I moved forward to grab his arm. If I could get him out and back up to the *Cherub*, back up to the air, everything would be okay, I thought. He could rest. I could get him medicine. Water. Hell, a doc to patch him up if it got that bad. But back up in the air, on the ship I'd have strength I didn't have right there.

I was reaching for his arm, looking in his eyes, and I swear I saw it happen. One moment, I saw my father there, his eyes large and haunted and full of fear. His posture weak and suffering.

The next moment, he Faded.

He convulsed, then shook his head again. He blinked his eyes, and when they opened, my father was gone. In his place was something else wearing his body. This thing had hunger in its eyes. Anger. Violent need. And his posture changed. Went rigid. The shoulders raised, the fingers curled. His lips skinned back from his teeth.

Eli Gold was gone. All that he was, all that he ever was, vanished in an instant.

My hand was still reaching out, and I wanted to grab him. I wanted to take him, whatever was left of him. I wanted to reach inside and stop him from leaving, stop him from drowning in the Bug. I wanted to save him the way he had always saved me. I wanted to pull him out of danger and wrap him in my arms and tell him it was all going to be okay, the way he had always done with me. I wanted to take him up into the air and away from everything terrible and scary and violent.

But I couldn't.

So instead my fingers curled around the chain that he wore. The one holding the Star of David. My gloved hand gripped a coil of the chain. And I pulled. It came away as I, even then, was turning and running for the door.

I didn't look back. I couldn't look back. I fixed my eyes on the door and thought about running through it. What was behind me was too terrible, too terrifying to contemplate. So I locked onto that exit and I ran, and then I was through.

I didn't stop running. I ran as fast as I could. All the way to the *Cherub*. And the moment I was aboard, I slammed the door shut and ran to the controls. I took her up and as fast and as far away as I could.

CHAPTER TWELVE

FROM THE JOURNAL OF MIRANDA MEHRA

Dear Ben,

They won't let me see you. Like I told you before, I know I have value here, so I tried to use it, by making a deal. I said that it would help me be relaxed and happy if they would let me see you, so they could assure me that you were alive and well and taken care of. I told this to Maya, the smirk only half hidden on her face. She said no. Just that. No. But that maybe if I was good, if they could start to trust me, maybe then they would let me see you.

Fucking cunt.

You know me, never one to take the first no as an answer; but I need to bide my time. Figure out what I can do. The Helix isn't going to give me information, so I asked Carmen and Dimitri if the Helix had leverage on them. Dimitri told me he had just been press-ganged, meaning forcibly pressed into service. They didn't have any of his loved ones. They just had guards.

There are lots of guards. This place is mostly Helix, but there are plenty of Valhallans here. We knew the two groups were allied, but I'm still unsure of the relationship. I've been watching them when I can, and they're more like contracted help. That is, the Valhallans don't seem at all interested in anything that the Helix is doing; and, if anything, they seem bored most of the time. Unless they get to threaten someone, or, worse, beat them.

There was a man, and I can't believe it but I forget his

name at the moment. We never talked, hardly ever interacted. I think I had my midday meal near him once and another time he dropped off a stack of papers at my desk, but other than that, nothing. But one day, he stands up from his station, and he says he's not doing anything. Not until they let him see his sister. Maya was there, and she didn't even say anything, just gave a look to her Valhallan thugs, and they moved in. They didn't even take him out of the room. One of the guards grabbed his arm and twisted it, forcing this guy to his knees. Then . . . well, they began to systematically and thoroughly beat him into what I guess was a coma. That arm they grabbed broke early on. His face was bloody pulp by the end. I'm sure he had broken ribs, multiple contusions, internal bleeding. And we all had to watch. And listen. It was a lesson, of course, of what happens when you get out of line.

In that moment, I had to revise my opinion of my own value a little.

Which brings me back to Carmen. So this man I just mentioned, he had a sister. I have you. Carmen has, of all things, a daughter. It surprised me when she told me, not because it's unheard of for someone like us to have a child, but, well, I don't know many. Not after my parents' generation. She said that she met a man, Matthew was his name, and while she studied biology, he studied technology and computers, and he would often help her out with her studies. He helped set her up with her own computer, and he was such a wizard with the stuff that she just fell in love with him. Madly. The way she tells it, she didn't really have much choice in the matter. They were both clean, uninfected, and both knew it, so . . . soon after, she was pregnant. She delivered safely, of course, with the help of the people in her not-commune, and she had a baby.

I asked her how she dealt with her daughter when she was out teaching people. Traveling across the country. " I took her with me," she said. " She's like . . . she's like a part of me. Her own self, of course. But a part of me. How could I not take her with me?"

" And you managed to keep her safe?"

There was a pause. "Yes," she said, afterward. " I've been lucky like that."

I chewed on all of this, my mind processing what she told me, and I asked a question that I maybe shouldn't have. I've never been good at that—not asking things—so I asked her. " And what happened with Matthew?"

She was silent for a while after that, and I wondered if maybe she had fallen asleep. It sometimes happens in the middle of conversation. They work us hard, and sleep is valuable. But after a while, she said, " I wasn't as lucky with him," and left it at that.

" So they have your daughter?" I asked. "Do they let you see her?"

" No," she said. I could hear the tears in her voice, even through the wall." But they sometimes send me notes. Or pictures. Not often enough."—she was almost sobbing now—" But I know she's alive." She cried some, after that. Then said, " I just wonder who's taking care of her. What they're teaching her. It drives me crazy."

To tell the truth, it drives me crazy, too. So I not only feel a renewed interest in getting to see you, but I want to help Carmen see her daughter. And I want to shut these bastards down so much.

So much.

Beck. That's what that man's name was, the one who got beaten by the Valhallans. As in " beck and call."

I wonder if he's still alive.

✳   ✳   ✳

I'm so sorry, Ben. I'm sorry. I don't—

You have to let me explain.

I pressed the issue with Maya. I had to. After hearing Carmen's story, I needed a note from you, something. Anything. I don't know that I've ever seen you write something, but just to hold something that you had written on would have been something. Some connection.

They refused the first time, telling me I didn't get to make demands. The second time, Maya set her jaw, then walked out. I didn't see her for the rest of the day. I even felt a little satisfied that I got her out of the lab for the day.

So stupid.

When I saw her the next day, she held out her hand. In it was a bundle of cloth. "Here," she said. "Take it."

I hesitated for a moment, unsure at first, but then of course I grabbed it. I unwrapped it, and it was one of your shirts. I recognized it immediately. The one with the red checks, faded now, into a kind of gray-pink. The one with the pocket flap that had come loose, which, I never told you, I sometimes had to force myself to stop staring at. For some reason it always distracted me.

Only this time the shirt was redder than I remembered. Stains, still wet. I dropped it when I recognized it as blood. I looked at Maya in horror. "What the fuck?" I asked.

She smiled at me. "Push me again, and next time I'll bring you a finger."

It was only because she said that that I didn't leap at her and break her neck. I know I could have done it. But I didn't know what they would do to you. Or maybe I knew exactly.

When they took me back to my cell, I wished that I had examined the shirt more, evaluated the volume of blood on it. Because I couldn't tell if they just gave you a bloody nose, or if they . . . if they did something else.

Now it's all I can think about. What they did. How you are. Are you still in pain? Did they at least stop the bleeding? I can't stop thinking about it. And the fact that I can't help.

I'm so sorry, Ben. Truly I am. I never thought . . . and that's just it. I never thought. I thought I had some leverage here, that they needed me, but they're the ones with the leverage.

They're the ones with <u>you</u>.

I hope . . . I hope you can forgive me.

✳   ✳   ✳

It's been days and I still can't shake this sense of panic. This sense that I'm mired in something inescapable and the monsters are at the door. There's so much I don't know. Which they use to great advantage.

I don't even know where I am. I never see outside the building, just the lab and my cell and the hallway between them. I don't know if I'm still on Tamoanchan or Gastown or halfway across the country.

I keep thinking about your shirt. The one with the blood on it, and the red checks. You left it in the house with me. It was maybe a day or two before the attack. You came to check on me and brought me some broth, because that was all I could get down at the time. I never really thanked you. It was so nice of you to sit down on the bed next to me, ready to feed me. Then I had a twinge of pain and jostled you and it spilled all over your shirt. Hot broth.

So you took off the red-check shirt and grabbed another one, one Diego had lent you, which was, of course, way too big on you but at least meant you didn't have to walk around shirtless, which I imagine would bother you more than almost anything.

That red-check shirt hung from the corner of my bed for

days. I think it was still there when they took me. It doesn't mean anything. But it's given me all these dark thoughts. If you were wearing it when they took you, or if they somehow got it from the house, then . . . they must have won. They must have taken the island.

I suppose I should be glad that you weren't killed. In the attack. But then I start thinking about everyone else. All my people. The labs. Rosie and Diego. What happened to all of them? How many people _were_ killed?

I think I had somehow convinced myself that everyone was okay. That they stole me away and then you'd won. But I have to come to terms with the fact that it's more likely that they took the island, using their Valhallan allies. And that a lot of people I know are probably prisoners. Or dead.

But you _are_ a prisoner. And while my compliance is keeping you alive, it's also keeping you a prisoner. Who knows how they're treating you. They won't say. So do I go along, hope for the best? Or do I try to resist in hopes that I can get free and get you free? Get you safe. Can I even talk about it here? Because if they find this before I'm ready, then they'll know. So just know that I'm thinking and I'm worried about you and, no matter what happens, I will do my best to find you.

✳   ✳   ✳

It's all my fault. Oh god, it's all my fault.

~~I was~~

~~I wanted to~~

I needed to try something. I had to. But I didn't know what that was. Then, I just . . . I had enough. Enough of feeling like I was in an experiment. An animal, caged, with a carefully designed maze. So I decided to leave, to try to find my way out of the lab and to figure out where I was and if there was a way out.

I'm not even sure that they have Ben at this point. They won't let me see him. You. But are they manipulating me? Or do they not have you? Oh, god, I don't even know who I'm writing this to anymore.

But I knew just running for it wouldn't work. One of the Valhallans would grab me and I would become another example. Beaten. Maybe raped. So, I needed a plan. For weeks I've been watching those around me and charting the movements of the lab. Recording them in my notebook in a cipher. It's run by scientists, so they keep everything on a schedule. Every morning they come to get us at a certain time, escort us to the lab, break for midday meal at the same time every day, then back to the second work session. Then, after the lab, either to wash or to exercise, then back to the dorm. I don't have any way to tell time, but it's like clockwork. I knew when the shifts changed. I knew when we had breaks. I knew when our guards and our Helix watchers would be distracted.

I sabotaged one of the machines, a trick I learned for, of all things, a prank back on Tamoanchan. On Crazy Osaka. I did the same thing here, I rigged one of the machines so that it would spark and catch fire. It took some doing. It actually took me days. A few minutes here while no one was looking. Another couple there. And so on. But eventually I had it set, and when the time came, I set it off and the box caught fire and there was . . . chaos. Delightful chaos. In that one moment, I felt like I had power again.

Using a path I chose because it had the most cover, I slipped out the door, staying low, moving as quickly as I could. There weren't any guards outside. The passageway on one end led to the dorms, so I ran in the opposite direction. The way they dressed us, in normal clothes, worked in my favor. Because as soon as I got some distance, I started walking normally, like I belonged there, and I headed for where I guessed the exit was.

I passed a couple of Valhallans on their way in, and I almost ran. But their eyes flicked over to me, and then back again, as if bored. They passed me, and I saw the door they had come through, and I moved as quickly as I could (without looking suspicious) toward it. And out into daylight. Glorious daylight. It was the first time I had seen the sky and the sun in weeks. I inhaled the fresh air, and it was cold and burned my nostrils. Something about the smell was all off. I wasn't on Tamoanchan, I knew that. Something about it reminded me of Gastown.

It was one of the more obvious options. That I was on the floating city. I knew that the airships are all lashed to the edges of the city, so taking a moment to orient myself, I ran, hoping to get to the edge as quickly as possible.

I saw flashes of Valhallans, which didn't really shock me much, since they had taken over Gastown, hadn't they? But I wasn't looking clearly. Something about the balloons above our heads was different. Something about the sky was different. The buildings. And I remember thinking to myself, have I really been gone that long?

Then, heedless of whether anyone was watching me or chasing me, just needing to get away, I neared the edge. Only there weren't any airships here. Just a simple rope band to protect people from falling over, anchored by posts. The planks swayed beneath my feet. I moved closer to the edge, and could see, down below me, buildings. A city.

I realized in that moment that I wasn't on Gastown.

I was on Valhalla.

I fell to my knees. There was no escape here. I heard footsteps behind me and turned to see Maya bearing down on me, flanked by four Valhallan guards.

"So now you know," she said. "There's no way out."

I don't know if I nodded or not, but I felt tears. I tried to hold them back—I didn't want to give them the satisfaction—but something leaked out. I searched myself for some kind of defiance and didn't find it.

For a moment, just one moment, I thought about jumping. It was at least some kind of escape. But that wouldn't help you. They grabbed me and dragged me back to the building I had escaped from. I struggled for a moment, but then a fist closed on my throat and they marched me back like that. I tried to take in a little of the city around me, even through my teary eyes. The structures were all similar, far more so than Gastown, and mostly better built, with better materials. The lab building, where we were headed, was impressive. Several floors, with windows in places, though of course nowhere that I had seen from the inside.

We didn't stop until we reached my cell, and they literally dropped me on the floor, like a sack of old junk. I didn't even look up at Maya.

"You want to know what that stunt cost you?" she asked.

"You going to torture me now?" I asked.

"No," she said. "That would be too easy."

"What then?"

"Wrong question." The barest hint of a smile touched her lips. "Not what. _Who_?"

Before I could even get to my feet, she left, the door closing heavily behind her. I wondered what she meant, who she meant, but it became obvious a moment later. I heard Carmen in the next room, heard her astonished cry, then her screams. Desperate and scared. I yelled at them to stop, and Dimitri joined me, but Carmen's screams continued. I heard the pain in them. It got to the point where I tried not to hear them, where I took my fists from the wall and jammed them over my ears, but the screams went on and on, louder, more desperate, shrieks of absolute pain.

Then Carmen stopped. Abruptly. For a moment all I could hear was the heaviness of my breathing, then the door to my cell opened and Maya stood there, blood on her hands, a scalpel held in her right one, the Valhallans flanking her. "Every time you step out of line," she said. "We'll kill someone. Probably someone you know. Almost always someone who won't deserve it. But it will be because of you. Remember that." She flicked the scalpel at me and the blood on the end splattered me, my face and chest. I flinched, out of habit, even while knowing that it wouldn't be infected, that she would never risk such a thing.

Maya smiled. Then she reached forward and grabbed my arm, dragging me out of my cell and into Carmen's.

Carmen lay on the floor, cuts all over her body. I was grateful for all the blood, for hiding some of it from me. On arm lay splayed out beside her, the hand curled into a claw, as if she were clutching at the ground for some kind of respite. But none came.

I felt empty. Drained of everything, of all my fire.

Maya grabbed the back of my head and forced me down. "Get a good look," she said. "Remember this." Carmen must have been beautiful. Once. But now she was just carved meat. The image is still frozen in my mind.

After Maya threw me back in my cell, I cried for a while. Cried for Carmen and cried for her daughter, a girl who would never see her mother again, a girl who might very well be absorbed into the Helix.

I didn't talk to Dimitri. What would I say?

Eventually I lay limp and awake on my sleeping pad, hollow. I am alone. I am a prisoner. They have me right where they want me.

And there is no escape.

CHAPTER THIRTEEN

I wake up and test my resolve. Is this really what I'm going to do? But I know that it is. Now that the thought has settled into place, I feel a kind of calmness. Like I've somehow come to rest and however strong the storm around me is, I can weather it.

I went through a stretch a while back in which I discovered books, novels, about time travel. I fell instantly in love. I read as many as I could get my hands on. It wasn't easy to find them—it's not like they were labeled—but I found books about books and then made a list and hunted them down. *The Time Machine. To Say Nothing of the Dog. Slaughterhouse-Five. The Anubis Gates.* Books like that. I could live in that mental space for hours and hours every day.

The obvious fantasy was going back to that moment when the Bug was released and stopping it. There are so many myths about how it happened. That it was an accident, an experiment gone horribly wrong. That it was a crazy mutation of some African virus. That it was a deliberate attack by terrorists from the East. Or by, well, insert whatever group you hate. No one I ever met knew for sure. What most people said was that they weren't equipped for it, that years of weak government and ignorance meant that when the Bug appeared, they couldn't stop it. It spread all over the world in a matter of weeks.

But whatever its origin was, I fantasized about traveling back to that moment, when the vial was dropped or the gas was released or that first patient sneezed, and I imagined stopping it. I imagined taking one act and forever changing the future.

It was only later that I realized that doing that would wipe me from existence. Without the Bug, without the Sick, my father and mother would never have met. That kept me up some nights, wondering if I would still do it. I've spent all of my life trying to stay alive. Would I throw my life away, even for such a huge thing?

In the end, I decided yes. Because of my father. Because of my mother. Because they would live lives free of the hardships that the Sick brought. They wouldn't have to spend their lives in fear of touching someone. Or breathing without a scarf wrapped around their faces. So that they could live in a world where they didn't have to worry about where their next meal would come from.

It was moot, of course. Time travel doesn't exist. I would say our current state of being confirms that. But that one moment was the biggest wrong in the history of our world. What Miranda was trying to do was to fix it. To mend that wrong. Years later, yes. And it wouldn't reverse everything. But it would fix that wrong, and that was (it took me too long to realize) a worthy and just goal.

The same applies to me, and my life. There are many, many (so many) wrongs written on that page, but one has stuck out above all others for years now. One is the King of Wrongs, that one bit of ballast I've never been able to drop.

Maybe, even years later, addressing that wrong is worth something.

Maybe it's worth everything.

So when I wake up, I don't reach for a bottle. I instead go to our water barrels, and the sponge and soap that have been strangers to me for at least several days (and probably longer), and I wash myself. I trim my beard. I dress in the cleanest clothes I can find. I pull on my boots. I strap on my holster. I shrug on my coat. I visit Claudia's stores of parts and gear and pull out a few choice electronic pieces. Only when this is all done do I make my way to front of the *Valkyrie* where Claudia is sitting. She likes to fly in a loose style. I slump a bit, but I'm usually straight in the chair. It's how my father taught me. Claudia will often lean to one side. Sometimes she'll throw one leg over the side of the chair. She seems to fly entirely by feel.

She looks up at me, then back at the windows in the gondola. Then back to me. "What's the occasion?"

"I need you to take me somewhere."

She sighs. A sound of utter frustration. I wish I didn't understand why. But I do. "What now, Ben?"

I inhale. Hold it a second. Then let it out. "It's important."

She turns to me and gives me a bitter smile. "Isn't it always? Isn't it a matter of life and death? Or a matter of personal honor? Or some wrong that needs righting?" Her face goes hard. "Or are you already out of booze?"

I close my eyes. "It's important now."

"Of course it is."

"Please, Claudia," I hear myself saying. "Just . . . please drop me where I need to go. Then . . ." I try to search for the right words, but instead grab the easiest ones. "I'll be out of your hair."

She narrows her eyes. "Where?"

"Utah." Pause. "The temple."

Her face turns angry. "Where your father Faded?"

I hold her eyes. "Just take me there. I . . ." I look away, then shut my eyes and shake my head. "I need to go. There."

"What for?" She throws up her hands, then points at me. "Jesus. That bitch got so far into your head that your brain is still choking on her shit. Tess was playing you, Ben."

"No," I say. "This is . . . this is what I have to do."

"Do what, Ben? Revisit the site of your biggest tragedy?"

"My biggest failure." Tears come as I say it through clenched jaws. Almost immediately I wonder if that's true. I think of the collapsed and smoldering house and Miranda. Then that guilt gets pulled into the whirlpool of shame and desperation that's churning inside of me.

"What do you want with that place?"

I don't know, is the answer. "Does it matter?" I say. "I need to go."

She shakes her head. "No."

"No?"

"No," she repeats. "I'm not taking you there."

"Claudia . . ."

"No, Ben. This is my ship. I don't follow your orders." She sets her jaw. "I never followed your orders. I'll drop you at the next stop, and you can make your way. But I am not taking you back to that temple."

"Claudia . . ." My voice is almost a whisper.

"No."

My eyes are closed, and I'm shaking my head, and tears are leaking from the shut lids. I vaguely realize that my right hand is resting on the butt of the revolver. I'm only slightly more aware when I pull it and point it at Claudia.

"Claudia." I say it short and clipped and as if through a heavy curtain of pressure. "I need. To go. Back. To the temple."

Claudia's look cuts me. "Are you going to shoot me, Ben?"

"Not if you take me where I want to go."

She smirks.

The bullet hits the console about four inches to the left of where she's leaning. She jumps at the sound and the impact so close to her. Her first instinct is to rise out of the chair and come at me. But I see her catch herself. She holds herself firm. "You just shot at me." Her lips barely move. Her tone is flat. Dead.

"To show you I'm serious," I say.

Her face grows darker, more dangerous. But she turns back to the controls. "Fine," she says. "Back to the temple."

A voice inside of me says "thank you," but it dies on its way to the light. I know I should feel bad. Part of me does, the part that thinks of everything that Claudia has done for me. All the many times she's come running. All the many times she let me back into her life. All the times she's saved my life. I wall it out. I drown it in this churning black soup inside of me. I drop a heavy weight on top of it and send it back down to where it came from.

I keep the gun out as Claudia flies.

Claudia is, almost surprisingly, good to her word. Not that she doesn't usually do right by me, but she has the tendency to overrule me when she thinks I'm doing something stupid. This time, she takes us right to where I want to be, and then she brings us down to the ground. Still, I keep the gun on her. "Walk me out," I say.

"Or else you'll shoot me," she says. Her eyes are narrowed.

"I don't want to," I say, but it sounds feeble, even to me.

"Yet you still have that gun out."

But she gets up, and together we walk to the exit ramp. It's true, I don't want to have to do this, but if I put the gun away, I'm afraid that Claudia will take the ship back up into the air or try to tackle me. I can't have that. So I make her, at gunpoint, walk me to the edge of the ramp, then I step off of it, onto the ground.

"Ben," she says.

"I'll be fine," I say. "I need to do this."

"No," she says, and there's so much of a growl in her voice that I turn to her.

Her leg lashes out in a kick that catches my wrist and sends the revolver flying. I raise my other arm to try to block, but she's already moving too fast. A punch hits me in the ribs, then in the face. I try to block her, but she's a lightning storm and I have no shelter.

A foot slides past me, and then I'm tipping backward. I hit hard against the ground.

"Don't take me back!" I yell.

Claudia stops, then looks at me like I lost my mind. "Take you back? Are you fucking kidding me? What would make you think that I would want. You. Back." She punctuates the last two words with kicks into my side.

I lie there and take it.

She stands over me, fists clenched, her face twisted in anger. "No more! No more coming to your aid when you need it. No more answering your call. No more pulling you up off the floor. No more cleaning up your messes."

She stalks over to the revolver and scoops it off of the ground. Her finger looks dangerously close to the trigger. Her eyes meet mine. Bore into them and through them. "I'm done," she says. "I'm completely done with you."

She lifts up the gun, then turns it to the side, regarding it for a long moment. Then, shaking her head, she tosses it to the ground next to me.

I sit up and watch as she turns away, walks back up the ramp of the *Valkyrie*, and retracts it behind her. Then, without fanfare, my oldest friend takes her airship up into the air and leaves me behind.

Where I wanted to be. The place that I've feared my whole life.

On the ground.

The place looks much like it did the last time I was here. A little more overgrown, sure. Wilder, maybe. I don't know. Maybe not. I guess it seemed a little different in my memory.

It wasn't "that place" until later.

The revolver is out, and down by my side. I'm on the ground, in the open.

Some habits are too hard to break. Nothing seems to be moving, so I do, treading out across the grassy ground.

I see some Feral spoor. Luckily, my father was a shit connoisseur. "This is dog shit," he'd say. "Look out for more. Don't want to disturb a pack." Or, poking at some with a stick, "Deer droppings. Better get the rifle." But the Feral shit was the stuff to look out for. "If they stopped to unload, it means it's safe territory for them. Not for us."

So they're still here, then. I shouldn't be surprised.

I used to think that it was the Ferals that were persistent, that it was they that were better suited to staying alive than we were. It always seemed a struggle for us, me and my dad especially. But Miranda taught me that it wasn't the Ferals, it was the Bug. Or the Maenad virus, as she'd call it. The Ferals were just . . . vehicles for it. Like the *Cherub*. Or any airship. A Feral body just transported the virus so that it could grow and escape its vehicle and infect another one. Ferals, in essence, were just side effects of the virus. They were good at eating and fucking and getting around. So the Bug thrived.

It was a real mindfuck.

Because of course Dad had taught me that it was always the Ferals that we had to fear. That we had to keep watch for. That we had to avoid.

Only he didn't end up avoiding them enough.

We thought we were safe. The Feral hadn't done real damage to my father. He didn't get clawed. Or bitten. Or even bruised, really. The Feral itself didn't do any damage.

But the Bug did. The Bug got inside him, and it killed him as dead as any bullet or knife or claw.

That's why I ended up coming around to what Miranda was doing. Sure, I'd killed Ferals. Bunches of them. Plenty. Not that I sought it out, though. I'd be more likely to run away from them than to shoot at them. But Miranda, she was trying to kill the Bug. The true enemy.

I reach the door of the temple and pull on it. The lock is still active, even years later. I'd suspected it might be, which is why I brought another portable EMP device. Claudia kept the parts just like I had, so I cobbled one together from her stores. That and the flashlight I took are her last gifts to me. Well, maybe not the last—my ribs hurt as I draw the EMP from the pocket of my coat.

I activate the EMP, and the lock disengages. I enter through the door, letting it shut behind me with a loud bang that sends dust swirling through the air. The place smells even worse than last time. I don't see any signs of Feral spoor, but I pick up the usual smells of aging and decay—mold, rust, a mineral scent. That I can't smell—or see—Feral shit is a good sign. I can't help but wonder why. We'd left the door open to the lower level. I'd think any Ferals would have wandered up. But then, I wondered how they got down there in the first place.

I pause at the picture of Ganesha, his form only a faint outline buried beneath the thick layer of dust. I pause to wipe some of it off, revealing some of the color underneath. I pay careful attention to his hands this time. One holds what appears to be an axe. Another holds a flower, a type I've never seen. The third is the outstretched one that I thought was telling me to stop. And the last is holding a bowl filled with what look like eggs. I notice the belly on the guy. He ate well, that's for sure. And there it is, in that one image. The outstretched hand of warning, the weapon signifying violence, the eggs or whatever they were, indicating the need to eat. The primal forces of the Sick.

Then what did the flower signify? For a moment I think of Miranda.

Fuck you, Ben. You're no preacher, no rabbi. Who the fuck cares what it means.

My mood darkens as I move down to the next level.

I have the revolver out, and I realize that I don't think I could put it down if I wanted. Those reflexes are wired right into the base of me. But it begs the question—what am I doing here? What am I searching for? Up until now, I've been acting on instinct. Autopilot.

My feet hit the floor on the basement level. Kick up the thick carpet of dust. The smell of mold fills the air—the Sick eating away at everything, minute by minute. I pause, waiting, listening, smelling, looking. The scarf and the goggles and the hat cut down on all the senses—the trade-off for protecting yourself. Again—you cover your front, you expose your rear.

There's no winning.

Nothing moves. I wait another moment. Still nothing.

I move forward. The lights inside have died, so I use the flashlight to look around. The beam isn't much light to see by. I keep expecting to see a Feral leaping out at me in every direction. Then the beam falls on a pile of bags, and boxes, piled haphazardly together. Our bags of haul. All the computers and other goods that we looted from this place last time. All that I left behind when I got my father out.

See, Dad? You had it wrong. I should have pulled out the gear and left you behind.

Then I stop.

I *did* leave him behind.

I could haul all of these bags and boxes and improvised carriers out of here now. Only I don't have a ship to take them anywhere. And whatever hold they might have had over me is gone.

The Feral's body, the one I shot all that time ago, is missing. Probably dragged away by others and eaten. I look for the blood spray, but with all the dust and dirt in here, I don't see anything.

This is the place. The point at which it all pivoted. In this holy place, it is a kind of holy place itself. A dark place.

I should leave.

Instead, I find myself moving to the door, to the lower level.

The air seems to get thicker as I approach. My *body* seems thicker. Heavier. It prickles, too. I tightly grip the revolver in my rigid hand.

I think I smell it then. The Feral stench. Then, there it is. The door. Still open.

We could have barricaded it.

He was right. There's a bookcase nearby. A refrigerator not too far along.

But would it have mattered? Dad was likely infected already by then. We would have gotten our haul, and we would have made for one of the bartertowns, and we would have hustled to turn all of that gear into food and fuel and the finer things in life. We might have been in a bartertown when Dad Faded. He could have infected others.

His words come back to me. *There* could *have been anything.*

I pass through the doorway. No signs of movement. No sounds that I can hear. I stand at the top of a stairway that leads down. It's dark, of course. That voice in my head, my father's voice, says that the flashlight is going to give me away to any Ferals that might be lurking below. Ferals still have human eyes, so they can't see in the dark, but they are better at using their senses, as far as I can tell. Still, I leave the flashlight on.

I start descending the steps. One. Two. The air seems to get thicker. Seven.

Eight. I wait for the Ferals to jump me and pull me tumbling to the ground. Rip into me with their teeth and nails.

Then, my feet hit the floor. It's a long space. Open. Lined with shelves. I move closer to one and shine the flashlight over it to see that it's covered in garbage. Boxes torn into tatters. Plastic wrenched and ripped apart. Food containers. As I shine the light over the next shelf, then the one opposite, then the far side, it's pretty much all like that. It makes sense. If the Ferals got in, they would have taken it all.

Just a few hours ago, I would have wilted at the sight of this. If it had been intact, it would have been a treasure trove. Some of it seems to be things like oil and salt and spices, all valuable. This plus the computers and other equipment on the upper floor would have been Dad's score. It would have set us up for years. Gotten us a second ship, even. Not that Dad would have wanted that. Me?

Maybe.

Something bothers me. There were Ferals here. There's dried shit strewn across the place. The smell is terrifying. Definitely more than one Feral. Where are they now? Did they just eat and leave? It seems like this would have been good shelter. It feels like it would have been comfortable. I think? But what the fuck do I know?

I move down the long room, shining the light in front of me. Over shredded bags and scraps of plastic, supplies made confetti by nails and teeth. More desiccated droppings. And there, at the end of the room, is the answer to the mystery. Maybe the ground shifted here, or there was an actual earthquake. Or maybe it was built upon shaky foundations. The wall, which seems to be solid and mostly intact, has fallen away from the building, leaving a big crack, almost a crevasse beneath it, which extends down into the hill. Some enterprising Feral must have discovered this entrance and gotten in.

That's one of the things I never understood, and Miranda never was able to enlighten me—what remains in a Feral's mind? Is there any scrap of humanity left, any knowledge or buried subconscious treasure still lodged in the mire of that Bug-addled brain? Is there memory? Or is it just curiosity? Because that's something Miranda talked about. That, in addition to the driving hunger and the violence, Ferals were, like our monkey ancestors, curious. Those things all together are why they run toward gunshots and engines and crashes rather than running away. That's why they're so dangerous.

I'm halfway down into the crevasse before I'm conscious of the fact that I'm doing it. The rock here is broken off in almost flat sheets, so it's not too hard to lower myself in, finding footholds as I descend. It wouldn't be hard to get up this way, either.

Further down this crack, I see why there are no more Ferals here. The rock gives way to dirt and, while there was probably a viable tunnel here for a while, it's now collapsed and filled in. I sit there, for a while, in the dark. Surrounded by cold stone and earth, like one of them.

I wonder what it must be like for Ferals. I was raised to believe that everything human in them was gone. That those things weren't people. But, if I'm honest, truly honest with myself, here alone in the dark, I can admit that I've had doubts. What if occasionally there are memories, fleeting in the chaos, but there after all. The memory of a smile of a loved one. Or the taste of something delicious in a world of rough eating. It doesn't change the fact that they're Ferals, or that they'll rip your face off, or that they should be put down as quickly and as efficiently as possible. Thing is, I don't know if it's better if those memories exist or not. What's more tragic—that they are haunted by their former life or that it's gone completely?

Ben Gold, philosopher in the dark.

I realize what I'm doing, squatting in the darkness, not just on the ground but under it. A piece of shit, stuck in the bowels of the world.

I climb back up into the storeroom, then up to the basement, and then to the ground floor. I don't know what I expected to find here—answers? Peace? None are offered. Ganesha's hands are actually empty.

I walk outside, and the sun blinds me. I should feel warmed, but instead I just feel exposed. The small, shriveled thing that is me is now laid bare to the world, and I find that prospect truly terrifying.

I wander around to the other side of the hill. Where I judge the tunnel would have led, and there, as I suspected, is a gash in the earth, the way into the temple that was probably until recently open and available to any Feral that might have come along.

Then, as I crouch atop the hill, eyes squinted against the sun, the heat beating down on me, I see my father.

CHAPTER FOURTEEN

FROM THE JOURNAL OF MIRANDA MEHRA

Dear Ben,

Have you ever felt like you're a passenger in your own body? Like a feeling of not fully being present, of being detached and untethered from what your hands and legs and even mouth might be doing?

Working in the lab is like that, rote but disconnected. You just focus on the work, on the data in front of you. Anything else gets too . . . defeating. I wake up in my cell, they walk me to the lab. There are brief interruptions—meal time (either next to the lab or in my cell), bathing time twice a week—but otherwise my life oscillates between two poles.

So when I was taken from the lab today and escorted to Blaze, it was notable. But also terrifying. What did they want from me this time? Was it some kind of new punishment?

My escorts walked me, without talking, to the second floor of the building, to a large office with windows overlooking the city. The guards left. Maya, too. Just me and Blaze. I'm sure there were others nearby, but for the moment we were alone, her standing behind the desk and me sitting in front of it.

I sat there and fantasized about escaping, about attacking Blaze, maybe even killing her. I started thinking about how long that would take. I thought that I could kill her before the guards got to me. I wouldn't last long after that, but surely taking down the head of the Helix would be worth it?

The thought was persistent. Mostly because I was scared. People don't see Blaze very often. I'd heard stories, of experiments she did on some of the people who didn't work out. Human test subjects.

Blaze is taller and more athletic than me. She might get the upper hand in a fistfight, and I didn't like those odds. I looked around for a weapon, somewhere, anywhere, but the closest I could find was the pen on her desk. That could work, plunged into the carotid. But I would have to be precise.

The moment passed. Of course I wasn't going to attack her. Not there. But if she tried something . . .

"You know why I don't fear for my safety?" she asked, as if reading my mind.

"No," I said. "Why?"

"Because I created this environment, I control the variables, and I've accounted for any possibility, including a threat to my person. Most people learn this quickly, either by the easy way or the hard one. Most of the time, I need not even bother to make a pretense."

"All of the variables?" I asked.

She stared back at me without saying anything.

"There's still chance," I said. "Entropy. You have the advantage in reach and weight and strength, but there's still a probability that I could overcome you, no matter how small that number may be. It's non-zero."

"True," she said, nodding. "But you're only seeing what's obvious."

I narrowed my eyes but said nothing. She held up one gloved hand, smiled, then formed a fist. Almost too quickly for me to see, a knife extended from her wrist, a good ten or more centimeters beyond her fist. "A special design," she said. "A bit dramatic, I'll admit, but certainly effective."

I nodded. With something like that, she could have killed me before I got close enough to do any real damage. She probably would have enjoyed it.

She grabbed the blade with her other gloved hand and retracted it back into its hidden sheath. "Just a reminder. You see only a fraction. You see the shape of the organism, but you don't see the brain, the nervous system, the limbic system. The complex systems below the surface that govern response and action. You see the guards, our visible security, but not the countless measures we built into our society here."

A threat. And an attempt to intimidate me. I wish I could say it didn't work, but there, with me sitting in that room, her standing up behind her desk, and all the space between us, I felt like she was in complete control. And me? I was power-less. "Noted," I said.

She smiled and it almost seemed warm and genuine. Almost.

"You've been here for weeks now, and you've been working, yes, but I know that you can do better than you are. Maya reported on all the work you did back on your island, the strides you made, even against our special cocktail, what you called 'Enigma.' Love those names, by the way. We tend to number our viruses here. It's more efficient, but I think I've shown that I have an appreciation for the dramatic from time to time."

She didn't seem to need a reply from me, so I didn't give her one.

"Threats can be useful. They keep people in line, but they don't engender enthusiasm. They don't stoke the fire, they stifle it. Instead, I'm going to make you an offer."

I stared at her.

"Miranda, I believe that we could accomplish great things together. I even think that you could come to see that, too."

The thought made me want to vomit, and I felt my morning meal come up in my throat. I swallowed it down, trying to keep my face blank. "What's the offer?"

Blaze placed her hands down on her desk, palms flat against the surface. "First, let me say that we're not monsters here. We're not the Valhallans, who threaten and bully pointlessly, even among their own people. I believe that minds work better with a little freedom."

I leaned forward in my chair. "You'll let me out? Into the city?"

Blaze nodded. "You'll have to be supervised, but yes. You'll come to learn that there's nothing you can do that would damage our operations; there's no way for you to escape here."

I wish I could say that I spit in her face, unimpressed by her offer, but the idea of weeks and months of my life alternating between my cell and the lab . . . it was wearing me down, little by little. On the commune, at Apple Pi, on Tamoanchan, we had labs, yes, but we worked outdoors a lot of the time. We walked outside to clear our heads and debate our work and feel alive. They had cut me off from all of that.

So when she held out freedom in her open hand, limited though it was, I wanted to grab for it. But I forced myself to remember the other hand.

"What do you want in return?" I asked. My voice sounded small and weak.

"Don't look so worried," she said. "What I'm offering you is a chance to do something you already want to do. I'm offering you a chance to work on a vaccine."

I sat back, stunned. I was sure she was going to put me to work on a new viral weapon. Or work on their weaponized Ferals. "A vaccine?" I asked, when I found the words. "For Maenad?"

She smiled. "Yes."

Once again I had to force myself to remember where I was, whom I was talking to. "Why?"

Blaze crossed her arms and gave me a deep stare. "I think you'll realize why," she said. "This is something we both want."

It was obvious. While we all worked with Maenad, we were still vulnerable to it. A vaccine would give the Helix free reign to work with Maenad without worrying about infection. I flashed back to being on Gastown, running scared like everyone else, as Valhallan ships, rigged with hooks, dropped bleeding Ferals onto the city.

"I want a vaccine for everyone," I said. "You would keep it for your people alone."

"Perhaps," she said. "Certainly at first. But . . ." She leaned forward and joined her hands together. "Once a vaccine exists, it exists. Once we crack that problem, it can be re-created." She shrugged. "Who's to say that you, or someone like you, couldn't take that and run with it. Make more. Spread it around. I don't think much of your chances, but they are . . . non-zero."

I sat back, still silent. Thinking.

"You know your best chance is with us. With our equip-ment, with our knowledge, as well as your own. You had an impressive operation, in your laboratory on that island, but ours is better. Our people are better."

"Bullshit," I said. I hadn't meant to, it just spilled out of me.

Something flinty came into her eyes. "You came from a commune, right? Some cobbled-together group of doddering old scientists trying to make the world a better place?" I could see something hot bubbling up behind her calm demeanor. "The people who started the Helix, they set their priorities early on. While the rest of the survivors were off raiding weapons depots for guns and ammunition, we were raiding hospitals and research centers. Our predecessors even raided the Centers for Disease

Control and Prevention." Her eyes sparkled, as if there was something more she wasn't revealing. A story there. "While people were fighting over scraps and finding holes to hide in, while your people were sitting in your fields or your schoolhouses, we were building laboratories, within which we were growing our own food, and planning, of course. Planning the future." Her gloved hand squeezed into a fist. "This is our birthright."

Somewhere in her pompous tirade I found a little heat of my own. "Yet you still don't have it. Your vaccine."

She inclined her head. "It has, so far, eluded us. But your detection test, that was groundbreaking. Using what you discovered, I think that we can bridge that gap. You can help us."

It was tempting. I'm ashamed to say it, but a _vaccine_. I've wanted one for so long. But the Helix killed my friend. They kidnapped me. They attacked Tamoanchan. They took Gastown. They have you, Ben. I wanted to scream in her face; I wanted to tell her to go fuck herself; I wanted to say that I would sooner die than help her and the Helix get what they want.

Instead I just said, " I can't."

Blaze sighed. She closed her eyes and shook her head. Then she shrugged. "Very well. I'm disappointed, but I can't force you. I expect you want to get back to your room?"

I exhaled and nodded. I had been expecting anger, a tirade, bullying . . . something. But she just came out from behind the desk and said, " Let me walk you out."

I stood up and she escorted me out of the room, surprising me by taking me into one of the adjacent corridors. " I'd like to show you something," she said. She opened a door off of the corridor and beckoned to me. It was clear this wasn't a request, it was a command. I told myself that if she wanted to hurt me, she would do it in front of the others. To make an example. I forced myself to walk forward and through the door. Blaze followed behind me.

I immediately smelled antiseptic, but something else. Something undeniably human. I stopped short when I saw the figure standing there.

A male Feral, naked and heavily muscled, held in a glass or plastic enclosure. It stood straight, barely moving. It didn't react to my presence, or Blaze's. I turned, scared, to look at Blaze. Her smile took up most of her face. "Isn't it impressive?" she asked.

"How?" was all I managed to ask.

"Careful training and conditioning. It took a while to get it to learn, but it's just another animal, after all. A social animal. That makes it easier."

"It's . . . larger than I've seen."

"Growth hormones and anabolic-androgenic steroids," Blaze said. "Administered regularly over a course of months. Plus more specialized training. We built an exercise course down on the ground."

I turned to face her, without turning my back on the Feral. "For what purpose?"

She smiled. "Control."

She walked up to the cage door, and, to my horror, opened it. "It's quite safe."

I stayed where I was. Then she came to me, put a hand on my arm, and walked me to the open door. "See?"

"Yes, I see," I said, trying to move away.

"See a little closer," she said. And pushed me through the door. It happened so fast. Next thing I knew, I was in the cage and the door was closed.

"Let me out," I said. I kept my voice even, scared that I would rile up the Feral if I was too loud. I stood sideways, trying to plead with Blaze but unable to turn my back to the Feral.

"Soon." Blaze crossed her arms. "I want you to see the level of our control."

"I get it," I said.

"Not yet." Her smile showed her perfect teeth. Then she held up a hand in a closed fist, palm facing outward, and whistled shrilly.

In an instant, the Feral changed. The stillness turned into a low crouch, muscles bunching, but even worse were its lips, which curled back from its teeth. A low sound came out of it, part groan, part growl, and it poised for attack.

I froze. I've worked with Ferals so many times. But this was something different. It went from completely neutral and still to ready to kill in just an instant. My whole body tensed up, waiting for it to start tearing me apart, and then—

Blaze whistled again. The Feral returned to its silent, still state.

I was shaking, no longer in control of my body. "Behavioral conditioning," I said, when I was able to form words again.

"Just so," Blaze said. "Strong conditioning. We can take it around anyone and it won't attack, unless we want it to. Only, we've never really tested the duration of the control. Whether it will hold indefinitely." She shrugged. "Until now."

Before the meaning of her words could sink in, she wheeled around and walked toward the exit.

"No!" I yelled, but then I immediately silenced myself, too aware, too afraid of the Feral so close to me.

"I'll leave the light on," Blaze called over her shoulder. "So you can at least see your companion."

Then she walked out the door.

Something that sounded like a whimper came out of my mouth, but I stifled it. I couldn't move. I could barely breathe. I was afraid that any movement I might make would attract its attention, would trigger its attack. Or that I might inhale some of its saliva.

I was too close to it. One lunge away. I froze in a standing crouch, unsure, unable to move, painfully aware of the Feral where it stood.

Eventually, I couldn't suppress the shaking, so strong that my teeth started to chatter, which I tried to still and which sent me into even greater shivers. I was rigid throughout, my eyes glued to the Feral's form but unwilling to meet its eyes.

That moment became eternity. It was like the instant right before a hammer meets the firing pin in a gun, that point at which the knife bends your skin before breaking it, only endless.

Somehow I moved away from the Feral. Fear of being too close to it won out, and I inched away. When that didn't elicit a reaction, I inched some more. But each movement brought on the fear again, that it would attract its attention.

Eventually, I reached the corner of the cell and pressed as much of my body into that corner as I could, keeping my eyes fixed on the Feral.

Hours passed. I don't know how many. They were all the same. Except for when the Feral urinated in one corner of the cell, sending me into another spiral of panic. (I later discovered that I had wet myself sometime during all of this.) The more time went on, the more my body started to scream, under the onslaught of the stress and fear in my system. My body cried out in pain from all the shaking and the position in which I was frozen. My brain was a constant alarm. And when I ran out of adrenaline, and the yawning fatigue set in, I couldn't relax or sleep. So I just lay there in a kind of fugue state.

Imagine your body screaming at its highest volume, your mind matching it, and having no escape from that. Imagine that this goes on, until you almost can't remember anything different.

I might have been there for years. I was there for years, despite what non-relative time would say.

Then, after eons of staying in that same position, depleting all of the resources and reserves my body and mind had to offer, a figure walked into the room, on the other side of the glass. Blaze.

"Please," I pleaded, in a whimper.

She walked up to the glass.

I raised my palms, pressed them against the glass as if I could somehow reach her. "Please. I'll do anything."

Blaze cupped her hand around one ear, as if she couldn't hear me.

I raised my voice, all the while expecting the Feral to come alive and rip me to shreds.

"Please," I croaked. "I'll do anything."

The next moment happened in a rush. Blaze opened the door, and I was scrambling through, and I collapsed at her feet as she shut the door behind me. I wrapped my arms around her legs. "Thank you," I said. "Thank you. Thank you. Thank you."

She bent down then, and tenderly stroked my hair. "You're safe now," she said. "You're safe."

Then the energy did drain out of me. And I could barely stand, could barely walk. Blaze grabbed my elbow and helped me out of the room and back down to my cell. I don't remember getting there, only that I woke up there in the morning, feeling like I hadn't slept more than a few minutes, the stress of my time in the cage still singing in my system.

The only thing I remember about that walk to my cell was what Blaze said to me. "We took it when it was young," she said. "We trained it for years. Now it's ours." She curled an arm around my shoulder. "Now you're ours, too."

✳   ✳   ✳

Blaze was true to her word about giving me some freedom and allowing me to try to develop a Maenad vaccine. After the first week of working on the vaccine, reviewing their data, trying to integrate it with what we had learned from the test we developed on Tamoanchan, Maya came to me to say that she would take me out into the city. "There's a speech," she said. "You should go see it."

I turned to her and was about to say, "Why?" but the lure of fresh air, and open sky, was in front of me. So I just said, "Okay."

She held out a jacket to me. "Take it," she said. "The wind can be cold."

So I took it and shrugged it on.

She led me out of the lab and outside, into the city proper. I had to squint my eyes against the glare, but I sucked in the fresh air. It smelled of cold and woodsmoke, and the faint smell of cooking meat. It made my stomach growl. They feed us very simply at the lab.

I realized as I followed her through the street that it was just the two of us. No extra guards. Unlike Blaze, Maya was smaller than me. It's possible that I could overpower her and run off. But where would I go, on a floating city surrounded by bloodthirsty brutes? No doubt they had people watching us, or Maya had some way of calling for help. That would have been the first thing they thought of.

I followed her through the streets, past shops and what looked like barracks and places that served food and drink. I saw mostly Valhallans at all of these, but every so often there was someone dressed in a jumpsuit or just with a calmer demeanor who was clearly a member of the Helix.

We arrived at last at a large theater, or at least something like it, with a large, raised stage at one end, and a large, open area for an audience at the other. The latter was filled with people already, mostly Valhallans, but with some Helix scientists scattered throughout.

A man stood in the center of the stage, and all eyes were on him. He raised his hands in the air, jowls quivering, to the applause of the crowd. His age hung on him, not like Sergei, but lined and sagging. He wore a breastplate, and a kind of armor made up of metal and leather, that he must have been squeezed into. The pale skin bulged at his armpits and around his neck. His hair contorted into a ridiculous crest that seemed dyed. And his face . . . it was bloated and discolored.

"Who is that?" I asked Maya.

"Odin," she said.

I'd heard of him. He rules here, and has done for a long time. I've heard some of the Valhallans speak of him like he's a war hero. Like he's the strongest, most virile person here. But seeing him on that stage, he just seemed . . . sad.

After the roars of the crowd died down, which took a while, he started to speak. The speech was a rambling, boasting mess. Half of it consisted of praising himself. The other half was telling people what I expect they wanted to hear—how Valhalla is the greatest city and culture left on Earth. How he will make a new world for his followers. How they can remake the continent, make it great again. The crowd loved it.

At one point he praised his right-hand man, this mean brute called Surtr, after some old white-person legend. You'd probably know all about it, Ben, from something you read. Did I mention he's mean? He looks mean, and the stories that they tell about him are mean. He does Odin's dirty work (because I can't imagine that bloated piece of pig's bladder doing anything himself) whether that's leading raiding parties or executing traitors or bringing him women to, well, you get the picture.

The rest of it was about all the settlements that they had taken or destroyed. So many of them. I had to fight to keep the tears from my eyes, thinking of all those people, afraid. Thinking that I didn't know about what had happened on Tamoanchan. This, I thought, was why Maya brought me here. To truly show me the scope of what we were up against.

It made everything seem futile.

After the speech, the whole crowd dispersed, the majority of the people moving to nearby bars and food stalls to celebrate. "We can have one drink," Maya said, dragging me to a nearby bar. "After that, things get . . . dangerous."

She stood opposite me at a tall table and passed me mead, a popular drink here. It was slightly sweet, made with honey, and I tossed it back, still imagining all the damage the Valhallans were doing.

"Blaze told me that you saw Herbie."

"I'm sorry?" I said.

Maya smiled. "That's just what I call him. We're not supposed to give them names, but. Well. I couldn't help myself." Then when she saw my blank stare, she said, "Our Feral."

Immediately I was back in that cell. Pain shot up through my back and down my arms. My hands started shaking, and I had to curl them hard around the cup of mead just to keep still.

Maya leaned in, the sweet honey smell on her breath. "What was it like? Up close?"

The memory started to return, and I tried to push it away, but it kept coming. Just the feeling of that moment. The pain and the fear. I was frozen there, in that time, in the past.

Nearby, some Valhallans knocked over a table and men started pushing each other.

"I'd like to go back now," I said.

Maya eyed the men, then looked back to me. "Yeah," she said. "I think that's a good idea."

That night, I lay awake on my sleeping mat, trying sleep, trying to stop shaking. Feeling unsafe despite the fact that I was alone in my cell. I ignored Dimitri's attempts to talk and just lay there, alone, yet feeling like there was a monster just waiting, over my shoulder.

✳   ✳   ✳

Two days later, Surtr visited the lab. I guessed it was a surprise inspection, from frantic air that hung around Maya and the Helix scientists. Even the Valhallan guards looked afraid. He came in flanked by his elite guards, draped in furs. He's tall, one of the most enormous men I've ever seen, and that includes Diego. He's bald, and everything about him seems hard. I tried not to make eye contact as he walked in, but he caught me once. He has a tattoo around one eye. A sword, wreathed in flames. But his dark eyes were hard and cold like asphalt. It sent a shiver through me.

Maya went to talk to him, very conciliatory. I could see the fear in her posture. It was in everyone's. Surtr talked to her as if she were beneath him, not even meeting her eyes. Instead, he scanned the room, a look of disgust on his face. Finally, he deigned to look at Maya and said something I couldn't hear. Her eyes widened slightly, then she turned and pointed at me.

I froze. I couldn't move. I felt exposed. I felt like I was back in that cell with the Feral waiting to pounce.

I just stood there as he walked over to me. I was forced to look up at him as he neared. He towers over me. He stopped in front of my station. "So you're the one," he said. His voice was dark gravel. I didn't know what he meant. He reached out a massive hand and grabbed my chin, raised it as he looked down at me, his face hard. He shook his head ever so slightly. "You're the one I lost men for."

I dimly realized that he was talking about the attack on Tamoanchan, but my mind was in a fog. I was too afraid to move. One twitch of his hand, and he could snap my neck. I was convinced of it.

"Are you worth it?" he asked.

I couldn't answer. My voice wouldn't work. I couldn't make the words come. And I didn't even know what I would say.

Then, as if seeing the fear in my eyes, he smiled, the grin of a predator. Then he dropped my chin and walked back to Maya. "Take me to Blaze," he said.

I was useless for the rest of the day. None of the diagrams or test results meant anything to me as I stared at them. One of the most powerful and dangerous men in this city now knows who I am, and lays the deaths of his men at my feet.

And I have this terrible feeling that, sooner or later, I'm going to have to pay for that.

✳   ✳   ✳

I am afraid of forgetting. Afraid of losing things in all of this. Of losing myself.

To help me, so that I'll always remember, I marked myself. Small cuts, on the underside of my arm near the wrist, so that they'll always be visible in the lab. I made three of them. The first for Ilaria, my mother, who I lost long ago to cancer, and who I will always be trying to emulate in one way or another. The second for Sergei, my second father, and one of the kindest people I knew. I failed him in the end when I couldn't cure Enigma, but I need to always remember that it was the Helix who ultimately killed him. The last is for you, Ben, wherever you are, because you gave me hope that there was something more than the fight. A chance for love, of all things. We'll never know if it would have worked, not now, but I need to remember that I felt that once. And even though it's so hard to feel anything now, except the fear, even if I can't remember the love, then at least I can remember that I once felt that. At least I can try.

CHAPTER FIFTEEN

T he thing that I'm staring at is not actually my father in any sense. It is a Feral. An old Feral, which is rare to begin with. It's moving across the grass slowly, but without any sense of illness or infirmity. Gray, curly hair, tangled into knots, falls to its bare shoulders. The Feral is lean, its skin tanned a deep brown. I can see curled gray hair on its chest and between its legs. But his height, his build, even the way he moves reminds me of my father. He would be the same age, roughly—his hair looks about the right length after all this time, taking into account the knotted, tangled mess it is. And it would be just like my father to become a Feral and still be dangerously hard to kill.

It's not him—it's probably some other old Feral that has lived here forever, that knows the area well enough to have stayed alive all this time.

And yet . . .

What are you doing, Ben? the voice asks, but I brush it aside.

I keep trying to get a closer glimpse of the Feral's face, keep trying to look beyond the beard and the hair. It's strange, because I spent a lot of my life inspecting my father's skin, examining him for scratches or bites or blood or spit. I did it over and over and over again. But it was in patches, under very specific focus. There are things about him I would recognize—his walk, his gestures, his eyes—but his body . . . Would any of those gestures or idiosyncrasies still remain in that thing? That vehicle for the Bug?

He moves out of sight, and I follow behind him. Keeping my distance, though. He seems more surefooted than me, even though his . . . *its* feet are bare. I follow it down and around the hill, keeping my distance, until it goes inside a building with the door hanging off of it. This structure is bigger than the others. Some kind of workshop or garage, maybe? I move closer, inching, crouching down so as not to be seen. I know it's not a good idea, but I can't seem to help myself. I feel driven to get a better look at this Feral. To see if it could really be my father. Or wanting to see that it isn't.

The building is large and dark. There are structures inside, haphazardly placed—furniture or machines long forgotten, or else things brought back by the Ferals, or collapsed bits of the building. It's hard to tell. The Feral I'm following moves to one corner, where he sinks to the ground, his legs curling, his head coming to rest against the ground. I see two female Ferals nearby. They look up at his approach, but they don't react much more than that.

The smell hits me a second later, if only because I was holding my breath. Unwashed human flesh, rotting meat, shit and piss and every bad human smell you've ever experienced. I once asked Miranda why it was that with all the shit and dirt and blood and whatever that Ferals came into contact with—not to mention uncooked meat—that they didn't just die off in droves from disease. She said that whatever it was that kicked their metabolism into overdrive helped to kill off infections before they could really take hold. She even once said that it was possible that the Bug kept them healthy by helping to kill off other viruses and bacterial infections so as to propagate itself and not them. It sounded perfectly ridiculous to me at the time. Now I've come to recognize that the Bug is far more nefarious than I had believed.

But the stench hits me, and then I scan the rest of the building and I see all of them. Ferals. Male and female, young and old, filling the space. Maybe fifty of them. Maybe more.

Ferals together is not an uncommon thing. They often hunt in packs. They get support from one another—warmth, for example, or the ability to take down armed prey. But it's always seemed like a precarious arrangement. Old Ferals are often killed off when they get to be too much of a liability, and younger Ferals will eat them. Challenges among the group are common, and fights can quickly break out.

But here's a large group. Taking shelter in this building. I wonder if they once took shelter in that basement, before it was rendered inaccessible by whatever earth-shifting force closed it off.

I continue surveying, to make sure I'm not spotted, but they all seem to be focused elsewhere, on the everyday lives of Ferals. Strangely quiescent. I've never seen them like this. But it's a blessing.

My eyes move back to the old Feral that reminded me of my father. Now that it's still, I can get a better look. It's hard to make out the facial features through all the tangled hair and the dirt. The nose looks like it might be his. But it's hard to say. The frame seems thinner, more wiry, but it would be.

Then it does something. Lying there, dozing or resting or whatever, it reaches one arm up and bends it, resting the back of its head against its hand. I tell myself that it doesn't mean anything, that it's a common gesture. That lots of people, and Ferals, and probably even cats and dogs and monkeys and whatever, make it. But it reminds me so much of my father that I have to blink my eyes to see for a moment.

You're being sentimental. Tess got to you, and now you're seeing what you want to see.

But am I? Do I want to see my father alive? It would have been so much easier just to accept that he died after Fading. That somewhere along the way something or someone dealt with him. That he didn't have to live long as one of those things.

Because that, I know, is what has been haunting me all this time. That I didn't do what I should have done and shot him, right then and there. That I didn't stop the Bug from running around in his body. That I didn't honor the memory of him and all that he stood for by killing one more Feral. One that was wearing his face. One that would go on to do unspeakable things, wearing him like an old set of clothes. Because I didn't, who knows what that body did. Who knows what it killed and what atrocities it committed.

Who knows what atrocities it might still commit.

My hand reaches down to the revolver.

I have a clean shot. From here, I could do it—shoot him, get off several shots to make sure he's dead for good. It would be easy. Of course, it would alert all of the Ferals in the building. I could run, but I couldn't escape them all for long.

Don't I owe it to him? Don't I have to put this right? Finally? After all of these years?

My vision blurs behind my goggles.

Images flicker through my head. Dad standing over me as I cleaned and loaded my first gun, offering criticism when I skipped a step. Dad and me taking apart one of the *Cherub*'s engines, doing repairs. Dad showing me how to bypass some burned-out solar cells, squeezing as much juice as we could out of the remaining series. Dad checking me for scratches and cuts. Dad sewing my first bullet hole closed. Then, Dad fishing out that same bullet. Even the memories are exhausting.

And I just left him. To become an animal in the wilderness.

Here, now, looking at this Feral that could very well be my father—maybe I can right this.

The goggles fog up, forcing me to push them up off of my head.

I raise my gun hand. I hold out my arm, keeping it as steady as I can, and I stare down the sights at the old Feral. At my father. At the thing that used to be him. At the thing wearing his body. I curl my finger around the trigger, knowing that the moment the others hear the shot, they will stream out after me, and they will tear the flesh off of my bones. I'll probably die with them chewing on me, eating my face and the rest of me. Just more meat.

But, still weeping uncontrollably, I hold my arm steady. I start to pull the trigger.

And the world splits apart around me.

The world tilts, disorienting me, until I slam into the ground, hard, on my side. The ground trembles beneath me, and then the sound. The booming crumple of an explosion nearby. My brain is screaming at me to look around and identify its source, but instead I get to my knees, the revolver still in my hand, and I raise it back in the direction of the door. But the Feral that may or may not be my father is gone. All of the Ferals are gone, pushed out by their alarm at the explosions. My moment is gone.

Crump. Crackle. Boom.

Another explosion, and this time I do look. A fireball rises into the sky, bright-red flame quickly fading to swelling black smoke. Then again. And again.

My eyes scan up to the ships. Three of them, moving in formation. Dropping bombs on what I can now tell is a nearby settlement. I move closer, walking to the edge of the hill, then down. Yes, a settlement. With fencing around it. A nice place, by the looks of it. At least the parts that don't resemble a burned-out, demolished mess from here.

I look back to the ships and almost certainly know what I'm going to see. And there they are—Valhalla flags, black with three white interlocking triangles on them. The fingers of my left hand form into a fist while my right grips the revolver tightly.

I move without thinking, heading down the hill as fast as I can, toward the burning settlement.

I think about all of the crimes I've been witness to that bear the stink of Valhalla. The attack on Gastown, using hooked Ferals to clear off the city. The taking of Apple Pi and the deaths and capture of the boffins there. The torture of Diego. The death of Atticus. The destruction of the *Cherub*.

Miranda.

Fire rages in my veins. Seething. Burning hot as those explosions. I half tumble, half slide down the hill in their direction. Scree and rock and dirt fly around me, bumps and jars that I can't feel through the fury that fills me. The need to do something, anything, overtakes me.

But as I hit the outskirts of the settlement, some hundreds of meters away from where the fence was, the Valhallan airships move away, leaving the smoldering corpse of the settlement behind.

CHAPTER SIXTEEN

I move toward the fence and as I do, the smell of burning penetrates my scarf. Burning wood. Burning plastic. Burning bodies.

I hit the fence at a run, easily passing through a large section gouged out of it by the explosions. I catch only a glimpse of the panels that make it up, but they appear to be sheets of stone held in place by metal frames. Tall enough to keep Ferals out.

But not airships.

The air is filled with smoke, and the sounds and smells of burning, and I can't hold back memories of Tamoanchan, the smoking, smoldering ruins of the houses there. Of Miranda's house. The smell of burning wood, the tang of gas and explosives. For a moment, something in me wells up, grabs hold of me, and wants to pull me down. Make me stop and curl into a ball. Make me stop entirely. But matching that pull is a push, a hot, fiery surge forcing me onward with the need for action.

I pass buildings, collapsed and on fire. Charred corpses, fallen in what pass for streets here, trying to flee burning buildings. Nothing seems to move except for the waving reach of the flames, greedily looking to consume everything it can.

What was this place? The buildings, at least those that still stand, seem well constructed. The layout feels good. Was this an old settlement, from the Clean, brought back to life? Or was it built here as a new start?

Fucking Valhallans. Preying on everything good and hopeful in the world. Cutting down everything green trying to claw its way up through the broken streets of yesterday.

I saw three ships flying away, three ships dropping bombs, but there might still be some around. They often send a ship down to mop up any survivors. I check the revolver, making sure its fully loaded and everything is moving smoothly after my tumble down the hill. I have to watch how much ammunition I'm using, too. I took everything I had with me off the *Valkyrie*, but I'm not liable to be able to replace it anytime soon.

Still, if I can find some Valhallans to put bullets into, it will be well worth it.

I run past a crumpled wooden bonfire and what looks like a house of worship still halfway standing amidst the wreckage. No religious iconography that I can see, just benches and some kind of stage.

Then I hear it—screams and what might be gunfire. It's hard to tell over the collapsing timbers and the cry of dying buildings.

I round the corner of the church, or whatever it is, and stop short. A group of people stand in front of a partially destroyed house. One has a hand out, holding a weapon of some sort, and others are arrayed around them. Is it a Valhallan? I raise my revolver and prepare a shot. But as I near, I see that I have it wrong. It's a handful of people, one of them armed, being circled by a small pack of Ferals.

I hesitate for a moment. Take the time to observe these people. Because if they're from Valhalla, I might just walk away and root for the Ferals. But they're dressed in simple clothes. None of them look, at first glance, like fighters—not the sort that I would expect on a Valhallan ship.

I target one of the Ferals and shoot.

It's a mistake. That Feral goes down with a hole in its back, but the others with it—five or six—turn toward me. Then start moving. Another pull of the trigger, and another Feral goes down, then they're on top of me, and I slam the revolver into one Feral's face and kick out with my boot at another. *Dammit, dammit, dammit, they're too close.*

"Shoot them!" I yell at the woman with the gun. I manage to break away from the three Ferals clustered around me, but an arm grips my leg and I fall to the ground. I raise the revolver. Squeeze the trigger twice. One bullet tears through the Feral's shoulder, and the other explodes its face.

Only two shots left.

"Fucking shoot them!" I yell again.

One of the Ferals lunges, and I blast it in the chest. But the one that's left scrabbles toward me and lashes out with its arms. I pull back from the blow, but it catches the revolver and sends it spinning away. Sensing that I'm helpless, the Feral jumps forward. I throw my arms up to hold the thing's face away from me, gripping the neck as firmly as I can. "Shoot it!" I try to cry again, but it dies as a gurgle in my throat as I struggle to keep the creature's teeth away from me. The

Feral's long nails scrape down my coat, and I hope the leather is holding. I bring my legs up to grip the Feral's body, trying to hold it in place. Slaver is running from the thing's mouth, but I'm holding it to the side, watching, and pushing as hard as I can, while a thin string of drool narrowly misses my face.

Then, in desperation, I squeeze as hard as I can with my legs and knees, bringing as much pressure as I can to bear on the thing's midsection. With my grip around the neck, I simultaneously squeeze and twist and keep that pressure up as much as I can—crushing and wrenching and using . . . every iota . . . of strength . . . that I have . . . until—

The Feral stops moving. Still maintaining my grip on its throat, I roll it to the side, where it falls to the ground, limp, its head twisted at an unnatural angle. I take a moment to make sure it's dead, and then I roll toward the revolver, grab it, and jump to my feet, head spinning from the exertion. I sway on my feet, but the revolver is out, pointing at the woman.

Who is pointing her own pistol back at me. For a moment I expect her to shoot, but she doesn't. Which is a good thing for her, because while she could take me down right now, I would almost certainly get off my own shot and make her pay for it. I'm also aware of the group of people, looking at me.

"Why didn't you shoot them?" I growl.

The woman shakes her head. "We don't know you," she says.

"I just helped to save you," I say.

"He's one of them," a young man with brown skin says. "He's one of *them*."

"I'm not one of the raiders," I say.

"Then where did you come from?" the woman with the gun asks. She has light-brown skin and long, dark hair that she tied back but which has come loose in all the activity. She wears a flannel shirt over a muddy t-shirt and jeans. These people are barely covered. Naked skin everywhere. *Fences*, I think.

I wave my left hand back in the direction of the hill. Then, in a gesture of what I hope is goodwill and trust, I use that same hand to raise my goggles and pull my scarf down. It certainly makes the breathing easier. "I was . . . I was investigating that temple up on the hill. I saw the explosions."

"Don't believe him," the young man says.

"Listen," I say. "I—"

I freeze as I feel something pointed press into my side. Very near my kidneys. I glance down quickly to see someone short—a kid?—with a wicked-looking blade pressed up against me.

"Give her the pistol," the woman says. Then, using the pistol for emphasis, "Slowly."

I nod, slowly, and adjust my grip on the revolver so that my fingers aren't near the trigger. Then I lower it and hand it to the young girl with cropped brown hair.

The girl moves her fingers to the grip and the trigger and holds the gun on me, not putting the knife away either, but just holding it in her other hand. The gun looks ridiculously huge, but it doesn't waver. She backs up slightly, covering me from the back as the woman covers me from the front.

The dark-haired woman moves forward. The gun is no longer outstretched. Her elbows are pulled in to her body, the gun still at the ready.

"So," she says. "The temple."

Now I hold both of my hands up, palms toward her. "Yes."

"Do you have an airship?" she asks.

I shake my head.

"Other transportation, then?"

I wince, then shake my head again. "Someone dropped me here."

"Are they coming back?"

I sigh. "It was a one-way trip."

"See?" the young man says. "He's one of them. Who would take a one-way trip out here?"

"Did you come looking for Phoenix?" This from a tall, thin, light-skinned woman with long, reddish-brown hair tightly pulled back, and glasses. Something about that reminds me of Miranda.

I think about lying. About telling them I was looking for Phoenix, but I don't know if that's a person, a place, or an animal.

"No," I say. "It's . . . complicated. But I'm not one of Valhallans. I hate them."

The dark-haired woman narrows her eyes.

Now that I have a moment, the appearances of the other companions sinks in. There are five of them all together. The dark-haired woman and the young man, the woman with glasses, and an older, tall man with light skin and gray hair, holding a club in his hand.

And the young girl holding my own gun on me. She can't be much more than a decade old, I'm guessing.

A Feral howl cuts through the air.

Shit.

"There are going to be more of them," I say. "Your fence may have kept them out, but it's torn to shreds. They'll be attracted to all the light and activity and noise. Are there any buildings left?"

The dark-haired woman's eyes don't leave me.

"We have to hurry," I say.

Again, nothing.

"Do you have any vehicles?" I ask. "Any airships or ground cars? Wagons? Bicycles? Anything?"

"It's all gone to shit," the older man says in a low voice. "It's all gone."

"Not all gone," the woman with glasses says. "The storehouse is still there." She points at a large building at one end of the settlement. It's hard to tell, it's obscured by smoke and flickering flames from the nearby buildings, but it looks like it might be intact.

"We need to go there," I say. "Now."

I can hear the howls. Closer. More of them. So can my new friends.

"You can't come," the young man says.

"I was trying to help!" I say. I point at the dead Ferals. "I took care of them."

"You were saving yourself," the dark-haired woman says.

"With no help from you!" I snap. "If you want to argue some more, can we please do it somewhere inside where more Ferals can't get—" Then we all snap our heads around, because we can see them running toward us. A big pack. Maybe the one I saw up on the hill.

Then we're all running, what we were arguing about forgotten, as we all make for shelter. I could run for it, try to get away, but where would I go? So instead I put my faith in their course, hoping that they're right, that one building escaped all of this unscathed. Besides, the little girl has my gun.

As we near the building, I see that it does indeed look like some kind of storehouse or something. Big, and blocky. The front of it is burned, scorched, but it appears as if the firebombs fell short of the mark and just splashed across the outside without doing any major damage.

A crater on one side supports that notion. But luckily the crater is out of our path. Our way to the entrance is clear.

We reach it at a dead run. There are two large sliding doors on the outside. My new friends all move to one and start pushing. It cracks open, but only a little.

"Well?" the dark-haired woman says. "You want to help? Help!"

"I wanted *you* to help," I say under my breath, but I move to the door and grip one of the large handles on the side, sharing it with the older man, and push with all the strength left in me. An agonizing long space seems to stretch on, but then it starts moving, wide enough for us all to speed in.

"Now close it!" the woman shouts and we all do the same, only in reverse. By now the mechanism has at least been loosened, and we're able to slide it shut with a resounding clank. The two women slide some latches into place. I finally let out my breath. I could see the Ferals coming toward us. See the numbers, their faces, the looks of greed, of hunger, upon them. So many.

So hungry.

I sink to the ground, exhausted.

The dark-haired woman turns the gun on me again. "Now tell us why you're really here."

I rub my face with my hands. That time in the temple, just a few hours ago, feels more like weeks. "It's personal," I say. "I have history at the top of the hill. I was . . . trying to reconcile it."

"Up at the temple?" the white woman asks.

"Yes," I say. "I was there once. A long time ago."

The woman with the dark hair crosses her arms, the pistol still held tightly. "And you had someone drop you here, all by yourself, with no way to get out?"

I meet her eyes. "Who said I wanted to get out?"

She shakes her head, her eyes widening. "So you're a crazy person."

"Let's just say it wasn't well thought out."

"You think?"

Scratching on the outside doors. Growls. Grunts. Screams of challenge.

I get to my feet and brush off my clothes. Dark Hair keeps the gun trained on me the whole time. "I'm here now," I say. "We're all here now. And we're all in a load of shit. So what say we put the guns away and work on getting out of here in one piece?"

Dark Hair, who seems to be the leader here, looks at her people, then back at me. Then she tucks her pistol away in the back of her jeans. "Fine," she says. "No guns. But—" She meets the eyes of her people. "You see him doing something funny, feel free to shoot him."

"Much better," I say.

She scans the room. "Look around for food. Or weapons. Or anything else that might help."

As they move away, I finally look around the place. I had been smelling it already. Grease. Dust. Mold. Machine smells. Chemical smells. Now I can see why. The space is big, and it's not completely full, but against the far wall is an assortment of machines, all in various states of repair. I see things that look like the remnants of ground cars. Parts of an airship. Several things that are probably large tool machines. A series of pulleys and winches. Engines. Motors. Fan blades. Smaller tools and parts resting on tables.

"A workshop?" I ask.

"Yes," Dark Hair says. "It hasn't been used much lately. But the idea was to see what we could salvage and repair from the nearby houses and shops."

I stare at her. "Is this your settlement?"

She looks at me in surprise and snorts. "Me?" She shakes her head. "No. I was just someone who lived here. Welcome to Phoenix."

The name of Mal's warship. Also a place. "Like the old city?"

She shakes her head. "Like the bird."

"You lost me."

"A myth. From the Clean. A bird that rises out of the ashes of its predecessor."

"Oh," I say, getting the symbolism. Mal always did have a poetic streak.

Her expression gets dark, and she runs a hand through her hair. "This place was founded by a man named Lincoln. He wanted to set up a place where anyone could come, a safe space. A place where the past would be forgotten. A new start. For anyone." Her eyes tear up. "And they killed him for it."

"The Valhallans."

She nods. She stares at me for a second, then shrugs. "I'm Coretta," she says. "The big guy is Tomas, the smaller one Buzz. Sondra is the one with the glasses, also a hell of a fine doctor. And the girl is Ellie."

"I'm Ben," I say.

"Well, Ben. What do you say we look around for something useful?"

I shrug. "Okay."

"Stay close to me, though," she says.

I nod—best to keep in Coretta's good graces for the time being, but I'm inclined to make her stick close to me. The first things I head for are the airship parts. There's no real hull to speak of. Or maybe some of the large plates might have been part of a keel, but there's what looks like ballonets, deflated, hanging from a rack. And some large tanks of lift leaning against a wall, which are probably hydrogen but may even be helium, judging by the look of them. They may even be from Gastown, before the Valhallans took it.

More exciting, to me at least, are the engines—propeller units—that are resting against the wall. They look like they're from a smaller ship. They wouldn't be enough to push the *Cherub*, or even the *Valkyrie*, but they look pretty good for what they are. Maybe a little dusty, but no signs of rust or deterioration. But there's no real airship for them to push.

"You have airships here?" I ask.

"Not really," Coretta says. "Some would come through from time to time, traders that we had relationships with, but nothing permanent. Lincoln intended this place to be a haven on the ground. Still, we had a few zeps who lived here. People who lost their ships or gave up the life for one reason or another. I think they were stockpiling parts to try to build into some kind of junker, to help us roam a bit farther."

I finger the ballonet skins. They're good, intact, but without a hull . . .

"Looks like they didn't get far enough."

We look some more, investigating some of the tools and machinery, before Coretta brings us back to the center and asks everyone what they found. Simple answer is: nothing useful. No food. No weapons, unless that means improvised clubs made up of metal rods or other bits of machinery. Already the grunting and shrieking outside sounds louder. That probably means more Ferals, attracted by the others, knowing that there's something good inside the building. Like a giant can of meat just waiting to be opened up.

"We're not going to be able to last long without food," Buzz says.

"The lack of water will get us first," Sondra says.

"So we need to figure out how to get out of this place," I say. "Unless we get lucky and the Ferals decide to leave on their own. But I don't expect that they will."

"We can wait them out for a day," Coretta says. "They may get bored and move on. Or some might, at least. I still have my gun. We have Ben's." I hadn't forgotten. "We have some other weapons. We can wait and fight our way out if we have to."

"And go where?" I ask. "Town's burned out. Ferals may be hiding anywhere. Do you know of any nearby settlements or places we can take shelter?"

"What about the temple?" Buzz asks. "You said you were there."

"There's no food there. Or water. And I'm not convinced that the Ferals don't have a way in there."

Buzz steps forward. "Or maybe you don't want us to go there."

I meet his eyes. "Honestly, kid, I don't care what you do. Go up there. Don't go up there. But—" and saying this makes me realize that it's true, "—I don't want to die, or get eaten by Ferals, so I'd like to get as far away from here as possible. Hopefully somewhere with food and water." I look at Coretta. "You have no vehicles?"

She sighs. "We had a couple of cars that were rigged up to drive, but they didn't survive the attack."

"You're sure?"

"Yes," she snaps. "I'm sure." She stands up. "I am the one who's lived here for the past year, and I'm the one who was here when the bombs fell."

"You checked everything?"

She gets in my face, her finger outstretched. "Who the fuck do you think you are? Coming in here, uninvited, asking questions? I can feel you working your way up to giving commands. You are only here for as long as we say you get to be."

"Coretta," Sondra says.

Coretta ignores her. "You're starting to piss me off, and I don't see why we shouldn't just toss your ass out of the door."

"Coretta . . ." More insistent now.

"In fact, why don't you get your ass up and get ready to run."

"Coretta!"

It cuts through the tension, and everyone turns to look at Sondra, wondering what's going on, but she doesn't need to answer. Because there's the sound of groaning, of something under pressure, and then a loud crunch as one panel of the warehouse falls inward, and suddenly the sound of Ferals gets louder.

I start moving toward it (wondering, even as I'm doing it, why I am), and Coretta calls out behind me. "Stop!" I look over my shoulder to see that she has the gun out.

"Shoot me," I say. "But I need to see what's happening."

When I get to the wall, I can see that this building didn't escape unscathed the way that we all thought it had. Something, the concussion from the detonation or something else, caused the wall to fracture. At least one thin crack runs up and down the whole panel, from the ground to the roof. There might be more. With the pressure of the Ferals against the wall, it's starting to shift. Already I can see shapes moving in front of the crack, near the ground. The Ferals can't breach it yet, but if they keep pushing . . .

"We need to stay away from this," I say. They might not be able to get in, but the Bug can. "There's a crack. And it might get larger. We need to get out of here. Now."

"How?" Buzz asks.

I return to the bits and pieces of vehicles. No airships, no, but there were some old hunks of vehicles. "Do any of those work? Or close to work? We would just need to get it moving and keep it moving. Steering is optional."

"Steering works," Tomas says, in his quiet, deep voice. "But they don't drive. No engines or fuel lines."

And of course we have airship engines, but no—

Wait.

"We should brace this crack," Buzz says. "Get things up against it."

Wait. Wait. Wait.

"Give me a hand," he says to someone.

We have the skeleton of a ground car. Or truck, rather, looking at it. No engine. But we have the propellers of the airship. And ballonets. It looks like there's fuel and . . .

The whole room creaks again, and the wall panel that was open just a hair a second ago now leans into the room, the crack even wider.

"What the fuck are you doing?" I stalk over to where Buzz and Sondra are, my hand automatically going to my holster, which is now empty.

Buzz moves forward, head out, aggressive. "We were trying to fortify the wall!"

"And how did that work out for you?" I shout back.

I'm thinking that I have no time for this fool of a kid when a hand, long-nailed and dirty, pokes through the gap between the wall plates, and I grab Buzz and pull him away.

He shakes free. "Get off of me!"

"Do you see the Ferals"—I point at the arms waving through the gap— "pushing their way through? Or are you too fucking stupid to get that?"

He shoves me, hard enough to force me back a step or two. The first thought in my head is, am I really going to have to fight this kid?

Then the little girl, Ellie, appears, and she puts a hand on his arm. "Stop, Buzz," she says. He seems to settle for a minute. I'm relieved, but I see my revolver tucked into Ellie's belt. I could probably get to it. It only has one bullet left, but I have more in my pockets. Not a lot more, but enough.

But then what, Ben?

The moment passes.

"We need to get out of here," I bark. "Now."

"How?" Coretta asks.

What I was thinking of before Buzz started fucking us comes back to me. "We build a junker. As quickly as we can."

"What?" Several of them say it at once.

"We have that truck—"

"With no engines," Buzz says.

"But we have the airship engines."

"How is that going to work?" Sondra asks.

"We use the ballonets," I say. "Fill them with as much gas as we can manage, attach them to the truck."

"Will that lift off of the ground?" Sondra asks.

"No," I say. "But it doesn't need to. It will lighten the truck, with all of us on it, and let us go quicker. It will also give us a way to rig the engines up. We can use something as a frame to mount them on and lift them with the ballonets."

"That sounds ridiculous," Buzz says.

"Maybe," I say. "But it should get us out of here. And moving. Does anyone else have a better idea?" I look around at all of their faces, blank or skeptical. "Please, if you have anything, speak up now, before the Ferals widen that gap and get in to kill us all."

"It's a stupid plan, Coretta," Buzz says.

Coretta nods. "But it might be all we have," she says. "How fast do you think it will go?"

"If I can tinker with the engines, and we're not worried about keeping them for very long, at least seventy kilometers per hour, maybe more."

"Is that fast enough?"

"It'll depend on acceleration. I'm used to being in the air," I say. "We'll have more weight, and while the wheels will help us a little, they'll provide some drag, so it will take us a little while to get up to speed. And the Ferals will be on top of us as we're trying." I shrug. "It won't be easy."

Coretta turns to her people. "I'm not your leader," she says. "You all need to decide if you want to do this. But I think this is our best shot. Who is with me . . . us?"

Ellie moves forward and stands next to Coretta first. Then Tomas says, "Me."

Sondra nods and stands up from where she's sitting on a wooden crate. They all look at Buzz. "Okay," he says. "But I still don't trust him."

"Noted," I say. "I'm going to need you all to help. If you know how to use tools, come forward now. I'll need some of you filling the ballonets, some of you helping me to rig up the engines and the structures. And we have to move quickly."

"Just tell us what you need us to do," Coretta says.

So I do. I split them up, assign them to tasks. I keep Tomas with me, because he's the strongest and because he knows his way around machines and tools. I assign Buzz to Coretta, because I think that he needs to be kept in line and she's probably the one to do it. That leaves Ellie and Sondra together. I put them on the ballonets. Ellie listens to everything that I say with a serious face.

"I take it that none of these people are your parents," I say.

She shakes her head.

"The attack?" I ask.

She looks at her shoes, thick black rubbery-looking boots that seem comfortable and practical. "My dad," she says. "My mom died when I was little."

I nod. "Same."

She lifts her head up, her chin jutting out defiantly, and meets my eyes. "I'm not going to let them kill me."

The trace of a smile lifts the corners of my mouth. "Same," I say.

Sondra returns from straightening out the ballonets and the connecting ties. I show them how to fill them and how to check for holes. There's enough extra to patch them if necessary. We're not going for permanence here, just enough to get us free and to some other mode of transportation or safety.

"So, a doctor, huh?" I ask Sondra.

She nods. "For all of Phoenix." Her face clouds over, and she returns to the ballonets.

"Well, I'm sure these people will be glad you made it," I say. "And I'm sure there will still be work for you to do."

"Isn't there always?" she says.

"You been here long?" I ask.

"Less than a year," she says. "I used to be in a settlement out east. Was a doctor there. Then . . . the Virus got in."

"Sorry," I say.

"I ran. Wandered for a bit. Then I heard about Phoenix. That it was welcoming newcomers. That it gave people a fair shot. I figured I could barter my way in. Been here ever since."

"They welcomed everyone?" I ask.

She nods. "As long as you were willing to work hard for the community. That was the chief guiding principle of the town, according to Mr. Lincoln. It didn't matter what you did before, what your past was, as long as you worked for the community and helped your fellow townspeople."

"And what if you didn't?" I ask.

She meets my eyes. "Then you couldn't stay," she said. "Lincoln was kind. He was generous. But he didn't tolerate troublemakers."

"Seems like I might have liked this man," I say.

"Everyone liked him," Sondra says.

I'm about to say something about the Valhallans, but I don't. It's clear that these people are grieving. Just being here feels intrusive somehow.

I make sure Sondra is doing okay with her part and then move on to Coretta. She and Buzz are working on the bed of the truck. Buzz glares at me as I approach, but he doesn't say anything. Coretta looks up from where she's bolting a metal rod into the frame of the truck. "Like this?" she asks.

"Looks right," I say. "You do any working with machines before?"

She shakes her head and wipes away some perspiration with her sleeve. "I'm more of an administrator."

"That get you very far?" I ask.

"Here it did," she says. "I was a teacher, I guess you could call it. Back where I started."

"Teaching what?" I ask.

She shrugs. "Reading. History, such as I knew it. Really anything I could learn."

I help her move the next rod into place. "Why aren't you still there?"

She holds the bottom of the rod as Buzz bolts it in. "They stopped valuing my teaching. It wasn't bringing in any food. Or fuel. And so I had to go."

"They kicked you out?"

She pushes a stray piece of hair out of her face. "Let's just say their feelings were clear on the subject. I wandered for a bit, like a lot of the people here, and then I heard about this place. Phoenix. And Lincoln Carter. He had printed these pamphlets and convinced some airship captains to carry them, couriers, too. He would give a bonus to anyone bringing new people in."

"He encouraged people to come?"

Coretta sits back. "He wanted to build something new. A place built on hope." Her face darkens. "I told him more than once it was a risky proposition, but he always convinced me that it was worthwhile. He brought me in to help plan the town, help set up a system that would work for us."

I help her with the next rod. "It sounds incredibly fragile."

She sighs. "In a way it was. But we made it stronger. The people who came here, they really wanted something new. Most of them, at least. Those who didn't, we dealt with as we needed. Lincoln gave everyone a second chance. Always. But after that . . ." She inhales deeply, then lets it out. "He may have been an idealist, but he wasn't blind to the world we live in."

"Sounds like a pretty great man."

"He was," she says, without hesitation, with complete conviction. "Which I guess is why they came for him."

"How did they even know about him?"

She hangs her head. "Lincoln and his pamphlets. At first it was getting people to come to Phoenix. But once we had our thriving community, he wasn't satisfied to stop there. He always said he wanted that feeling of hope to spread outside our walls. He saw other settlements being terrorized by the Valhallans, saw what they were doing everywhere. He . . . he started speaking out against them."

"Oh," I say.

"Some of our people warned him not to. Said we shouldn't attract their attention. But Lincoln wouldn't listen. He said we should stand up against tyrants." Tears fill her eyes. "And, God help me, I agreed with him."

I put my hands on her shoulders. "This isn't your fault," I hear myself saying. "The Valhallans are evil. They're terrors. And they need to be stopped."

She wipes her eyes with the back of her hand. "Yeah. Well. Who's going to do that?"

I don't have an answer for her, so I leave her to her work and return to Tomas.

✳   ✳   ✳

Tomas and I work on getting the engines hooked up and suspended from a frame that will sit on top of the rig that Coretta and Buzz are putting together. "You know engines?" I ask Tomas.

"A little," he says. I'm getting the impression that he doesn't talk much.

"What did you do before coming to Phoenix?"

He looks up at me, his face mournful. "Not a lot of good," he says, then returns to his work. I shrug and go back to it too. Then he says, "I done some things I'm not too proud of. Did what I thought I needed to do to survive. But it ate at me. Then I hear Lincoln. The word he's spreading. And it seems like he's offering, well . . . a second chance. A chance to . . . to move in a different direction. So I came here." He shrugs. "Now things are different."

I nod as I digest all of this. "That's great," I say. But I'm wondering what that means for him now. If this place and that man gave him that second chance, that new life, what happens now that everything's fallen to shit?

We don't talk much more. We just work. The storehouse has an acetylene torch, which we use to weld the frames together. It's really the one thing allowing this to all come together. I work with Tomas, who seems to know how to use it, and together we build the frame and attach the engines. It's an ugly construction, solar panels bolted on in places, fuel lines hanging free. Thankfully, there's some fuel here that works in the engines. They kick up quite a bit of noise, and it revs the Ferals into a frenzy, but they work and that's all I care about at the moment.

Holding this thing together is going to be tricky. We have the welder and bolts and some industrial-strength glue, and I intend to use all of it. But none of these pieces of metal were meant to be joined together, and who knows what stresses this is going to put on them. We'll give it the night to set and then test it out in the morning.

We all come together with our separate pieces. First I help Ellie and Sondra bring the helium-filled ballonets over to the frame, and we all lash the ballonets to it until it's suspended in the air. That's the easy part. Then we float the frame, complete with engines, over to the truck bed and join that together. In the end, we are left with a vehicular monstrosity: part truck, part airship, all ugly. We've stripped the truck down to essentials, the wheels, axles, body, steering wheel, seats, and flatbed in the back. If all goes according to plan, Coretta and Buzz will sit up front with the rest of us piled in the back. We even rigged up some sides to provide defense. And the front . . . It's a mess of spikes and jagged metal, angled away to protect the drivers. It will slow us down, especially if Ferals get stuck on it, but it's protection.

Which we'll need.

For tonight, though, we'll rest. Let the night play out. Make our start in the morning.

We huddle around a small heater, more of a stove, really, but it's hooked up to the solar cells and it's putting out heat so that's all that matters. We try to ignore the howls and barks and screams of the Ferals that continually come in through the crack in the wall.

Buzz is sitting off to himself, playing with, or working on, a metal pipe. I think he's going to use it as a weapon. I saw him wrapping one end in strips of something. Tomas was doing the same thing earlier, taking that wooden club that he carries, which might be a baseball bat, and hammering nails into the far end.

I guess it's weapon time, because Coretta is cleaning her pistol. Sondra, who seems unarmed, sits quietly with Ellie. But then Ellie comes over to me.

"I think you should have your gun back," she says.

I stare at her face, so young and yet also so old at the same time. I shake my head. "Why don't you hold onto it for a little longer?"

"Will you . . ." She looks down at her worn boots. "Will you show me how to use it?"

So I do. A little girl like that, stuck in the Sick, deserves to know how to use a gun. So I show her how to load it, how to clean it. How to treat the weapon with care and respect. Then I show her how to hold it, and how to aim. "You want to aim for the largest part of what you're trying to hit," I say. "It's okay if you don't kill it, as long as you slow it down or stop it. Don't try to go for the head or the legs, or you're asking for trouble. Your best bet is to hit something. Misses are just wasted ammunition."

"And always keep track of how many bullets you have."

"That's not too hard," she says. "There are only six."

I smile. "Maybe," I say. "But when you're in the middle of a fight, or when a pack of Ferals is chasing you, it's easy to lose track. I like to picture the number in my head. I think it helps. Can you read? Do you know your numbers?"

She nods. "Coretta taught me."

"That might help you. Just find something that works. Stick to that."

She nods again.

Looking at her, I'm reminded of myself. She's got more to deal with than I did. I at least had my father. But she's got these people. There are worse places to be. Still, I recognize something in her. Some set of the jaw. Something in the way she stands. As if she feels the weight of the world on her, but she's determined to stand up despite it. Memories flood into me. Standing nearby as my father negotiated a deal and the room suddenly grew tense. The feeling that they were going to kill him and I would be on my own and in their hands. The relief as he grabbed my hand and pulled me away, and then the return of that fear as we started moving faster and gunshots rang out behind us.

The blind terror that time when someone snatched me, just grabbed me and held me tightly in their arms, and ran. The screams I let out. The sudden glimpse, as we turned a corner, of my father running after me. The fear that he wouldn't get to me in time. The terrifying panic of thinking I would never see him again.

A Feral on top of me when I was close to Ellie's age. Knocked down and pounced upon. It reared its head back, roaring in triumph, and I knew it was going to kill me. Or else the Bug would get me, reach down to me despite all the coverings I wore. The fear was made all the worse when my father plowed into it, stabbing it with a piece of glass. Those horrific three days we waited to see if either of us were infected.

I reach out and put a hand on her arm. My eyes blur for a moment. "Keep practicing," I say.

I curl up in an open space on the floor. I hope for sleep, but it doesn't come. I toss and I turn, and I listen to the Ferals and the voice inside my head, not knowing which one is worse.

At some point in this whirling storm of shit, there's another wrenching, squealing sound and another crunch as the wall collapses inward. I jump to my feet and see arms reaching through the crack, and then a head and body wriggling through.

"Everyone, get on board now!" I yell. "We have to get out!"

They all get to their feet, reaching for weapons, for clothing, and scramble on board the junker that we decided to name "The Monster," after Frankenstein's creation, a similar construction of disparate parts. I hope our monster treats us better.

The Ferals are pushing their way in as I reach up to two switches that start the engines. They're not situated in the most convenient place, but we didn't have a lot of time or materials to work with. As I'm reaching, Tomas comes up behind me and lifts me up where I can kick them both into gear.

One of the problems with our plan was the need to get the doors open. If we had two people do it (and it would need two at a minimum), they would be torn apart by Ferals. And even if they weren't, it would be hard to catch up to the Monster. So we had to come up with an alternate plan.

When we tallied up what was left after building the Monster, we realized we still had a few tanks of gas. The thing about gas is that it is held under intense pressure. When that pressure is released, it can pack quite a force. I once saw a pressurized gas cylinder used as a torpedo. All you need to do is to shear off the regulator, and the cylinder will take off like a rocket. We lined up three of them, held in place by some extra metal. Another piece of metal, long and thin, had been rigged to fall down on the regulator ends.

I turn to make sure that everyone is on board the Monster, and as I do a Feral wriggles through the crack and drops to the ground. Like a worm. Or something being born.

I reach for the chain that's rigged to the hanging metal and yank it. The metal falls down, straight and hard on the regulators. One of them stays attached, but the other two shear off, and two metal cylinders take off for the door as if fired from a gun. Both hit the door and tear it from the tracks that hold it in place. The door falls to the ground with a clatter, landing on many of the Ferals standing in front of it. Then I leap aboard the truck and hit the brake release. We shoot forward into the breach.

CHAPTER SEVENTEEN

FROM THE JOURNAL OF MIRANDA MEHRA

I know I haven't written for weeks. For a while there was nothing to write about. I worked on the vaccine and it was slow going. Maya came to me. "You could be doing better," she said.

"I'm doing the best I can," I told her. "This is complicated work."

"It's all complicated work," she said. That evening, as she escorted me back to my cell, she took a detour. Back into the hallway that led to their conditioned Feral. She didn't open the door, but as soon as I saw it, I couldn't breathe. I felt lightheaded, and my heart pounded in my chest. I almost fell over. Maya had to help me get back to the cell. "We need results," she said before closing and locking the door.

So I redoubled my efforts. And it must have paid off, because a few weeks later, Maya took me aside to say that the Helix was pleased with my progress. "What would help you move more quickly?" she asked.

I had to think about it for a while. They didn't often ask my opinion. "More eyes. More hands," I said. The next day, there was a new face in the lab. He was an older man, gray-white hair on his head, gray-black hair in his beard, a scar on his forehead. He wore a few pens clipped to his shirt pocket. He seemed serious but had kind eyes. "This is Dimitri," Maya said. "You tell him what to do."

He said hello and walked with me to my station. I couldn't help but grasp his hand, hopefully where no one could see.

I'm sure they know we're friends, that we sleep in the cells next to one another. Still, I had to force myself to hold back. I was afraid that if I showed some enthusiasm, they would take him away from me.

Now I have my extra set of hands and eyes, and it's hard to not think that I have an ally now, alongside me. Someone whom I've shared things with for months now, who has shared with me. We talk about the vaccine in the lab, and at night, we talk about our fears.

My latest is that because of our progress, I'm already looking forward to the next stage. The testing. We can use animal subjects, but, knowing the Helix, that won't be good enough. What's to stop them from using as test subjects any of the people that the Valhallans capture? What's to stop them from using whole settlements as test cases?

"Don't think about that," Dimitri tells me. "That day isn't here yet. For now we just have to focus on getting through today. Tomorrow will be a new day, a new challenge. We just have to focus on what's right in front of us."

So that's what I'm trying to do.

✳   ✳   ✳

Our progress also warranted another outing, escorted once again by Maya. This time, they allowed me to bring someone with me. So I chose Dimitri.

Maya took us to one of Valhalla's bars, a place called Utgard. Yet another mythological name that means something to the barbarians that run this city. The drink of choice again is mead, so Dimitri and I sat and sipped ours, surrounded by cutthroats and thugs.

Surprisingly, Maya wandered about the bar, keeping an eye on us but not listening. Leaving Dimitri and me some privacy.

"Thank you for bringing me," he said.

"You've been a big help to me," I said." And not just in the lab."

"I could say the same," he said. Then he looked at my face, my expression." What's wrong?"

I stared into the mead." Things are proceeding so quickly. We keep getting closer to the vaccine."

"That's good, isn't it?"

"Is it?" I asked." Once they have it, they'll be practically unstoppable. And I can't figure out a way to halt our progress."

I took a long gulp of the mead.

"Unless I stop myself."

Dimitri leaned forward." What?"

"I seem to be the one making the progress for the vaccine. Maybe without me . . ."

"Miranda," he said." You can't."

"Why not?"

"Because—"

But he never got to finish the sentence.

Because Surtr and his elite security force walked in, sending a ripple through the room. The whole bar quieted and stilled. I instinctively moved closer to Dimitri. Maja returned to us a moment later.

Surtr walked up to the bar and ordered a drink, and everyone in the bar relaxed a bit. But the atmosphere changed while he was there. He only had the one drink, and he talked quietly with his companions. Dimitri, Maja, and I barely spoke. I couldn't take my eyes off of Surtr.

Then, as he turned from the bar, he saw us. I considered running, but instead I stayed at my seat. He walked over to us.

"You," he said, staring at me. His voice carried the hint of a growl." No longer hiding with the other fleas."

Maya stood up, but Surtr reached out and pushed her down in her chair.

"Out here among my people."

My heart hammered in my chest, sending waves of pressure rippling out through my body.

His lips curled back from his teeth. "This is my city." He raised a hand and made a quick gesture, and all of the Valhallan guards in the bar drew their weapons. Stood at attention. All eyes were on me.

Surtr turned, smiling, and grabbed a knife from one of his men. He turned it back to me. Began tracing the tip over my face, my neck, my chest.

Everything in me screamed at me to run. But I knew that was what he wanted. So I put all of my effort into standing still, keeping my breathing as regular as I could, and not moving beyond the shaking I couldn't suppress.

He lifted the tip of the knife to my chin, gently pushing against it until the tip pierced the skin and I raised my head toward him under the pressure. I swallowed, trying to keep the movement small, still feeling the knife point in the soft flesh. He removed it.

"You should smile more," he said, lowering the knife.

I just stared at him.

His mirth disappeared. "Smile."

I closed my eyes for a moment, seeking some kind of centering. Then I opened my eyes and smiled. I tried to let it come naturally, imagined seeing my friends again. Seeing Ben again.

His smile returned. "Good," he said. It sounded like an engine rumbling. "You look so much better when you smile."

The knife returned too, the point scraping down the skin of my collarbone and to the top of my chest. "Maybe next time . . . next time we'll get better acquainted."

Then he handed the knife back to its owner, did another

hand gesture that had all of his men put their weapons away, and walked out of the bar.

I sank to the stool, my legs no longer able to hold me. I raised my finger to my chin and felt the bead of blood there. Dimitri offered me another sip of my drink." No," I said." Take me back."

Maya stared at me.

"Take me back!"

So she did. I couldn't even speak to Dimitri on the return trip. I just collapsed into my cell, like I had so many times before, and huddled on my sleeping mat.

Wondering when this nightmare was going to end.

✳   ✳   ✳

For three nights, I barely slept. I lay awake, thinking about how I was helping the enemy and running my fingers over the scars on my wrist. I knew the tactics they could use. The thought of being tossed into the Feral cage still sent me into fits of shaking, and yet at least that would be an end. An end to the fear, to the pain. After that, they couldn't use me anymore. Maybe they would find the vaccine on their own. But they wouldn't do it with my help.

The decision was easy in the end.

So when they came to get me the next day, I didn't get up. I didn't walk to the door. I lay on my mat, like something broken. Something dead. Maya screamed at me. Then she ordered the guards to take me. They picked me up by my armpits and then dragged me to the lab, where they shoved me into my seat.

I didn't work, though. I didn't flip open the lab book. I didn't pick up my pen. I just sat there.

The first hit by the guard knocked me out of the chair. I fell to the ground, writhing in pain. _It's only temporary,_ I told myself. Then a kick knocked all the air out of me. Then one of the guards picked me up by my hair. I remained limp. Uncooperative.

"Stop!" Maya said.

The guard looked at her like she had spoiled his fun. But he lowered me to the ground.

Maya bent down to me, put her face in front of mine. "Are you sure you want to do this?" she asked. "You know what the next step is. Do you really want to see Herbie again?"

Even the name she had given the thing sent me into panic. I hadn't been intending to respond, but I met her eyes. And smiled.

That cage was actually my best bet. Even if the Feral didn't attack me, it was still a Feral. I could still infect myself. I could still render myself useless to them.

Maya searched my eyes, my face, and frowned.

"Take her back to her room," she said to the guards.

"No," I said. "Take me to the Feral." The guards came and lifted me up. "What are you afraid of?" I screamed at her. Because I had seen it there in her eyes. Fear.

They dragged me back to my room, threw me roughly on the floor, and then locked the door. My face hurt, my ribs, too. But I felt like I had won the round.

I was so stupid.

Maya came to my door later. With the guards again. They came and dragged me out of my room. Only they didn't take me far. They brought me to the door next to mine. Dimitri's door.

Maya gave me a hard look, then opened the door.

Inside, a naked Dimitri hunched over himself, his left arm wrapped in a sling.

"No!" I screamed. "What did you do?"

Dimitri looked up. Dark circles ringed his eyes, and his skin looked waxy. I saw cuts on him. What looked like burns. And the nails on one of his hands were completely gone. Just angry red wounds where they used to be.

I gasped, and my hand went to my mouth as tears filled my eyes.

I tried to go to him, but the guards dragged me out, throwing me back into my room.

"Do the work," Maya said." If you don't, others will suffer. Maybe Dimitri again. Maybe even your dear Ben."

"You don't have him," I said.

She gave me a grim smile." Do you really want to take that chance?"

The truth is, I don't. I can gamble with my own life. But not with Dimitri's. Not with yours, Ben. Not with anyone else's.

They've won. They do own me.

I see no way out that isn't covered in blood.

CHAPTER EIGHTEEN

The Monster lurches forward into the night and hits the door, now lying on the ground. The impact jars the whole junker and throws me off my feet. I grip tightly to the railing I've been leaning on and only just manage to keep myself from flying off. The engines are kicking up speed now and with steady force we slam into the Ferals gathered beyond the fallen door . Several at the front go down in a spray of blood across the ballonet skin, and the wheels crush them beneath us. I hope that Sondra, up front in the steering position, is free of the spray. But the Ferals are all around us and we're not going fast enough yet. They're reaching for the edge, trying to pull themselves onto the platform.

With my one hand still firmly around the railing on the side of the truck, I reach down for my revolver. My hand closes on air.

Ellie still has my gun. I look over to her, on the other side of the flatbed. A Feral tries to pull itself up that side. Ellie raises the revolver and fires. The recoil knocks her back a bit, but the Feral falls away.

Good girl.

As I'm processing this, a Feral clambers up the side of the Monster, pulling itself up by the same railing that I'm clinging to. Its dirty, blond hair streams behind us, even as the engines rev up even more.

I lash out with the only weapon I have left, my boot, but I miss the face and instead hit the shoulder.

Its clawed hands close on my other leg, by the ankle, its mouth open like it's ready to clamp down on me. So with it on my leg and my hands on the railing, I lift myself up, my other leg coming up and coming down hard on the thing's head. Once. Twice. The third shot smacks its face against the floor; it falls away as we move on.

All around me, others are repelling similar would-be boarders. Buzz swings his metal pipe, and Tomas his baseball bat. Ellie and Coretta both fire down at the oncoming Ferals. Sondra is, thankfully, at the steering wheel, where she has all the light, and she's more protected than the rest of us, but that depends on us keeping them from climbing aboard.

Good enough.

I use my boots as much as possible, slamming them down on fingers and wrists and arms. I kick in teeth and noses and try to break bones wherever I can.

I spare a look behind us, at the back of the Monster, and see the mass of Ferals there, trying to keep up but unable to. That means we just have to contend with the ones still clinging to the Monster.

I step to the edge and sight down at one, bald and scabby, trying to keep its grip. Then, thinking better, I turn to Tomas. "All clear?" I call.

He nods.

"Lend me your bat?"

He nods again and tosses it to me. I catch it, take a moment to feel its heft, then swing down with it at the bald Feral. I catch it in the head, in the back, and the arm. It falls away as well, tumbling in our wake, narrowly missing the crush of the wheels.

I shake off the bat, then turn to hand it back to Tomas. I step forward, not wanting to toss it to him with the Feral blood all over it. Tomas graces me with a rare smile.

"Thanks," I say, holding it out.

He reaches out, and then suddenly falls back, and I see the Feral clinging to his leg. They both go spilling over the side, and out of the flatbed. As I rush forward, still ready to extend the bat to him, the Feral climbs atop him and bites into his cheek in a hot spray of blood. Two more stragglers who were chasing us fall upon him. Buzz next to me is vibrating with rage and sadness.

"Ellie!" I yell, and hold out my hand. She slaps the revolver into it and I bring it up, aiming behind us, where Tomas fell. We're moving quickly, but I do my best to sight, and fire off three shots before we're too far away, hoping that at least one of those bullets finds Tomas.

Then we roll on into the night.

After a frantic round of checking for cuts and scrapes (with none obvious) we take the main road in town out to the fence, and then out to where it reaches the nearest highway. Coretta is familiar with the area from trading and outreach trips, so she guides us. But Sondra is the first person to ask the question we've all been wondering. "Do we know where we're heading?"

Coretta stands up from where she'd been huddling with Ellie. "If we stay on this route," she says, "we should find another town. Something. Somewhere we can forage and try to figure out our next move."

"If the road holds," Buzz says. "If there isn't anything blocking it off."

"We'll just have to take our chances," I say. "We can steer this thing. Or stop it if we need to."

"And if we disturb another pack of Ferals along the way?" Buzz asks.

I shake my head. "What do you suggest, Buzz?" I ask. "I'm sure all of us would love to hear your better plan."

He scowls at me but then turns away.

I address everyone. "The engines will last a while longer with the fuel we have on board. Assuming we don't spring a leak in the ballonets, we should be good for another half day. Also assuming, as Buzz said, that we don't hit some kind of obstacle. But I agree that the best bet for us is to continue going until we see a settlement or structure where we can find shelter and forage, or maybe even find some better kind of transport."

No one says anything, so I continue. "We should take the opportunity to get some rest. If you can. We can have two people keep watch while the others sleep, or just give your bodies a rest. One in front on the steering wheel and one in back. We only have the one flashlight, so the person in front gets that and uses it if they hear something or need to check out any potential obstacles. Yes?"

Some of them shrug. Others nod. Buzz looks away.

"If anyone sees something, they have to let us all know." I make sure I meet them all in the eye. Each one. Even Buzz. "You saw what happened to Tomas. It can happen like that." I snap my fingers.

I see Ellie flinch, and I feel shame for doing that, but this is important. Normally I would be scoffing at entrusting my life to these strangers. These optimists. These idealists. But I don't want to see any more of them die. Not even Buzz.

Not any of them.

I move to Coretta. "See if you can get Ellie to sleep. I'll take the first watch."

"Me, too," Buzz says.

"Okay. The rest of you get some shut-eye, if you can."

Coretta looks at me doubtfully, but she takes Ellie by the shoulders, and they move to the center of the Monster. "I guess it's just me and you, then," I say to Buzz.

"I want the front," he says, in his usual, surly way.

"You need to use the flashlight," I say. "Can you do that?"

He just gives me a look that says, *of course I can, shithead.*

"You have to let me know if you see anything."

He meets my eyes and just sets his jaw.

"I get you don't like me," I say. " I don't give a shit either way, but if you endanger the rest of them because of some grudge you have against me, I will make it a point to make sure you get your brains blown out before I go."

He looks at me, incredulous. "You think that I wouldn't . . . *You're* the stranger. We barely know you."

I walk a step closer to him and put my face in front of his. "None of that matters. Our lives are tied together now. Our survival depends on one another. Each one of us matters. You. Ellie. Sondra. Coretta. And yes, me. You're just going to have to take all that disappointment and choke it down, like an under-cooked piece of rat meat, because that's what's going to get you through to tomorrow."

He clenches his jaw so hard, the muscles flex in his cheeks. Then he grabs the flashlight from my extended hand and moves to the front of the junker to relieve Sondra.

After talking all that toughness, I move to the back of the junker and hope that Buzz doesn't get us all killed.

My watch passes without incident. I'd like to say that I let Buzz be the big man up front, but the truth is that every so often I move to the front to make sure everything is okay, that he hasn't fallen asleep, or that he isn't missing the barricade or a crack in the road that would derail this whole thing. But everything seems okay. He deploys his flashlight periodically to check out something to the side of the road. Then, when I am satisfied that it isn't anything threatening, I slink to the back unseen and resume my watch, which isn't eventful. Hell, I can't see much, even with my vision adjusted to the dark. But I listen. And I smell. And I hope that I'll be able to pick up the presence of any Ferals. Or wild animals. Or anything.

I stay there for a while until someone taps me on the shoulder—Coretta. Already the dark of the sky is lightening to a grayish glow all around us. "You're relieved," she says.

I nod and stand up. "Did you manage to get any sleep?" I ask.

"Something in the general area." She shrugs. "It was better than nothing."

I nod to her. "Buzz did well."

"Not a surprise."

"Ellie?"

"I think she slept for a bit."

"Good."

"Go do the same."

"Yes, sir."

So I move to the center of the junker and I lie down on my side, cradling my head in the crook of my arm and curling my legs to fit them into the space there. Buzz takes up position on the other side. I think about saying something to him, but then I think about his reaction—a sneer or something like that—and instead I close my eyes and hope that I can dig up something resembling sleep.

I lie in that position for a while, my eyes closed, trying to find sleep. Hoping for it. Hoping for some kind of rest. Thinking of rest makes me think about the temple. And the settlement. The idea that I was going to put my father to rest. Put myself to rest. Place the ending on the story. Wrap up the loose ends and close all the doors.

Then all of this happened. In that moment that I saw the explosions, I had a thought. That I hated the Valhallans. That they were to blame for everything that had gone wrong. Or if not everything, enough of it. Enough for me to hate them. Enough for the world to be a better place without them in it.

I think, there, in the predawn dark, that if I don't fall into a crevasse or get chewed on by a Feral or starve to death, I'll find a way to do something. To hurt them. Even if it's just one of them. Even if it takes me out in the process. Because that there's the real revenge. Not Tess. Tess, if anything, was just a pawn. Someone trying to play both sides. That came back and bit her, and that's done and gone. But the people behind most of the evil in the world were the Valhallans. And the Cabal. They deserve a little pain for their sins. No. They deserve a lot of pain. But if I can deliver even a little, that's something.

A knife to the gut in the dark.

Something like sleep comes over me some time later. Until the cries wake me up.

I sit up straight and clamber my way to the front of the Monster, thinking that maybe we hit an obstacle or the road had fallen away ahead of us. Instead, I see Buzz pointing off into the distance. There, on the horizon, and on surprisingly flat ground, is a settlement of sorts. Coming up fast. I get a glimpse of tall walls. And towers.

"I'll slow us," I say, then I rush to the back where the engines are, and with the trailing engine controls dial us down to a less breakneck speed at which we can consider our next move.

As we slow, I see something in motion on the side of the wall; and a moment later, a ground vehicle, a truck of some sort, pulls out of the side and starts moving straight toward us.

I don't like the look of it. Dark metal and fluttering flags and . . . is that a cage bolted to the back?

Coretta is by me in an instant. "I don't think—"

"No," I say. "Turn us away!" I call. I start dialing the engines' speed back up, past where it was before, to hopefully give us a quick boost. Then we swerve, and I move to the other side to try to keep the new vehicle in my sight.

It's still coming toward us, and I can see it more clearly now as it emerges from a cloud of dust and grit that it just kicked up. It's the front part of a truck, the cab area painted all black; but on top of the flatbed behind it, they've bolted a large metal cage. On the side, there are platforms with men and women crouching on them, two on each side. One set sits off of the top of the truck, while the other sits just below the level of the flatbed. "That doesn't look like a welcoming party," I say.

"What do they want?" Buzz screams.

"Us," I say. "What we have." I turn to look at everyone. "But we're not going to let that happen."

The voice comes back to say, *how are you going to stop it?*

No time to think about that. I put the engines to maximum power, which is dangerous because they could die on me, but we need to put as much space as we can between us and the truck, and we're in a cobbled-together junker and they are in a ground vehicle from the Clean, probably nicely topped up with fuel and with better steering and acceleration.

"Grab that bat!" I point it out to Buzz. "Everyone grab what you can!"

The Monster is kicking up huge dust clouds now that we're off the road, which helps in that it obscures us, but it also makes it very easy for our visitors to see which way we're going.

"How many bullets do you have left?" I ask Coretta.

"Five."

"Get 'em ready."

I check the revolver. Six in the cylinder. I count the bullets in my pockets. Or where I think the bullets are. Then I remember. I gave them to Ellie.

I'm moving toward her, the revolver down by my side, when the bullets start flying.

"Get down!" I call out and then follow my own advice, ducking back behind the engine casing. I sneak my head around, deafened by the roar of the engines, and see the people on the platforms raising rifles. Sparks fly off the engines next to me. They're not shooting at us. They're shooting at the engines.

I pop out from my cover and take a bead on one of the shooters, squeeze the trigger. Only once. I stop the second pull. Can't go through the bullets too fast.

Of course my shot misses, and then they start firing at me. I drop back into my cover.

They clearly want us for something. No use wasting bullets and fuel on killing a bunch of stragglers. And the junker isn't worth anything to them. Not if they have a working truck. So they want us.

And there's that cage on the back of the truck.

Slavers. Again.

I look back at Sondra, trying to take cover behind a railing, the bat held firmly in front of her. Coretta crouches just past her, automatic out, trying to get a clear shot at someone.

Slavers.

I inch my head and arm out around the engine, and try to hold my arm steady, which is impossible with all the bumping and jostling. The driver's too well covered—I can barely see him—but if I can take out enough of the men on the outside, they won't have anyone to board us or take us down.

I line up on one side, try to compensate for the movement, and fire. Three shots this time.

One of them finds the mark and the shooter falls limp, but now I see that the shooter is still attached to the truck. Smart. The shooter bangs and bumps and twists on its platform, which temporarily distracts the other shooter on that side.

Good.

Only two bullets left and then I'm dry.

Now what, Ben?

Slavers. They don't want the junker. They want us alive. They'll probably be okay with shooting me to make it easier to take the rest, but they'll want to keep the others intact so they can sell them off. Which means we have a little bit of an advantage. Because I want to kill all those fuckers.

So I move back to the engines and turn down our speed. It will allow them to get closer, but that will give me a better shot at them. The trick is turning the speed down just enough so they don't get on top of us.

Then, as I watch, the remaining three platformers put themselves flat against the side of the truck, like they're hugging it, and the truck shoots forward. Too far. Too fast.

I pop out and fire twice for the windshield, where the driver should be sitting, but the first shot hits an overhang of armor, and the second one hits the armored front.

Fuck. "Reload!" I yell, and slide the revolver over to Ellie. She catches it neatly, nods, and starts fishing bullets out of her pocket.

Then the truck leaps forward and slams hard into our backside.

For a moment I'm thrown into the air from the impact. Gunshots ring out from the truck and I get down, but bullets hit one of the ballonets, and it becomes a limp rag. Only four left, which gives the engines more work to do as the weight of the truck increases.

One of the people on the side of the truck detaches herself from the side and runs across the hood of the vehicle and onto the back of the Monster. I move forward, only to realize that I don't have the revolver back yet and I just gave the bat to Sondra. I grapple the woman before she can reach the engine controls. She's wrapped in tight fabric, a hard helmet and visor over her head. She slaps my arm away and slams me hard in the face.

For a moment I can't see from the stinging pain. A bat swings out by my head—Sondra—but the slaver catches it on an arm. If it hurts her, she doesn't show it. The slaver throws Sondra back and moves toward the engines. I try to intercept her, grab for her wrist, hoping I can overpower her. Though it doesn't look like I can. She elbows me in the chest, and I lose my grip and then—

BANG.

I duck instinctively, only to see the slaver fall back from the Monster and onto the hood of the truck. I reach for the engine controls and turn them back up. With a lurch we pull away from the slaver truck. "Turn!" I yell. We curve away from the truck, and I'm thrown against a railing.

I turn to see Ellie, still holding the revolver. "Thanks," I say. She just nods back to me.

Really like that girl.

The slaver truck takes a moment to reorient back on us, but it quickly closes the gap. We're moving slower now, with some of our lift gone, and the engines are pushed to the max. I'm worried that they'll overheat soon, and then we'll be done. We need to lose some weight. And we need to find a way to stop the slavers.

I look at Coretta and Ellie, even Buzz, these poor idiots who tried to find a better life and now are the only survivors. I think about how people like me are better suited for this world and how fucked up that is. The world could use more like them.

I beckon Buzz over. I'm forced to yell over the sound of the engines, but I point up to the controls and explain how they work. "I'm going to slow us down again," I say. "But then you speed right back up. Push them to the max until you have a decent lead, then keep them somewhere in the middle. Don't want them to overheat or give out on you."

"Why are you telling me this?" he asks.

I just smile at him. "Give me the bat," I say. He holds it out to me. I take it. "Thanks."

I turn to Ellie and bend down to her. "Good shot before," I say. "Keep shooting like that, and you'll be better than me in no time."

She presents the revolver to me, holding it by the trigger guard so the grip is toward me. I feel a lot of things in that moment—incredible affection, admiration, pride, but also an undercurrent of momentous sadness. I push the revolver back gently. "You keep it," I say. "Use it well." I rise back up. "Remember what I showed you." I place a hand on her head and give it a little tousle. "Take care of these guys for me."

Then I hit the controls to slow us down. The truck speeds up, once more looking to ram us. "Get ready!" I say to Buzz. Then, when it's just about to hit, I jump across the gap between the vehicles.

My feet come down on the hood of the truck and then slide, and I have to drop to my hand to stabilize myself. I try to get a swing off at the windshield, but in my position it just lands weakly without doing anything.

The truck swerves, and I shift to one side, but I reach out, see the free strap hanging there, and grab it, swinging out and to the side. I dangle from the strap, slamming into the side of the truck. A hand, from a person on the platform below, grips my leg, pulling me down, yanking on me. I hold tight to the strap, but only with my left hand, fingers rigid. With my right hand, I swing downward with the bat, as hard and as wildly as I can.

The hand lets go for a moment, and I manage to pull myself up onto the upper platform. Making sure I'm in a stable position, or as stable as I'm going to get—legs curled beneath me, strap wrapped around my arm—I swing the bat again, this time aiming for the driver's window and whatever else I can hit. I feel impact as the bat strikes metal but nothing else. My arm is already aching from the reverberation of the hits.

Another hand grabs for me from above, aimed at my face; it grabs my chin and starts pulling. I look up to see another of the slavers on top of the truck, trying to pull me off. My neck protests in pain as my head is pulled back. I think about just jumping off of the truck and trying to roll away. But I still need to buy the Monster time to lay down some distance.

I brace myself on the platform. With one hand, I pull on the slaver's arm. With the other, the one grabbing the strap, I wrap that strap around the arm, tangling it as much as I can.

The slaver tries to pull his hand away but can't. The hand is trapped. I ready the bat and—

I'm pulled down again by the slaver beneath me and I fall. There's a mad moment of chaos as I tumble out into air, but I scrabble and manage to hold onto the slaver, trailing him and then holding onto his leg. The bat goes whirling off behind us. We're still moving at speed, and we both slam into the side of the truck.

Then he slips, and I slip, and my feet scrape ground for a moment until I climb back up his legs, then to his waist. He's holding on to the strap with both arms, so I use his clothes and his harness to climb up. One. Limb. At. A. Time. He takes one hand off of the strap to try to shake me loose. I catch sight of his gun beneath him, strapped around his chest. But I can't reach it, not tangled up underneath him. If only I had a weapon . . .

Holding onto his shoulder strap, I get one arm around his neck, pulling it back. I fumble at the gun straps, trying to pull it free. Trying to . . . just . . . re ach . . . for . . .

The truck suddenly stops.

I jerk forward, without an anchor, and fly through the air.

I hit the ground—hard— and I try to roll, but everything feels broken.

I hear the truck door open and raise my head to see two sets of boots walk toward me.

I manage to get my head up further and then force the rest of my body to follow. Everything hurts, everything feels battered and crushed, and I can barely breathe, but I shakily rise to my feet.

I feel like I'm in thick soup. One of the men, wearing a cowboy hat and a white mask made up to look like a skull, wades in. I try to move aside as he raises his fists, but one slams into my stomach and I drop again, coughing and spitting.

"You son of a fucking bitch," he says. Then, "Get him up."

The other guy comes around and jerks me up from behind, holding me by my armpits. I want to say something, mouth off. My mouth is the only weapon I have left, but I can't figure out how to make that happen. Then Skull Mask's meaty hand closes on my throat and my breath starts to fade.

Missed your chance, Ben. No last words for you.

Then, sudden pain in my neck, down near my shoulders. I catch sight of a syringe pulling away. Skull Mask removes his hand from my throat, and it trails other hands behind it. An endless flutter of hands following him as he backs up. I feel my head swim and my legs go liquid. I try to hold myself up.

Why?

What?

. . .

CHAPTER NINETEEN

When I come to, I'm in the back of the truck. I'm sitting up and my hands are bound behind me, looped into the cage. I'm not alone. The cage is full of people. Men, women; light, dark. They all look bedraggled, but mostly unharmed. There are a few bruises and scrapes, but nothing serious. Nothing that would mark down value significantly.

Next to me is a man with dark hair and a thin, tan face. He has bad skin and a couple of days' growth of facial hair. His face is completely uncovered, which unnerves me, but then all of the people here are. Myself included. I don't know what they did with my goggles and scarf and hat.

My head is pounding, the aftereffects of whatever they gave me to knock me out. But I try to push my brain to functioning. That we're all here, tied up, means we're going to market. Either to be sold, or else to deliver on a promise. I can't really discern any pattern in the people here. A couple of them are on the bigger side, but not by much. And no one here is well-fed. Probably market, then. Where the more depraved and wealthy individuals of the Sick will barter for people.

Dad and I didn't come by slavers too often. That's one of the benefits of living in the air. Most of the time, you're more worried about pirates or raiders. Even then, they'll just take your ship and leave you to die.

But down on the ground? That's another story. I'd heard about slavers when visiting a trading post or settlement, but they were shadowy concepts, fodder for my imagination when I was young. I remember asking Dad who would buy slaves. Most people barely had enough food or water or fuel for themselves. Who had enough to buy whole people? His answer was simple and straightforward. "Life is cheap," he said. "You can own someone for very little."

And there are those who would be considered rich in the Sick. People sitting on stockpiles of food or weapons or materials. People with rare skills that are in demand. People who start their own settlements and make free with their settlers' things. For people like that, they can almost barter for anything they want. If what they want is a person, well . . .

The trick, at least as far as I see it, is being able to enforce that slavery. Someone might barter for me, to use as a sex slave or labor or, hell, for target practice, but they have to be able to hold me. Restrain me. Buying a slave that you then have to keep under watch and guard all the time hardly seems worth the trouble. There are . . . ways, of course. Horrific ways that I've heard of. I don't like to think of them. But they're the extreme cases.

If you want to keep a slave around for a while, then you have to keep them fed and watered, let them live in a place that isn't covered in shit (or risk disease). That's a lot of capital to spend.

So, yeah, I guess I don't really understand the whole slave economy very much. But I have a feeling I'm going to get an education very soon.

The ride passes mostly in silence. Occasionally someone coughs. Every so often there's a grunt. A sniffle. But no one says very much.

Until one of the men in the group starts screaming. It starts as a slow grunt that builds into a growl, and then rises in volume and pitch until he's in full-on scream mode. One of the others tells him to shut up, but he just continues. Then he starts pulling on his bonds, straining at his bonds until his face is red. After a few minutes of this, the truck rolls to a stop. Only, Screamer doesn't stop. His face is bright red now, his wet mouth is open, the cords on his neck rigid.

It's annoying as hell, but I'm more curious than anything. Has this guy really lost it, or is this some kind of play? If the latter, I want to be ready in case all hell breaks loose. My hands are tied behind me. But my legs are free. That's something.

Two of the slavers come to the back of the cage, one with a shotgun in his hands, ready to fire. They wear mostly black, or clothes that used to be black and are now gray from all the dust. Unlike us, they wear masks. One of them has a bandana around the lower side of his face and a kind of hard, black helmet like a beetle on his head. That's the one with the shotgun. The other one has a full cloth face mask with eyeholes and a mouth hole cut out of it. That one moves to Screamer's wrists and unties them. Then he moves to the door of the cage and opens it. He climbs up into the cage, a small pistol down by his side. He walks up to Screamer, who is still screaming, but now also wiping his hands together, like he's washing them, but there's no water.

"Stop," the slaver commands in a gravelly voice.

Screamer doesn't. He looks up at the slaver with wide eyes and a red face, but he doesn't stop. By now he's sucking in lungfuls of air between screams, and there are tears in his eyes either from the effort or from emotion, and he's still wiping his hands in front of him. Then he lowers his head and rocks back and forth, still screaming.

The slaver doesn't repeat himself. Instead, he bends down and hooks his free hand under Screamer's armpit and pulls him to his feet. He guides Screamer to the door of the cage, showing surprising care in helping him off of the truck. The other slaver, with the shotgun, swivels smoothly to cover the man. The slaver with the pistol pushes Screamer to his knees, places the pistol to the side of his head, and shoots.

The screams stop.

The slavers lock up the cage and disappear.

A moment later, the truck continues on.

I try to sleep. There's nothing much else that I can do, restrained like I am. Oddly, restrained gently—not with metal cuffs or even plastic, but with something softer, like cloth. I'm guessing it's so they wouldn't cause too much damage. Or risk the loss of stock.

If I'm going to try to make my escape, it's going to be when we get to where we're going. As long as I don't scream or make too much trouble, they will keep me alive until we get there.

That's the theory, at least.

So I try to sleep, and I get to something mostly resembling it. The bumping and swaying of the cage actually hits a rhythm, and while I don't fall into a deep sleep, I fall into a trance. Images flicker behind my eyes, images of people. Of places. My father. Claudia. The gone-but-not-forgotten *Cherub*.

Miranda.

That's the one I try to shy away from. To close my already-closed eyes to. But that's the face that comes back. Miranda. Her hair tumbling out in front of her glasses. A half smile on her face as she looks up at me. The tiny patches of freckles across her face.

I miss you, Miranda.

As if acknowledging that unlocks some kind of door, I see them all, then. All the boffins, particularly Clay and Sergei. I don't even tense up at the appearance of Clay's face. Then Diego and Rosie. Mal. Tess. Cheyenne. Even Lewis from Tamoanchan.

Haunted by ghosts.

Restrained in that cage, I can't escape them.

It goes on like that—images from the past in half-dreams of shadowy darkness until the truck stops, and we're all released from the cage. One of the slavers barks out to us, "When the door opens, walk out and stand in a line. Do you understand? Try anything, or don't do as you're told, and you will be punished. Is that clear?"

He doesn't wait for an answer. Instead, he moves to the door and opens it. Through the bars I can see maybe eight slavers. All armed in some way. All prepared for some kind of resistance. They look like veterans—they've no doubt done this many times before. So we do what they say. It becomes a kind of calculated gamble. You can try to make a break for it now, when there are eight and possibly more slavers who have seen all of the tricks in the book. Or you can wait to see if you're bought, and maybe try something on the other side, when you're with someone who might not be as savvy and might not have the guns or the numbers on his side.

Then again, maybe that works against you as well.

Me, I've decided to bide my time. Unless shit starts blowing up. But for now, I'm content to go along with this. Until I can make a better move.

I follow the others to the door of the cage and carefully climb down to the ground, where I get in line behind the guy with the slightly scarred cheeks. As I slowly take in where we are, and what's in front of me, I recognize it. I never saw it from this angle—not on the ground—we were smuggled inside the first time. But I did take off from it, with the *Cherub*, and I did move around inside of the place. I remember the color of the walls and the pipes that raced along them from one room to another. There's no other place this could be. I do the mental calculations in my head, and it's right, geographically. Based on the time we've been traveling, it would put us right there. At least as close as I can guess. Yes, it has to be. I have to be right.

I'm back in Gastown's helium plant.

CHAPTER TWENTY

FROM THE JOURNAL OF MIRANDA MEHRA

Days have passed, and I'm back at work on the vaccine. Between that and sleep, there's little else. Dimitri came back to the lab yesterday, his arm still in a sling. Some of his wounds are starting to heal, though. But he won't meet my eyes very often. I think he still holds it against me, the torture—how can I blame him?

It wasn't the Helix this time, either. Not Maya. It was the Valhallans. True experts in torture and sadism.

To say I had little hope, little sense of anything good in the world, would be an understatement. I felt like I wasn't in control of anything anymore. I wasn't even a person. I was just a number in an equation.

Then someone new just walked into the lab.

He was delivering a bag full of supplies, and at first I didn't look up, but then he dropped them off at the next station from mine, and I glanced up and saw him.

Clay.

My Clay.

Here. On Valhalla.

Something surged inside of me. Something that I didn't realize I still had. I had felt bloodless, like a corpse, but suddenly I had a heart again and my face flushed.

But I couldn't say anything. Not there. Not in front of everyone.

He looked different—his hair was longer, and he was wearing

a beard. But I would recognize that earnest expression anywhere. I gave him a little nod. "I'm Frederick," he said.

"Miranda," I said back. Very polite. Both of us pretending
we were meeting for the first time. Then he left.

I haven't been able to think of much else since. Was he
also kidnapped from the island? Or was he press-ganged? The
last time I saw him, he was on Tamoanchan, still there as the
Helix and Valhallans were attacking. Does this mean they took
the island, then? Or does it mean that he left?

One thing I'm sure of: Clay didn't join up willingly. Of all
the people I worked with, back at the commune and afterward, Clay was the most ardent. He approached science the
way religious people approached their religions. It was one of
the things that used to rub Ben the wrong way. But it was
something I always appreciated about Clay. I think he loves
Science more than I do.

What if I never see him again? What then?

Will he be able to see me again?

I don't know where he is now, or what he does here other
than deliver supplies. Or if he'll be back.

But when he is, I'll be waiting.

✳   ✳   ✳

A week passed, and Clay didn't reappear in the lab. My hopes
sunk, thinking that maybe his presence here was random, and
that he couldn't find a way to get back. That brief moment of
color in my bloodless world started to fade again to gray.

Instead, he found his way to my cell. Someone knocked at
the door, then it opened, and it was Clay.

"Clay!" I said, then caught myself.

"It's okay," he said. "I was able to get the guard to give
us some privacy."

"How?" I asked.

He shrugged. "I'm one of them. That gives me some power."

"One of them? How, Clay? Why?"

He looked behind him, then moved forward. He grabbed my hands, rubbing them. "Miranda . . ." His eyes were shining, then swelling with tears. "I thought you were dead. We all did."

I shook my head. "No. They took me here. They must have planned it."

He nodded slowly. "They wanted your knowledge and experience," he said. "That's how they operate."

"I know."

"They look for people to join them, recruiting, or else just kidnapping them to increase their ranks."

"I know," I repeated.

"I just . . ." he said. "After what happened to you . . . or what I thought happened to you. Hell, Miranda. I wanted to do something about it. Things at the island, well . . ."

"What?" I asked.

"The island got hit hard. The labs, all that we built . . ." His jaw clenched. "A man named Malik came to our rescue, and—"

"Malik? There?"

He nodded. "You know him?"

"Yes," I said, remembering being pulled out of the ocean by his people. Being a prisoner on his boat. The dinner where I got him drunk and made my escape.

"Well, he came and fought off the Valhallans. Afterward, there was a lot of rebuilding and restructuring, and Malik's people stayed on the island. They halted most of our work while things were figured out. So . . . I left."

"You?" I said. "You left the work?"

"It wasn't the work anymore," he said. He shook his head. "I needed to do something. I thought where better to get back at them than from the inside? Why not learn their secrets and their weaknesses? We had lost so much of our data. So I made my way to a settlement I knew of, and I asked around, and eventually I joined up. I started out on Gastown, but then they moved me here."

I shook my head, trying to digest it all. "Clay," I said. "So much has happened."

"And yet our paths brought us together again."

I nodded. Then it was my turn to get teary-eyed. He pulled me close, in his arms, and in that moment it felt so good to be with someone I knew, someone safe. He even smelled like I remembered. I laid my head on his chest, and he cradled it there for a while. Then he gently raised my face to his. "I'll have to go soon," he said. "Before they get too suspicious."

"Will you come back?" I asked.

"Of course," he said, as if there would ever be an alternative. "I'll be back, and I'll get you out of here."

"How?"

"I think I can get access to a ship. I just have to figure out how to get you on it. In the meantime, you sit tight here and I'll visit when I can."

"Okay," I said. Something changed in me then. For months, the Helix had been breaking me down, stifling me until my fire had guttered. There, with Clay, I felt something spark inside of me. For the first time in a while, I felt something resembling hope.

Clay turned to go.

"Clay," I said, before he walked out. "What do you know about Ben?"

He turned back to me and his face and neck were red, even in the dim light. "I knew you would ask me about him."

"And?"

"When I left, he was in a cell," he said.

"The Helix did get him?"

"No," he said. "He was in a cell on the island. He survived the attack."

They didn't have him after all. All this time, and they never had him.

"I'd heard that he and Malik had some history," Clay said.

"Yes."

"I don't know much. Only rumors, but . . ."

"What is it?"

He met my eyes, then looked away. "I think they were going to execute him."

My breath caught in my chest, and the tears returned. I nodded. It wasn't a surprise that Maja had been lying to me all these months. I think I suspected it somewhere in the back of my mind. Only I couldn't take that chance. But then to learn that they didn't have him, that he might be dead . . .

"I see." I nodded again. I smiled a smile I didn't feel. "Thanks, Clay. Make sure you come back soon."

"I will," he said. "I promise."

Then he walked out and shut the door.

Afterward, I cried for a while, now knowing exactly everything I was crying for.

✳   ✳   ✳

Clay has returned four times now. Each time he brings me something. Some kind of treat. Something to eat, or a special pen, or a new notebook. Every time he does it so that we're not noticed. When we're together, we talk about the old days, about our friends, about better times. Through it all, Clay holds my hand, and I hold his hand back, as if that physical connection helps reinforce our emotional connection. As if we are anchored to one another.

Clay's still planning our escape, but he has to work some more on the plans. Getting me on the ship will be the trickiest part. Getting the ship out without anyone noticing I'm there will also take some planning. But once we solve that, we should be home free.

"But what about Maya?" I asked him, the second time. "She knows what you look like. She was on Tamoanchan."

He nodded. "That's partly the reason for the hair and beard. I thought it would help to disguise me."

"I recognized you," I said.

"Not everyone knows me as well as you do," Clay said. "But you're right. The less she sees of me, the better."

"Which makes it riskier with her always being around."

"We'll find other places to meet," Clay said.

I shook my head. "Don't you get it? They're always watching. I start meeting with someone suddenly and they'll investigate. If they start pulling on strings, it all might unravel."

"I'm willing to take that risk." He grabbed my hand in his and it was rough, and warm. "What else can we do?"

I leaned my head against his chest, once more comforted by something familiar. I didn't feel confident, but I let his confidence buoy me. I clung to him, the only bright and good thing in my life.

"We're smart," he said. "We'll figure it out." Then he threw his arms around me, and we stayed like that for a while.

What I didn't say to him before he left is that I'm not entirely sure that the people watching us, the people keeping us, aren't smarter.

CHAPTER TWENTY-ONE

We're in an inner yard of sorts, some place where they can bring in vehicles. We're in our line, still, the slavers in front of us, half of them with guns, the other half with long metal rods. They're soon joined by other people, rough faces, rough expressions, most likely out of Gastown or Valhalla. Some of them are wearing furs.

That confirms it, then. We're back at the plant that I visited with Claudia and Rosie. Where I rescued the *Cherub* from, only to sacrifice her to save Tamoanchan. The first attack, I mean. I didn't have a *Cherub* to sacrifice the second time.

You sacrificed something.

I brush the voice away, if only because I can't indulge that kind of thinking now. If escape was hard before, it's impossible now. The number of people guarding us has not only increased, the competency of those guards has multiplied. I've seen these people execute their workers. Without hesitation. They've probably all seen some kind of combat before. This place, this plant that still provides helium to Gastown—and, by extension, to Valhalla—is essentially an armed camp.

So my hopes crash as quickly as a downed airship, my dreams burning like a hydrogen fire.

Poor humor. But it's all I have left.

I was wrong—it's not a market. The transaction had already been made. We were being hand-delivered.

One of the Valhallans, a tall, muscled, pale man with a shaved scalp and some missing teeth walks up and down the line, inspecting us. One of the slavers stands close to him. Looking expectant, even behind his mask.

Baldy opens his mouth and hollers at us. "Do any of you know how to work machinery?"

I keep my eyes straight on him, but can feel some of the others looking at one another in the line. One woman calls out, "I once worked on a metal press and I've used other machines from the Clean."

Now I look over. Baldy comes and pulls her out of the line, and she goes to stand by one of the other Valhallans.

"Anyone else?" Baldy calls out.

No one says anything.

Baldy walks the line again. "You are all *here* to work for Gastown," he says. "*This* is the Gastown helium plant. The plant provides *helium* that is sold in the city. *You* are here to help us *operate* this plant." He talks forcefully. I can see the spray of his spittle as he barks at us. "Do a *good job*, and you may well be rewarded. Food." He meets some eyes. "Smokes." He meets others. "Sex." A broken-mouthed leer. "*Refuse* to do as you're told, or do a *bad job* . . ." He trails off.

Two more Valhallans step forward, eyeing the line. I fight the urge to meet their eyes and instead look neutrally into the distance. It only takes a moment, but then they move forward, grabbing a man out of the line and pulling him forward. The man whimpers.

"Refuse to do as you're told, or do a bad job," Baldy repeats. He removes an axe from his belt. More like a hatchet, but with a cruelly sharp-looking blade at its end. In one smooth motion, he buries the blade into the man's head. There's spray, but it goes wide of Baldy, and his people are out of its reach. The man from the line falls to the ground, his feet kicking and twitching.

"Am I clear?" Baldy cries out.

There are some assorted affirmatives and mumbled yeses.

"*Am I clear?*" Baldy roars.

The whole line says yes, and I only realize afterwards that I am one of them.

"Good," Baldy says. "You'll each be taken for a debrief, and then you will be assigned to jobs. You will be housed here on the site, fed, clothed. Excel at your tasks, and you will be well cared for. Cause problems, and . . ." He gestures to the body on the ground.

Then Baldy walks away to talk to the slavers, and each one of us in line is taken to a room with tables and benches, and we're each sat down with someone from the plant. These aren't Valhallans, though. Not even raiders. Maybe workers from the plant or even Cabal. It's not easy to spot them.

"What skills do you have?" the thin, reedy woman with reddish-brown hair asks me while tapping a hand on the surface of the table.

"I'm a pilot," I say. "Airships. A forager."

She looks me up and down, but clinically. Almost absently.

"Ever worked with machinery?"

"No."

She writes something down on a paper in front of her.

"Any physical problems?"

I meet her eyes. "I get this crick in my back every so often."

She sighs, then writes more on her paper.

"Any technical training at all?"

I spread my hands out on the table. They haven't restrained us, but there are plenty of guards and there's little to no chance of doing anything in this room. "I told you," I say. "I'm a pilot. A forager. A zep. I make my living by finding things and flying them away. I can repair an engine. Mostly. But I've never worked in an operation like this, ever."

She makes a few short strokes on the paper, then says. "We're done."

They throw me into another cell. This one is a bare room, large enough for a lot of people. There's a smell here. Human waste, I think, but covered up by some kind of antiseptic, some kind of super-strength disinfectant from the Clean.

I start to have a sneaking suspicion of why they need to hire slavers for new labor. I think back to my last time here and a man named Atticus, who helped lead me out of it, or at least most of the way out of it. He ended up dead. Because of these people. If they're as bloodthirsty here as they are elsewhere, I'm sure they've chewed their way through a lot of the people they had working here. Especially after I escaped with the *Cherub* and took out a few people along the way. I later heard from Tess that there had been a big reaction to what we did, and I wonder if that heightened things for everyone else.

More blood on your hands, Ben. More wreckage in your wake.

For now, I'm the only one in the cell, though. I guess everyone else has something that would make them useful here. Everyone except for me. What does that mean? Does it mean I'm going to be put to work sweeping up or cleaning shit? Or does it mean I'll do labor, carrying things or moving things? Or does it mean my value isn't worth them feeding me and keeping me around? My chest starts feeling tight, and I feel like I might throw up, despite the lack of food in my system.

The doors to the room open up and a guard walks around the cage. I recall this one from the yard, but he's wrapped up. Large, with a knit cap low on his head and a red plaid scarf wrapped tightly around his mouth. Dark shades and protective gear on. The guard stares at me. I stare back, not saying anything.

The guard uses a key from his belt to open the door. He enters, then closes the door behind him.

I hold my hands loose at my sides. I don't see any reason why he would be in here with me. Unless this is where he's going to kill me. I'm reminded of the antiseptic smell that lingers here.

But he has a key to the door on him. The currently unlocked door. There's nobody else here. I could try to overpower him and make my way out. He's big, but I fight dirty. Is this what they have planned? Make it look like an escape attempt so they can dispose of me quickly? Is this a test?

The man moves toward me. His weapon isn't out. He seems relaxed, almost casual, but there's a set to his walk, a way he holds his back and shoulders that makes it seem like he's prepared. That he could drop into a fighting stance at any moment, or draw a weapon and fire. But there's also something familiar in that walk. Something I can't place.

The man stops in front of me, and I have to look up at his face. All I can see are hints of brown skin around the shades and the scarf. That tells me nothing.

Then he tugs down the scarf, pulling it away from his face, and I see a full, dark beard. Then the shades are pulled off.

And I almost gasp.

"Diego. What—"

Then the massive fist comes up and punches me in the face.

* * *

The last time I saw Diego was during a dark time in my life. I had lost Miranda. *Just* lost her. Tamoanchan had been attacked. In force. Not just ships, but mutated Ferals, dropped on the island. Tearing through it. Killing people and causing fear and terror. Blood and fire and ashes. And just when things seemed like they couldn't get worse, just as I was lost, and frantic, wanting to run, to get up into the air and away from everything, where I could find a safe patch of sky (up in the Blue) and cry and grieve and fall to pieces, that's when Mal appeared.

I never figured out if he tracked his ship, the one I stole, or whether he had found out from Tess—it was something I didn't think to ask her before I killed her—but he found the island. The supposedly hidden island. And he found me. On the beach. Still shattered from what had happened to Miranda.

He wanted revenge. Of that I was sure. As he stood over me, in the sand, his eyes seemed to burn with it. Not only had I left him for dead, all those years ago, but then I returned to offer him his chance at a reckoning. Only I escaped. And I had stolen one of his ships to do so.

I didn't do it alone, of course. It was Miranda who rescued me. Sweet, smart Miranda. But Mal blamed me, and his desire for revenge must have only grown. That's how it looked on the beach. I expected him to do it then. To pull out a gun, or better yet a knife, and end it there. To sink the blade in, with his own hands, feel the hotness of it, the immediacy. I was ready for it. I almost felt like I wanted it in that moment. It would have spared me all those horrible, terrible feelings that were spewing up inside of me.

Only, he didn't do it. Instead, he had some of his men take me away. First to his ship, then later . . .

Well, I'm getting ahead of myself.

Mal arrived in the middle of the attack on Tamoanchan. On an island already devastated by the Enigma virus. The island had been caught by surprise. But the thing is, Mal came in force, too. He brought his whole group with him—the warship, carefully reclaimed and restored to full working order, and the airships that moved with it. His mercenaries and pirates and forager friends came too. They were looking for a home. And they had found, along with me, an island that was already set up.

So it wasn't a surprise that Mal made a quick decision, and, using his warship and his airships and his weapons, helped to push back the invading Valhallan/Cabal/Gastown forces. I remember being pulled aboard the ship as the cannons went off, and there was a tremendous sound, like the sky breaking open, and then airships, in the distance, exploded into fiery pieces.

A part of me cheered at that, even as another part of me cringed.

With Mal's help, the assembled Tamoanchan defense ships, once they were able to mobilize, were able to push back the attacking ships. Mal's people, along with the Tamoanchan defense forces, were able, with some casualties, to kill all the mutated Ferals that had been sent to attack. Mal helped save the day. And Tamoanchan, I later discovered, loved him for it.

But of course I didn't see all of that, because they threw me into a cell. If I ever get a tombstone, maybe that should go on it—*Ben Gold, From one cell to another, now in his last.*

As cells go, it had been one of the worst. Mal's good humor, his sense of honor, had been all but obliterated. They threw me into a dank hole, dripping with water, smelling like shit, with no clean place to sleep. Nothing to piss or shit in. Sweltering. Hot. Humid. Like the inside of a toilet.

While I remember knowing where I was—and I remember every horrible, stinking detail—I don't remember much else. They left me alone there for a while.

I knew what was going to happen. At some point, whenever Mal was ready, they would pull me out, and there would be some kind of ceremony—a mock trial, or a proclamation, or a celebration—and at the end, Mal himself would order my death, either by his hand or by hanging or drowning or whatever. He once threatened to keelhaul me, which meant tying me to the bottom of the ship and scraping me against the bottom of the ocean.

I knew that was coming, and I had resigned myself to it. This was the natural end of my story. Everything had led to this. All my past crimes had caught up to me, and this was where my trajectory had tossed me.

So I waited. And I lingered there in my own piss and shit, and I waited for the end. I looked forward to it.

They didn't really come to see me much. Mal certainly didn't. Someone would shove in some food from time to time, and sometimes I would eat it. I seem to recall a couple of times one of Mal's people coming in and force-feeding me, shoving food down my throat. Sometimes I would vomit it up. Other times

I didn't. From time to time I would wonder why they didn't just let me die, but then I realized that Mal wanted it to be a big deal. He had been imagining this day for years. He wouldn't just let me wither away in a cell. That wasn't his style. He needed to see it happen. He needed me to know that this was his revenge. He needed others to know it.

One day the cell door opened, and I didn't bother looking up because I had stopped doing that. A voice said, "My god."

Then . . . "Oh, Ben." It was said almost in the same way that Miranda would have said it. But she was dead. And it wasn't her voice. It was Diego's. Even then I didn't look up at it.

A presence drew closer. I felt the strange urge to scuttle back away from it. But I didn't. I didn't do much of anything back then. Then, louder, I heard Diego's voice. "Ben. It's me. Diego."

I mustered up the motivation to roll on my side, toward him. He was crouching, one hand on my arm, looking at me intently.

"Is it time?" I asked. My voice sounded strange in my ears. I hadn't heard it for a long time.

"Time for what?"

"What else?" I asked. "The end."

He frowned. "They let me see you," he said. "I had to pull some strings, but they let me."

"Mal?"

He nodded. "Since the attack . . . the Council welcomed him with open arms. Those that survived, that is." He looked down. "He's been appointed Protector of Tamoanchan."

I didn't bother asking him what that meant. It hardly surprised me. Mal had saved the island. He was a natural leader. He had a forceful personality. Of course he would quickly take a leadership position here. I found I didn't care.

"He wants . . ." Diego's hand faltered for a moment before coming back to my arm. "He wants to execute you. He's managed to convince the Council that you were the one who led the attackers here. That it was all of your actions that got them here."

I didn't disagree with that.

"We'll figure out a way to get you free, though," he said quickly.

I didn't say anything.

One of his hands moved to my chin, lifted my face. "You don't look so good," he said. "Are they feeding you enough?"

"They feed me," I managed to spit out.

"This isn't right. They can't keep you like this. Don't worry. I'll do something about this."

I was about to tell him not to bother. That it didn't matter. But then he was standing up again and by the door. "Don't worry, Ben," he said. "I'll fix this."

Then he was gone. Pretty soon afterward, I forgot about the visit. But some time later, I can't remember how long, someone came to the cell, and they pulled me out and they dumped me in some water and cleaned all the shit and dirt off of me. They gave me some decent food and changed my clothes and threw me back in a different cell. This one was cleaner, and there was a sleeping mat in one side that had cushion, and a blanket. And they gave me two buckets—one for liquid waste, one for solid—which they changed on a daily basis. It was only later that I realized that I probably had Diego to thank for that.

But it didn't really matter to me at the time. It was all pretty much the same, just the long wait before the end.

One day, that end came. Two guards came to the door, and they pulled me up, tied my hands, and marched me out of my cell. I didn't look at them, just shuffled where they directed me. I remember being conscious of the lack of smell once I had left my cell. Or maybe of the smell of other people and things, not just my own stink, which I had become accustomed to. Then we were out into the air, and I remember bracing myself for sunlight and instead exiting out into the dark. They pushed me down the street this way and that way. I kept thinking that Mal must have come up with a truly big spectacle. Something at night with lit torches and a bonfire. Maybe they were going to burn me alive. Or maybe they would hang me by starlight.

At one point we stopped, and my guards went to talk to someone. Or someones. I don't remember. All I remember is sinking to my knees and taking a moment's pleasure in the cool night breeze that blew across me. Now, recalling it, I remember the sound of the waves in the distance and wondering if they were going to execute me on the beach.

One of my escorts, or I thought it was, moved back to me and pulled me toward a dark patch on the ground. Then the guard turned to me and I saw that it was Diego.

"Ben," he said. He seemed as if he were waiting for me to respond, and when I didn't, he said, "I'm going to get you out of here."

"What?" I asked.

"We have to move quickly. There." He pointed to the dark patch. "It's the *Valkyrie*. Claudia is here."

Nothing he was saying made sense. I was supposed to be going to my execution. "Is she here to say good-bye?"

"What?" Diego said. "No, Ben. She's going to get you out of here."

It took a moment for the words to sink in, for me to realize. He meant off of the island. He was trying to rescue me. Steal me from my fate.

"She's waiting. We just need to get you on board, and you'll sail off." He paused and looked off at the ship. "Don't worry about me. I'll figure something out to tell the Council."

He turned back, holding out his hand.

That's when I jumped on him. I was weak from eating so poorly and living in cramped conditions. I hadn't had much exercise, and my muscles were wasted. But I flailed my limbs, all of them, and maybe because of the surprise of the attack, I managed to get Diego down to the ground, where I started pummeling him. He tried to get his hands up to protect his face, but I was a wild man. Desperate. I was screaming at him. It's a bit of a blur in my memory, but I knew that I didn't want to leave. I couldn't leave. This was what needed to happen. This was what was supposed to happen. It couldn't go on anymore. I couldn't let it. I was shrieking, like that poor sap in cage on the back of the truck. Only I was letting loose with everything. Diego didn't know what to do.

Until he did.

He threw me off of him, his superior size and strength making that easy. And maybe to shut me up, or just to stun me, he smacked me hard in the face; I wavered for a minute, and the screaming stopped. Before I could gather up what meager wits I had left, he pushed me to the ground and leaned on top of me, using his weight, putting one arm down to bar my chest, the other pinning one arm to the ground.

"Put me back," I said, with a huge effort because his arm was pressing on my lungs. "Put me back. Please." Tears leaked from my eyes as I pleaded. "Put me back."

Then, spots in front of my eyes. My vision going dark, and then . . . nothing.

When I came to again, I was back in the air. That much I could tell with the lifelong sense of a zep. I was aboard the *Valkyrie*, in the gondola, with Claudia at the pilot's chair. When she saw me stirring, she said, "It's all going to be okay, Ben. You're free. You don't have to go back there. You never have to go back."

I just sat in the corner, tears of sadness and rage rolling down my cheeks.

Diego's arm across my chest is eerily familiar to that last time I saw him. Only that time his face was creased with worry and concern. Now it's just angry.

"Diego," I gasp. "I can't breathe."

Spots start again and I grab at him with weak, ineffectual hands.

"Diego."

He eases back up, relieving the pressure, but he doesn't get up. I suck in air greedily.

"What the hell are you doing here?" he hisses from beneath his teeth.

"What am I doing here? What are *you* doing here?"

He pulls back, rocking back onto his heels. In one smooth motion, he stands up and then bends to pull me up. Then he slams me back against one wall of the cage, knocking the air out of me and catching my head against the metal. "I will not let you fuck this up for me," he says.

"Fuck what up for you?" I say. "Diego, how are you working for them? After all they've done?"

His face screws up into a disgusted scowl. "You don't know anything." He shakes his head. "You don't know what they've done. You don't know what *you've* done."

Ouch. "Diego . . ."

"You want to know what I'm doing here? I'm here because of you. Because I tried to help you. That poisoned *everything* for me back on the island. I had to get out of there. I couldn't stay, not after what I had done. So . . . what would you have me do? I couldn't take the *Osprey*. So I had to jump another ship, and take whatever employment I could find."

"But here, Diego? After what happened on Gastown? What they did to you? What they did to Miranda?"

He flinches at that last one but quickly regains his composure. "You think you know everything, but you don't. You never did. You have no idea of what's really going on out in the world. You live in your own head. Ben Gold, always concerned primarily *with* Ben Gold."

"Diego—"

"Fuck you, Ben," he says. "I should kill you right now."

The scary thing is that as he says it, I believe him. I could never believe before that Diego could legitimately try to kill me. That he would want to. But right now, I'm surprised that he's not trying to.

I hold up my hands. "I'm not trying to do anything," I say. "I won't do anything to fuck up whatever it is you're doing."

"I'm supposed to take your word?" he asks. "Isn't that what you said in the beginning? That you wouldn't do anything to mess with my shit? And what always happens? What happened when I vouched for you on Tamoanchan in the first place? You bring a live Feral to the island and ruin my chances of being on the Council. What happened when I went with you to Gastown? I got captured and tortured. Then, you get me to help you bring Miranda's people back to the island, and that goes all to shit. Then I try to *save your life*, and that gets me kicked out of my home, separated from my sister, with nothing to show for any of it." He's roaring now, overcome by rage. "Things started going south from the moment I met you," he says. "How many times have I almost died because of you? How much do I have to give to help you?" He shakes his head. "You're not worth it, Ben. You've never been. No matter what Miranda thought of you."

That sparks a fire inside of me, and I snarl at him and push him back. "Don't say her name."

"Why?" he asks. "I'm not the one who got her killed. That was you."

Something snaps inside of me, and I step forward, swinging at him. I want to take him down. I want to bloody him. I want to unleash all this rage inside of me onto him. For caring about me in the first place. For betraying himself by working for a bunch of bloodthirsty, raging maniacs. For telling the truth.

He blocks the first blow with his forearm, then lets the second sail past him, and he grabs my arm and pulls me to him, wrapping one arm under my armpit and grabbing it with the other, laying his iron-like forearm across my neck. This time he's really pressing on my windpipe, and it doesn't take long for the black spots to streak across my vision. I kick and claw at his arms and try to move my neck, but he has me firm and he presses tighter and I can't breathe and I'm gasping for air, except I can't gasp and my chest strains and I can't breathe and—

I black out.

And fall, apparently. Because when I open my eyes, still sucking for air, still floundering like a fish on land, gulping for oxygen, desperate to breathe, I'm on the bottom of the cage. Alone. The door is closed. Diego is nowhere to be seen.

I'm alive, but I am truly friendless, and in the hands of the worst people I have ever seen.

What else could go wrong?

CHAPTER TWENTY-TWO

They put me to work doing manual labor, as expected. There are areas of the plant that need maintenance, and those tasks need extra hands to get it done. I'm put under the command of a woman named Jean, who is in charge of our crew of four people. They don't give us a guard at all, but Jean has a device called a cattle prod, a metal rod that can deliver a shock if necessary. It's possible that we could overpower her, but a guard is never too far off; and, if found, we would be killed on sight. Still, I think about taking Jean out, but I don't know my fellow workers (an older man named Carl and a woman named Racine) that well and so I don't trust them to have my back. For all I know, if I try something, they would turn me in to benefit themselves.

So I continue to bide my time. To be honest, I'm hoping to see Diego again, because I still can't figure out why he's here. He says he needed a place to live, something to do, but I can't see him choosing *this* place, no matter how badly off he was. Could he be working an angle? If so, what? Some kind of revenge? The Gastowners fucked him up good, so is he trying to do what I was trying to do? Is he interested in causing some damage? If that's the case, then we could act together. Assuming he would stoop to that again.

I wouldn't blame him if he said no.

I spend my days helping to fill cracks in the walls and replacing the screws on some of the equipment and cleaning and sweeping and picking up debris. In some areas we shore up the structure with wooden boards, and in other places we use stone. We replace toilets and sinks, some of which actually have running water because some enterprising member of the plant designed a plumbing system that draws from wells and other water sources, and we help keep that alive by replacing pipes and pulling things out of drains and, occasionally, wading through the muck. It's not great work, but it's not the worst I've done. And Jean isn't too bad of a leader. She makes us do all the hard work, but she's helpful when necessary and she doesn't use the cattle prod on us, though she mentions it often enough.

Every day after we're done with the work, a guard escorts us back to our cell, which we share. Everyone from the slaver cell that I came in with is here, with one or two exceptions. Those people, we guess, were taken to a different part of the plant to work in other operations. Diego is never one of the guards who brings us back or one of the guards who escorts us to Jean in the morning. I haven't seen him since he choked me.

Days pass, and I work for these reprehensible parasites and bide my time. But that little voice in my head keeps piping up.

What are you doing, Ben? What is your plan?

And every time it asks, I don't have an answer.

But I think about my goal. I want to hurt these people. The Valhallans. The destroyers of everything good in the world. I want to damage them. And here I am, in one of their most important resources. Where better to do a little sabotage? So far I haven't been able to do anything, but if I wait long enough, an opportunity might just present itself; and if I'm ready for it, I might be able to strike a blow.

But what opportunity?

Most of the work we do isn't near any sensitive systems, at least from what I can tell. I don't think taking out the plumbing, for example, would be a significant blow to the plant, though it might clog things up for a short time.

Getting loose and killing a few people might be gratifying, but it also wouldn't impact the Valhallans' operations significantly. Presumably they'd just send more people down from Gastown or Valhalla, or find some new slaves (not that I would kill any of the slaves—I'm not a monster).

So how long will you wait, Ben? Helping these people you hate?

It's about a week into my stay at the plant, and all I've come up with are some weak and tentative ideas. I've managed to smuggle a few old nails back to my cell with me, and they're mostly sharp, but they're hardly a weapon. They're a little too thick and stiff to work on the lock. So they're currently sitting there. I've memorized the routes to various places in the plant and marked, in my head, the exits, both real and probable. I've decided that whatever I do has to be done while I'm out of the cell. The best I've come up with to date is to make a break for the armory or some storeroom and find some explosives and set them off.

Not a very satisfying plan.

As I'm sitting in the cell, trying to avoid my fellow prisoners, who have gotten on my nerves after our confinement, and thinking about all this, I hear noises in the plant. Yells. Ominous thumps. What I think is a muffled boom.

The others in the cage are standing up now, pressed against the bars, trying to figure out what's going on. They remind me of animals, test subjects I remember from my time at Apple Pi with the boffins. Or, even more disturbing, Alpha, the captured and caged Feral that we kept on Tamoanchan (I wonder what happened to it). Despite those associations, I join my fellow prisoners at the bars, trying to figure out what's happening, making sure my three nails are tucked into my pocket. Then I hear it. Gunfire. Unmistakably. Nearby.

I press myself against the cage, worming my way between two of my cellmates, and try to get a glimpse. Nothing by the door. No guards, though, either. More gunfire, this time automatic, and yells.

My first thought is that it's Ferals. That the Cabal are keeping some here and they escaped, and now the Valhallans are hunting them. If one gets in here, I don't know what we're going to be able to do. The cage bars are good enough to keep us in, but not enough to keep the Bug out. Our captors don't give us much in the way of protection against the Bug in here, mostly because there shouldn't be a real risk of exposure for us. That is, unless a Feral, possibly mutated, bursts in to the room, full of spit and blood.

I flinch when the door opens and a large figure steps into the room, slightly illuminated by the light from the hall behind. But I can make out its clothing, and that belies the idea that it's a Feral. Unless they're clothing them now.

The figure stalks over to us, fully covered, with a submachine gun slung across its body, one hand on the grip. As it nears, I recognize the walk. The movement of the shoulders. Diego.

He stops, looks for me, and finds my face in the cage. He has a bright-green bandana threaded around his bicep. "I'm not doing this for you," he says. "I'm doing this for them. Get them out of here."

Then he tosses me the keys to the cage and turns and walks away.

"Diego, wait!" I call after him. But he ignores me and stalks back to the door, getting into a combat stance as he reaches it, swiveling around the corner.

For a moment, everyone just pauses, overcome by the shock of what's happening. But then that bubble breaks and everyone in the cage realizes that I'm holding the keys. They all move to take them from me, reaching for and grabbing my hands.

Using my elbows and knees, I try to keep the others away from me, keeping my hands close to my body.

"Let me get to the lock!" I say.

I fight, tackle, and shove my way to the front of the cage. You'd think that we'd have developed some camaraderie during our time in the cage, but the truth is, we all just want to be left alone. I push to the front, bruised and battered, but I reach the keys out and into the lock, and I manage to turn them. The door unlatches and swings open. I'm pushed out by the swell of excited prisoners behind me.

Okay, Diego. I got them out.

The other prisoners move to the door, and I have no choice but to follow them. The sounds of combat and fighting are still present, but they seem a little farther away now.

Everyone hesitates at the door, not sure what to do. I move to the front and, gathering up my courage, I look outside, ready to duck back in if I see something hostile.

The hallway is empty, save for one of the guards, who's slumped on the ground in a bloody heap. His clothes are covered in his blood, so I don't think about taking them, but his submachine gun is lying next to him. I pick it up quickly, throwing the strap around my shoulder, and I check the clip. Not full, but near enough.

"Stick close to me," I say to my fellow prisoners, but some of them are already running down the corridor the other way. A few of them trail behind me. One guy named Roland. A blond man whose name begins with a *D*.

The corridor ahead turns right at a ninety-degree angle. I move to the corner and look ahead. Two dead bodies on the ground, but no rifles visible. Both are shot up, geared up for a fight, but one of them has a bright-green strip of cloth wrapped around one arm. Some kind of revolt?

I bend down to untie it.

"What are you doing?" Roland hisses.

"It's okay," I say. "Don't worry about it."

"We have to keep moving."

"Just give me a second." I almost have the green strip undone now. I can feel it coming loose.

"Fuck you," Roland says. He grabs for a pistol in a holster on the other dead man. "Come on," he says, but to Blond D, not to me. Then they run off down the hallway.

Are you sure you know what you're doing, Ben?

I finally get the strip free, and then I tie it around my own arm, up near the top where it will be visible to anyone who sees me.

I just hope it doesn't make me a target.

Once that's done, I move to the end of the corridor and out the door into the yard.

And straight into a firefight.

I take shelter behind a large pile of mortar sacks and try to get a sense of what's going on, the submachine gun ready in my hands. People fire at each other across the courtyard. Some of them are easily identifiable as Valhallans. The Valhallans are firing at a couple of people taking shelter behind some kind of lifting vehicle. Sparks spray off of the metal from the gunshots, and the whine of bullets fills the air. The air smells heavily of smoke and explosives and cordite.

I crane my head around to try to see the people pinned behind the big yellow rig, but I can't see anything from my current angle. I inch my way around the pile of mortar bags to try to get a better look. I'm just nearing the edge when mortar flies everywhere as bullets strike the bags. A sharp spray of it hits my neck and when I put my hand up to it, it comes back wet and red.

I crouch down, then pop out and fire a couple of short bursts toward the Valhallans; that pressure helps give the pinned-down couple (because I can now tell there are only two) some space to shoot back themselves. As the larger one shoots, I see the bright-green bandana on its arm.

That's enough for me. Now that I know that they're ostensibly on my side, I pop off another couple of rounds against the Valhallans from my current position. As they're reacting, I race around the pile of mortar bags to the other side, where I have a better drop on the Valhallans. As they're taking fire from my green bandana brethren, I fire on them from the side. Two of them go down, leaving only three left.

Bullets rip up the mortar bags where I'm hiding, and I drop to the ground, worming my way to the other side as mortar sprinkles down on top of me. Three of them. Three of us. Only, they have better cover. If only I could . . .

I move around to the side closest to my allies (or who I think are my allies) and I wave to them, hoping to get their attention. I try to indicate, with a combination of raised fists and pointing, that they should wait for me. Then I move back, positioning myself squarely in the center of the pile of mortar bags, and I prepare myself. I check the clip to make sure I still have enough ammo (I do) and make sure the safety is off (it is) and the strap isn't tangled (it's not). Then, on the count of three, I stand up and haul myself atop the pile of mortar bags. It's a dumb move—I won't have any cover—but I will be high enough that I can get a better angle down onto the Valhallans. I hear gunfire as my allies start shooting, and the Valhallans start shooting back. Then I've reached the top of the pile of bags, and I'm firing down on the Valhallans, and a tall black woman goes down to my first burst. I move forward, trying to get a bead on the next one, trying not to be a stationary target, but the bags start to shift, and my footing starts to give way, and the whole front section of the pile starts to topple over.

And I go with it.

Bullets explode into dust all around me even as I fall through the air, the gun forgotten as my arms go up to try to brace my fall. I hit the ground, and I grunt. Or, rather, I hit the bags that have fallen. There's no time to figure out if I'm hurt. Instead, I pull the rifle closer and start firing at the two remaining Valhallans. They're standing up now, and any second they're going to tear me into bloody meat. Then someone strides up behind them, a pistol outstretched, and fires three shots into the back of one Valhallan and two into the head of the other.

Breathing heavily, I get to my knees, my hands held above my head. My body feels battered but nothing feels broken, at least. The woman (because I can tell now that it is a woman) still has the pistol out. "I'm on your side," I say, through my ringing ears.

The woman, who is wearing a worn baseball cap and a thin, gray scarf, tugs the scarf down. It takes me a moment to realize that I recognize her face. Rosie. Diego's sister. Who I had last seen on Tamoanchan as we tried to kill the mutated Ferals the Cabal dropped on us.

"What the fuck?"

She lowers the pistol, then moves forward and grabs my hand and pulls me up.

"What are you doing here?" I ask.

"I'm here with Malik," she says. Her face is set. She doesn't seem happy to see me, which I kinda get, but she doesn't seem unhappy either, so that's something.

"Mal? What's Mal doing here?"

She looks around. "Give me a hand with Diego," she says, before grabbing a rifle and a second clip off of one of the downed Valhallans.

I go back to where they had been taking cover and see Diego huddling behind the yellow vehicle, cradling his arm.

I bend down by him. "Are you hit?"

He looks up to Rosie. "What is he doing here?"

"Leave it," she says. "He helped get us out."

The surreality of them both being here hits me. "What the fuck is going on?" I ask. "Why are you here?"

"I told you," Rosie says. "I'm here with Malik. He's attacking the plant. I got word to Diego, and he helped us from the inside."

My mind reels. Malik is attacking the plant. He was set up as head of Tamoanchan, or at least its "Protector," and now he's attacking Gastown's helium plant.

I sit back on my heels. It's a good move. Gastown and Valhalla, and the Cabal, know where the island is now. They'll keep attacking. Taking the fight to them is the right thing to do.

"His people are here?" I ask.

"*Our* people are. His and Tamoanchan's forces." Rosie pulls out a roll of bandages. She kneels by Diego and looks at the wound. "It just grazed you," she says. "You got lucky."

"I'm fine," Diego says, trying to shake her off.

"Let me take care of it. Don't want it to get infected."

"It's a good plan," I say.

"It is," she says.

She doesn't ask me why I'm here. How I got here. Either Diego said something, or else she doesn't care. A coin flip as to which one is true.

"So you're taking the whole thing?"

She nods again. "Or else we're taking it out."

Also a good play. If they can't hold and keep the plant, the best thing to do would be to take it away from the Valhallans. It would mean no more helium. Back to hydrogen for all the pretty ships. But at this point, I would take that over leaving it in its present hands.

"What happens when Gastown comes down to try to take it back?" I ask.

Rosie shrugs. "Then we hold it. We'll have some advantage here. They can always bomb us, but then they lose the plant, too. Either way, we win. But if you ask me . . ." She stares me in the eyes. "We'll take Gastown next."

She says it with such conviction that I feel a thrill at the statement. Because despite the history between us, despite Mal wanting me dead, despite the bitterness I feel toward him, if anyone can take Gastown, now, it's Malik.

"Good," I say.

And I mean it. Because anything that can be done against them is smooth sky, but I'm also realizing that Mal, who just kinda fell into this whole situation, has already done a lot more than I've managed to do.

But I realize in that moment that Gastown is not my target. Gastown is the western outpost of Valhalla, yes, but the source of all of this shit, of all of this blood and tears and murder is *in* Valhalla. And we're all running around trying to deal with the symptoms, as Miranda would say, and not the underlying disease. Until we do that, there can be no cure.

It's one of the few times in my life that everything seems to fall into place. Thoughts and fears and plans and desires, fractured like broken glass, spinning and tumbling through a cloudy sea of doubt and pain and self-pity settle down, fitting back together, showing me a way forward. Showing me what I have to do.

It's funny, this moment—some would say that I was led here for a reason.

That some kind of force, God or Fate or whatever, made this happen. I don't believe in any of that shit. But I do believe in opportunities, believe that when the dice roll comes up in your favor, that you seize on it. So that's what I'm going to do.

I have to take the fight to Valhalla. And I know exactly how I'm going to do that.

I could join in the fight here, strike a blow, but I'm just one more pair of hands. And in the end, when Mal or his people realize that I'm here, I'll go back into a cell where I can't do anything. But if they tie up Gastown's resources here, and that sends a shockwave back to Valhalla, well . . . now would be the time to strike.

I grab Rosie's arm. She looks at me, her face hard. "He'll be all right?"

She nods. "It's only a scratch."

"Good. I'm really sorry," I say to both of them. "I'm sorry for everything I've done. For all the shit I've landed you in. For all the pain that I've caused."

Rosie's eyes widen, then narrow. She's trying to figure out my angle. To try to see how I'm working them. Only I'm not. Maybe for the first time, I'm not.

"What are you doing?" Diego asks.

"Trying to set a wrong right," I say.

I stand up.

"Ben—don't even think about—"

"Good luck," I say. "I hope you take it all. I hope you bloody them, and send them packing to whatever holes they came from in the first place."

"Ben!"

"I have to go."

Rosie catches my eye, then gives me a nod. "Good luck," she says.

"Thanks."

Then I run off, deeper into the plant.

CHAPTER TWENTY-THREE

When I was here last time, I wandered into an open area while looking for my ship. There, in this large storeroom, was a relic from the early days of the Sick. A Firestorm bomb. One of the weapons the government dropped on towns where the Bug was starting to spread, in an effort to contain it. Obviously, they failed at containing the Bug; but they did leave numerous areas of devastation across the country. I can remember flying over areas that had been hit. Even with regrowth you could see the craters and the burnt surroundings. Down on the ground, the few times I had seen the results, everything seemed melted like wax. When I asked, Dad explained to me how it happened.

I remember being horrified at first, then reaching some sort of under-standing. By then I knew how terrible the Bug was. Burning down a whole town to stop it was a choice I could almost understand. *Almost*, because they failed in their attempt and it meant that the Bug still existed, and there were whole areas that we couldn't forage in because they were wreckages of twisted steel and plastic and stone.

When I first found it, I almost took the Firestorm bomb. I didn't. But if it's still there, it will be perfect for my plans. How better to hurt Valhalla than to shove a Firestorm down their throat?

So I run for that storeroom, relying on my recent knowledge of the layout of the plant and my hazy memories of my previous trip to get me there. I run through hallways chaotic with firefights, hugging the walls and ducking into rooms so as not to be noticed. I want the plant taken down, but I can't waste time joining in the fight. Besides, Mal's people would just want to take me prisoner.

I head to the service tunnels that I took before with Atticus and Rosie. That's what led us to the room with the explosives, and it should be out of the way of most of the fighting. I move as quickly as I can, practically running through each stretch of tunnel until I reach a door, and then pausing before heading into the space afterward.

Finally, I reach the door leading to the room with the Firestorm bomb. At least, it used to be. Last time I was here, I cleared them out of a lot plastic explosives, so it would make sense if they had moved things. Or put them under lock and key. Or maybe they had even used the Firestorm to bomb some place like they did back at Phoenix. That hadn't been a Firestorm, but, then again, Phoenix hadn't been a large settlement. I wouldn't put it past them to drop those things somewhere else that threatened them, or even just offended their sensibilities.

Beyond the door is that large room where the Firestorm was. But that room had also contained guards. Now that the place was under attack . . .

Only one way to find out, Ben.

I pull open the door, and the room looks much the same as it did before—stacks of equipment and cases, in different configurations—and a Firestorm bomb, in a large square case, right where it was last time. Except, this time, there's a group of Valhallans and guards right in front of it.

For a moment, they all stand there, heads turning toward me as I enter, necks craning around, and hands reaching for weapons.

But my gun is close at hand, so I snap it up and press down hard on the trigger, spraying the group standing in front of me. The Firestorm is right behind them, and I know the danger, but if I wait, if I hesitate, they will turn me into a bloody stain, and I can't allow that.

Three of them go down, and the rest scatter, moving as far away from the bomb as they can—they know the danger they're in with a crazy person shooting so close to it.

Two dart into the open, out of cover, and I take the opportunity to mow them down. I start moving forward. Toward the Firestorm. I take up position right next to it, above the bodies of the people I just dropped.

I'm hoping that they're not as stupid as I am, that they're more concerned with surviving this firefight. The thing is, I am, too. Maybe a few weeks ago I would have been content to go out in a giant fiery explosion, but not today. Not yet. There's still too much to do.

As I take shelter behind the bomb's case, a box about a meter and a half on each of its sides, I see two things: that it's raised on top of a kind of cart with wheels for transporting it, and that it's not alone—there are two more bombs stacked next to it on the cart.

Mother. Fucker.

Bullets whizz over my head, but none close enough to hit the Firestorms. Or me.

I hope.

The bombs are big enough that it's hard to see around them, hard to pin down where the Valhallans are. The room is filled with crates and piles of equipment and possibly explosives. I'd guess they've taken up positions behind these. But I think I know generally where they are, so I start to move the bombs, pushing the cart that they're sitting on, trying to angle it so that it protects me from groups on both sides.

The bombs are heavy enough to be unwieldy, and I'm only one person, so I have to pump hard, pressing my feet down against the floor, using all of my weight to push the damn thing forward. Then it's suddenly rolling and I'm lagging behind. Bullets rip up the floor next to my feet.

It's tricky, keeping the cart moving and taking cover behind it, so I do a little shuffle-push combination, moving it and running alongside it in little bursts. All this momentum is starting to catch up with it, and I need to move faster to keep up.

Movement out of the corner of my eye, and a Valhallan appears, rounding the bomb with a long curved ax in his hand, ponytail streaming behind him. The ax is already coming down as I whirl and shoot, and despite the barrage that tears through him, he tumbles toward me, and I'm forced to stumble out of his way, back from all that blood. I practically run into the other Valhallan coming at me from the other side.

She holds a straight blade of some sort, and it's all I can do to raise the submachine gun to try to deflect it. The blade slides against the black surface of the gun, and the tip jams into my chest and tears upward as I lift the gun.

Pain sears through me, and I gasp. That strike could have killed me. I bring up my knee and catch the woman in the midsection, slamming my forehead into her face.

I feel crunching. My whole head rings with the impact, but her hands fly up to her face and the blood splattered across it, and I jam the muzzle of the submachine gun into her midsection and fire a short burst.

With the bomb cart still sliding across the floor, I duck behind a stack of crates and wait for a beat. Another Valhallan appears, rounding the moving bomb, and I take a second to line up a shot that will take the burst clear of the bomb. My chest and shoulder are burning from the knife cut, but I ignore that for the moment as I aim down the sights and pull the trigger. Then I run to the far side of the bomb, sliding to the ground as I clear it and quickly pan the gun until I find another Valhallan and squeeze. The Valhallan drops even as the SMG trigger clicks empty.

I drop the gun and run back to the bomb and the downed Valhallan and quickly try to free the gun strapped around his back; that's when the other Valhallan climbs up over the top of the bomb and drops straight on me. My head bounces off of the ground.

I spin. I reach. I . . .

Something hot sinks deep into my leg, and I scream as pain spikes through me. My ringing head goes white and I shake my head to clear it.

I'm staring at a large, bald man over me, his hands locked around my throat, all of his weight atop me, immobilizing me. My breath is cut off and I'm already seeing spots at the corners of my vision.

My hands are stuck down by my sides, but I can feel the pain in my left leg, the sharp something embedded there. I reach for it with fluttering fingers, and, luckily for me, the grip is wrapped in something like leather and I can grab it, even with my fingers losing their strength.

My vision narrows, and I pull hard with what strength I have left. The pain almost makes me pass out, sends vomit boiling up into my constricted throat, but before I black out, I angle the blade toward the man on top of me and push as hard as I can. There's a movement, away from the bite of the blade, and I shift, trying to roll, the man still gripping me. I find the blade again and push harder.

This time he lets go, reaching down to the blade now inside him, and I gasp and scramble away.

A large hand grabs the back of my head by the hair, and I'm sucking in air, vision still flickering, pain playing out a symphony in my body.

But I remember that I have legs, and I kick down with the one of them. Once, twice, and the grip lessens and I pull away.

I get to my feet, swaying, blood leaking from my chest and my leg, possibly my head.

My enemy rises as well, a long, bloody knife in his hand. He's pale, taller and bigger than me, his face and head shaved, his mouth stretched in a rictus grin.

I have no weapons. I have less reach. Less strength.

I can't reach the fallen Valhallan's gun. Not before this beast could stab me again.

My left leg shakes. I feel like falling to the ground and lying there for a long while. No weapons. No tricks.

No. Wait. . . .

My hand reaches into my pocket, fingers blindly grasping at the three sharpened nails there. *Right, Ben. That will help.*

He's moving at me, large and strong, and the blade darts out, quick, like a snake, and I just barely get my hands on his arm and twist it so that his knife cuts through the fabric of my coat and shirt and not my skin.

His other fist slams into my face and I teeter back, the world spinning. I almost fall. Then he kicks my feet out from under me and I do.

He comes in for the kill, the blade coming down, my blood and his on it, but he's a little too eager. A little sloppy, and I manage to roll away from him. He takes a moment to reorient with the knife, and I roll back to him, one hand on the knife arm, the other with a nail in it. It's as long as my little finger, and I jam it into his ear as far as it will go. A jerk of his head is the only response, until I take my left hand and grip his neck, knowing that I'm exposing myself to the knife, and I jam the next nail into his eye.

This time he reacts, throwing his head back, shaking it.

I slam my right hand—which, until recently, held the first nail—into his ear. Again. Again. The eye. The head. I roll on top of him, punching the throat. Kneeing the groin. One hand on the wrist that holds the knife. His eye is a bloody mess, and the nail head is barely visible. I slam the back of his head into the floor. Repeat that. Repeat it all. Hits. Punches. Mete out the pain.

Then he's lying still and I'm breathing hard. My leg is on fire. My head feels like it's been split in two. My chest is carved up. I pry open his fingers and pull out the knife. Then I take the monumental task of getting to my feet and looking for a new gun.

One bright spot for me is that there don't seem to be any other Valhallans here. None alive, at least. I must have gotten them all, or else they ran for it when I was otherwise occupied.

No matter.

There's no one to stop me from arming myself, grabbing extra ammo, and trying to staunch the bleeding. My leg is the worst. The wound is deep. I tear off some strips of cloth from the dead Valhallans, because that's my only option, so I make sure to grab for cloth that isn't directly against the skin. Not going to put sweaty cloth against an open wound.

When I'm reasonably sure that I won't pass out from loss of blood (yet), I work on getting the bombs moving again.

I push the cart right up against the doors. Outside are probably more Valhallans. Outside is also freedom. My enemies, and the opportunity to hurt them.

No time to waste.

Having the Firestorms on wheels helps, but moving the cart by myself isn't the easiest. It's not like this thing is small. Last time I was in this room, we took the service tunnels to keep moving, but the cart is not going to fit in there. I have to use the larger doors to the right. The ones that lead out into the center of the plant. I get the Firestorms right up to the doors, run around to open them, make sure there's no one hostile on the other side, then push the whole cart out into the open.

The plant has a series of inner courtyards that are open to the sky. Through these I should be able to get the airship landing, but my knowledge of this area is hazy. As prisoners, we had walked through some of the courtyards to do some of our repairs—even worked in one of them—but we had taken the inside corridors to get to them.

This particular courtyard seems clear—even untouched by the fighting—though I can still hear the sharp report of gunfire and the occasional yell of an order nearby. From time to time I hear booms that must be coming from explosions. But right now I'm clear, so I push the Firestorms forward, taking some time to overcome my inertia and get this cart moving, so I can round the corner easily and get them to the next open space.

And there, ahead of me, *is* the firefight. Numerous combatants—some of Mal's people and some Valhallans—spread across the space. I see some atop stairways, shooting down. Others taking cover behind machinery, and one group behind a simple wagon.

From my approach, they are on either side of me—Mal's people to the left, the Valhallans on the right. If I try to run down the middle, I'll get cut to pieces, and who knows what will happen to the Firestorms (though the thought of taking this place down with me is not the worst one).

I need to get beyond them with the Firestorms intact. Waiting for the firefight to end is not an option—Mal's people won't let me through if they control the area, and the Valhallans will just kill me.

I leave the Firestorms where they are for a moment, and then I crouchrun to the nearest of Mal's people. I still have my green bandana on, and this person doesn't know me. At least I don't think she does. The woman—short-cropped hair and a broken nose—looks up at me in alarm but doesn't shoot me. Thankfully.

I take cover with them, my new SMG held forward.

"I need your help," I say.

"With what?"

"See that?" I gesture to the Firestorms. "Know what those are?"

We're cut off by a barrage of gunfire on our position. Broken Nose pops up and fires back, and I join her before dropping back to cover.

"Some kind of bombs," she says, reloading.

"Big bombs. I need to get them to the airship landing."

She frowns at me. "Why?"

"Orders from the top," I say. "Malik wants them."

She chews on this for a second. It's ballsy and perhaps a little dumb, but these people don't know me. I don't think that anyone I know would buy anything I said at this point, but this woman doesn't know that.

"Contingency," I say. 'If we need to drop one. Or all."

Her eyes narrow. "Who are you with?"

"Rosie," I say. "I've been waiting on the inside."

She looks me up and down. After a moment, she nods. "What do you need?"

"Cover fire," I say. "I'm going to try to run it past their position, but I need you to pin them down so they don't get me. Or the bombs."

She nods again. Barks orders to her crew. "Get ready," she says.

I nod and run back to my position.

I get behind the bomb and crouch, ready to push as hard as I can. I need to get this thing moving as fast as possible, as quickly as possible.

If this doesn't work, I'll be a wet mess in the middle of the courtyard.

"Go!" I hear. Probably from Broken Nose. Hopefully from her. Because I'm moving. Pushing my legs as hard as I can. My left leg is screaming, but I lock the pain away for later. I have a little bit of space to build up momentum before I get to the killing grounds; we start picking up speed and then we're there and I'm pumping and pushing and the cart is moving pretty well. And then the world becomes a storm of bullets and gunfire and screams and shouts.

Mal's people are good, though. Firing at once, keeping the Valhallans pinned down so I can sail through the space. I hear a couple of shots from my left—maybe a few adventurous Valhallans who are willing to brave the hail of gunfire—and I do hear a few bullets (maybe ricochets) flying past me. But I don't have time to think about any of that. Just move. Push. Fly.

The barrages lessen and the ground is eaten up behind me as the Valhallans unload, but I'm already through the gap, and I swerve around the corner into the next space and the next danger. But, through a clear path ahead, I see it. The first of the plant's airship landings.

A way to get back into the sky, into the Blue.

So I rush ahead.

✳ ✳ ✳

The trickiest part of my plan will be to get close to Valhalla, and that means looking nonthreatening. The best way to do that is to fly a Valhallan ship. Luckily for me, there are plenty of ships here. It doesn't look like many of the Valhallans have abandoned the plant. Not yet. There aren't any combat dirigibles here. The handful of ships moored here are cargo ships, which is exactly what I want.

I size them up. The blimp won't work. The rigid zeppelin is out as well. I've flown a few, and I hate the way that they handle. Out of the remaining choices, that leaves the large one that might have been white once but now looks like dirty snow. It's big, but it's one of the newer designs from the Clean, which probably means it's faster than its comrades, and that's what I care about right now. It will have more than enough room for the Firestorms and, judging by the animal face painted on the front of the envelope, it is clearly a Valhallan ship.

It doesn't look like it has the same kind of VTOL engines as the *Cherub* or the *Valkyrie*, though, no lowering the ship straight down to the ground, so I'm going to have the haul the Firestorms up. Which isn't my preferred way of doing this, but it will have to do.

I need to move fast.

I leave the bombs where they are—no other choice—and locate the ladder that leads up to the ship that I decide to call the *Beast*. It's been a little while since I climbed up one of these, especially into a strange ship. But while it sets every part of my body on fire with pain, it also sets my mind alight with excitement. The anticipation of getting back into the air, getting back behind the controls of an airship. I occasionally helped Claudia fly the *Valkyrie*, but that had been happening less and less frequently (for which I don't blame her).

It takes a while. Every time I reach up to the next rung, my chest wound feels like it's widening, spilling pain out from an ever-wider pool. Every time I pull up my legs, my left leg screams in protest and I have to make sure my arm is wrapped around the ladder so I don't slip and fall. But I muscle my way up, so close to escaping this place, and reach the gondola, hauling myself in. I ready the SMG as I enter, just in case someone is already up here.

The gondola is surprisingly small. This isn't meant for living or for a large crew. There's space for maybe four people in the actual command area. I take a quick inventory of the controls, and they look mostly familiar. I don't think I'll have any problems with them. It has automatic ballast control. Decent fuel management. The engines should be adequate for the job. Assuming that they've been kept in good shape.

Whoever owned this thing could read, though. I know this because carved into a piece of wood, mounted above the pilot's seat at the front of the gondola, is the name "White Wolf."

"Hello, *White Wolf*," I say. "We're going to be friends. At least for a little while."

Having made my quick assessment, I move to the cargo area, which is huge, and I lower the winch and the cables to secure the bombs, using them to get a quick ride down to the ground. But as I'm descending, I see someone waiting down there, next to my bombs. With one hand securely around the descending rig, I aim down at the person through the sight of the SMG.

She's just standing there. Armed, but not aiming up at me. Then I recognize the baseball cap on her head.

"What are you doing here, Rosie?" I ask as I hit the ground, wincing at the pain of landing. "I thought we said our good-byes."

"That was before I heard you were taking bombs with you." She pats one of the Firestorms.

"I told you I wanted to hurt them," I say. "Now I have a big-enough gun."

"You'll never get close enough."

I shrug. "I think I will. I have something in mind."

She shakes her head.

"Is it the bombs?" I ask. "You want to keep them for Mal?"

"No, you idiot." She shakes her head again. "You are one of the dumbest people I've ever met."

"What?"

"You made some really idiotic choices," she says. "And you ended up hurting people along the way. I see that you're starting to get that. But in your typical boneheaded way, your response is to go over the top. Make a statement so big and so bold and so . . . stupid, because that's all that you can think of."

I just stare at her.

"Did you ever think about just . . . helping people? One at a time? Making up for your past by doing little things? Saving one person. Lifting up one soul who needs it."

I think about Ellie, back on the junker, and the life she's going to face, and I'm forced to look away from Rosie. She's right, there are other paths I could take. Good I could do. Take the slow, steady climb back out of the muck. But . . . my course is already set. I feel it. In my bones. In the pit of me.

"I have to do this," I say, meeting her eyes.

She shrugs. "Don't think I'm not happy to see you go. You are one of the most frustrating people I've ever come across. And you're always getting my brother in trouble. But . . ."

"You'll secretly miss me?"

She smiles. "Like hell." She sighs and shakes her head. "Godspeed, Benjamin Gold. I hope you find what you're looking for."

I nod, grateful. "Tell Diego . . . Just take care of him."

"I always do," she says.

She helps me rig up the container of bombs and then, with a quick wave, I hit the button to pull us back up to the *White Wolf* and into the sky.

CHAPTER TWENTY-FOUR

FROM THE JOURNAL OF MIRANDA MEHRA

I pushed Clay today. He came to see me again, in the lab, when Maya was on a break. We have to be creative with the ways that we meet, and how we spend our time, so that no one sees.

"Any news?" I asked him, as he perused some results.

"I think I'm close," he said. "No ship yet, but . . ." He looked at me directly. "I think I can get a message off of the city."

I frowned. "A message? Saying what? And to whom?"

He looked around, but no one was taking an interest in us.

"If we can't get off, maybe someone else can get in."

"That doesn't make sense," I said.

"We need something to help us," he said. "A distraction. An open door for us to leave through."

"And who do you think will do that?"

"The island," he said. "Everyone thinks you're dead. I could get word off, let them know you're alive. That we're here . . . I don't know if the others would organize anything, but maybe if you sent it to one of your friends . . ."

The first person I thought of, at course, was Ben. But I had given up on the thought of him being alive. I didn't see Malik postponing things. I pushed the thought away. I had been doing that since Clay had appeared. I couldn't really let myself sink into that despair. Not now that there was some hope in my world.

But there was another answer.

"Diego," I said. "If there was anyone there who could figure something out, and who I'd trust to, it would be him."

"Good," he said. "That's good. I can work with that."

"But why would he believe it was real instead of some trick?"

Clay thought for a moment. "Give me one of your note-books. If he doesn't recognize your handwriting, someone else on the island will."

It made sense. That's why I started writing them here in the first place—to get a message out. I nodded and told him I'd get him one.

"We still need a plan, though," I said. "We need to get out of here. Every day I help them get closer to a vaccine."

"I know."

"If I could get back to the island, I could tell them about this place. What they have. What they're doing." _And I just need to be out of here_, I thought. _I need to be gone._

"I'll do what I can," he said.

I grabbed his hand, down below the table where people couldn't see. "Thank you," I said.

He looked back at me, eyes shining. Then he leaned forward and kissed me. I was . . . shocked. We were there in the lab with everyone watching. But I didn't pull back or push him away. I kissed him back, and there was something hungry and desperate beneath it.

He pulled away, his face red. "I'll see you soon," he said.

Then he left me to the strange whirl of emotions that I was feeling.

✳   ✳   ✳

Well, that escalated quickly.

Clay found a way to visit me a couple weeks later, at night, in my cell. He knocked at my door and opened it and we both sat on my sleeping mat and talked, and laughed.

"What did you bring me this time?" I asked.

"Two things."

I looked at him expectantly. "Well?"

"The first is just that . . . I've found out a way to get us off of Valhalla."

"What?" I said. "Clay!" I hugged him then pushed him back. "How?"

"I've arranged to go on a supply run. My supervisor put me into contact with the ship captain who's taking me out, and I told him I was going to load up with empty cases to fill up on the trip. All we need to do is get you into one of the cases, I get it on the airship, and then we sail away."

"Then what?"

"Then we make a run for it whenever we set down. Find transport somewhere else. And they'll never see us again."

I considered it. Assuming all went well, it seemed like a straightforward plan. "When can we leave?"

"Not for a few days at least. The run has to be planned, a site determined. I'll have to assemble the cases. But not too long. I'll make sure of it."

I hugged him again. "Thank you, Clay. I knew you'd come through for me. For us." I was overcome with a surge of hope, for the first time in a while. Then I remembered what he had said. ". . . You said two things."

He smiled and pulled out a small bottle, and two cups. "Took me some time to barter my way to this stuff, but I think it's probably decent." He twisted off the top and poured some amber liquid into the two cups. He held one out to me with a slightly trembling hand. "Cheers," he said.

I clinked his cup and tipped the contents back. The alcohol burned as it passed my lips and down my throat. It had a harsh edge to it, but also a pleasant flavor. Almost vegetal. "Good," I said. He nodded.

We drank some more, and talked, and I felt something close

to real happiness. It felt like a stranger, but I welcome it. A feeling of home. Of all the memories I had forgotten.

Clay brushed a piece of hair from my face, his hand resting on my cheek, and leaned in to kiss me. I kissed him back, happy to be in that moment, happy for that feeling, that familiarity and also that spike of excitement. I grabbed the back of his head and pulled him to me, our lips pressed together, first soft, then hard, then fast.

We fell back onto the mat and peeled off our clothes, kicking and pushing at them until we were naked. There, again, a sensation I had missed. Naked skin on naked skin. The heat beneath it. We fucked with an intensity that surprised me.

Clay said everyone thought I was dead. I think, in a way, I have been. Taken from everything that matters to me, made to live in a crazy place in an insane world, I've been sleepwalking through the days. But in that moment, I felt alive. Truly alive.

I wanted to make it last longer. I wanted to stretch it out and drain it of each second and millisecond. But Clay had to leave. It wouldn't do to be discovered. Not with the plans that we were making. Not with the risk involved. So he put his clothes back on and left.

But before he did, he turned back and said, "I love you, Miranda. I always have."

I smiled back at him. He walked out the door.

I tried to hold on to that feeling as tightly and as long as I could.

✳   ✳   ✳

Three days after we fucked in my cell, Clay met me in the lab. "Tonight," he said. "We leave tonight."

I grasped his hands, making sure that it wasn't seen. "You're sure?"

He nodded. "I made all the arrangements. We're due to arrive at the site in the morning. I'll get you on board in the storage case, and you can hole up in the cargo bay. Then, when we land, you get back into the case, and when the time is right we'll make our break."

Then a thought occurred to me, one I hadn't really considered. I was about to leave Dimitri behind. In this horrible place. After getting him tortured.

"Can you get someone else out, too?"

"What?" he said. He looked around. "Who, Miranda?"

"Dimitri," I said. "He's trapped here, too. He was press-ganged. He's been a friend to me all these weeks. They tortured him because of me. I can't leave him behind."

"Miranda, this is going to be hard enough, just the two of us. I haven't prepared to take another person."

"All we need to do is get him out," I said. "He can hide in another of the cases. We can all make our break together."

Clay shook his head, clearly frustrated with my request.

"Clay, please . . . This isn't just about me. This is about saving who we can save. It's riskier, yes, but we stand to gain so much more. Another person. Free of this terrible place."

He looked away.

"Please, Clay."

Clay turned back to me, his face tight. He said, "Okay. We'll get Dimitri out as well. But he has to be ready tonight. And he needs to follow my lead."

I smiled. "He will. I'll make sure of it."

"Okay. Wait for me tonight, after you're back in your cell. I'll come for you."

"I can't wait," I said.

But of course I had to. Until I was off of the city, I was still doing Blaze's work.

✳   ✳   ✳

I've been thinking about the first time I met Clay. Back when I was looking for others like me, I was so worried that I wouldn't be able to find anyone. It took some doing, and talking to some people whom Sergei knew, but then the word started to spread and scientists started coming to us.

Clay seemed so young when he joined us, just as we were starting to put Apple Pi together. I'm pretty certain he's around my age, but he seemed so much younger, so full of energy, but also so rigid. He told us that his grandmother had done something (my memory fails me) for the Centers for Disease Control and Prevention. She and her people had kept trying to fight Maenad. Later, as they had families, they enlisted their families in the fight. I knew from talking to him that Clay wanted, or rather needed, to finish that fight.

I know Ben didn't like him. Not from the first time they met. I often wondered if that was because they were so different, or because, deep down, they were similar. Or maybe it was because of me. I'm no psychologist.

So looking at him, stretched out on the table, cut and torn and beaten, his skin already pale, his eyes blank and staring, I didn't believe it was him at first. I mean it _was_ him, I could tell by his face, what wasn't covered in blood and bruises and cuts. But Clay had always been filled with such fire. I'd found it sometimes a little much, I have to say. But that was Clay. This . . . corpse couldn't be him.

But of course it was.

He lay on a table stained with blood. Next to me stood Maya, and beyond the tables, wiping his hands clean with a towel, was Surtr.

"You were warned," Maya said. "You were given an explanation. Nevertheless, you persisted."

219

For a moment the words didn't make sense. They entered my head, joined the swirl of words and thoughts there, and just spun. Beneath that was the spiral of emotions, but I was too scared to even delve into those.

Maya walked forward, arms crossed. " I should have recognized him. From the island. Even with the beard and the hair." She reached out a hand and trailed her fingers through his beard. " But he was good. He kept out of my way."

Surtr walked forward, too. " He held out for a little while," he said, his voice deep. His dead eyes bored into me. " Even after I started using the blade. But he soon gave up the identity of the captain, and what your plan was." He smiled, and the fiery-sword tattoo seemed to writhe. " He was good sport."

I wanted to scream at him. Lunge at him. Him and Maya and all of these psychopaths. But I just stood there. Like a mute statue. I couldn't move. Couldn't process. Couldn't even cry.

" Three weeks," Maya said. " On restricted rations. And don't forget, we still have Dimitri."

I took the words unsurprised and unmoved. I let them lead me back to my dorm, all the while not speaking, not feeling. Just . . . numb. I replayed the image of Clay's body in my head. Counted the number of wounds I had seen, categorized them. What for? I don't know.

Then I sank down to the floor on my mat and just sat there, staring at the wall.

" Miranda?" Dimitri called.

" Not now," I said. The first words I had uttered since they took me to see Clay.

Not now. Not ever.

What now? They've taken all my options. There's no escape. No getting out.

I'm trapped here forever.

CHAPTER TWENTY-FIVE

Airships dot the sky above the helium plant. Armed airships, Mal's people, I would guess. And here I am flying a Valhallan ship.

Nothing to do but run for it.

I pivot the airship toward the largest patch of sky I can find and aim right for the center of it.

From the gondola window, one of the ships turns toward me, begins to move in. I can see the large gun in its belly even from this distance.

You did not make it this far, Ben, to get shot down in the sky.

I lean forward, gripping the controls, ignoring the pain in my body, and I push the *White Wolf*'s speed to maximum. At the same time, I dump ballast from the nose, putting me on a course that should take me up above the other ships and at the very least out of the reach of that belly gun.

The ship starts shuddering at the sudden change of course, but that should pass.

I hobble to the gondola window to see what the other ship is doing. It's far too close. And matching my attitude. Gunshots rip through the air around me.

Ahead of me is a patch of cloud. High up. Higher than I should be taking the *White Wolf*. But what other choice do I have? I dump all of my ballast, making the ship as light as I can, willing the engines to stay with me.

The whole ship vibrates and I have to grit my teeth against the pain in my leg, have to grip the controls tightly and hope that my head won't split apart.

A quick glance out the back window shows my pursuers still after me.

My hand hovers near the gas distribution controls.

We pass through the outer layers of cloud. I start counting. *One, two three . . .* In my mind I'm estimating the distance between ships, making assumptions of speed and bearing.

When I hit twenty, I vent gas from the forward cells, then cut the engines on one side. We dive, like an injured bird, and I push us into as hard a turn as I can. The *White Wolf* moves with agonizing slowness. The ship shudders. I feel the shakes reverberating throughout my body, and each one sends pain rippling after it.

But I hold course.

As soon as I complete the turn, perpendicular to my original course, I put all the engines back on line.

Red lights flicker as the engines fail to start.

C'mon, damn you!

Any second now the other ship will figure out where I've gone, and now that I'm below it, that belly gun will be all the more effective.

I stab at the controls again and let out a whoop as the engines rev to life and we shoot ahead. I let us drop some more before letting the gas distribute and take us level.

By the time the other ship figures out which direction I've moved in, I'll have put valuable meters between us. They'll have to decide whether to follow me or to stay close to their companions at the plant.

The last glimpse I have of the ship is it turning back toward the plant.

I continue on, heading east.

Thankfully, there are maps aboard the *White Wolf*. Maps with Valhalla clearly marked on them. It's not a quick trip, unfortunately. I'm not concerned with preserving these engines for very long, so I estimate that, at maximum speed, I can reach the sky city in about two days. That's a lot of time, and plenty can go wrong. I could run afoul of raiders or pirates. I could experience an engine failure. I could hit a massive storm.

I also neglected to check if there was any food or water on the ship before I left. It didn't seem like a priority at the time, and I don't want to stop to barter— not that I have any barter to begin with.

So, after I set my course and am sure I'm not being pursued (which I'm not—I wonder if I have Rosie to thank for that), I look through the gondola to see if there's anything there for me.

I find a storage box with a few things in it. Plenty of jugs of water, more than enough for this trip. And some old fruit that's somewhere past ripe, but somewhere before moldy. It should be enough to get me through, if not to satisfy me. I've eaten worse.

The real treasure is the parachute packed into the cargo hold. I've only seen one once before, with my father, aboard another pilot's ship. He liked to take it down, parade it around. Show off how lucky he was to have something so valuable and useful. Some other time, this would be an exciting find.

The more important discovery is that there's an emergency medical kit here. Bandages. Even a little of what I'm hoping is antiseptic. It's not labeled, but it looks right. I rinse my wounds in the water and squeeze some ointment into them. There's even a needle and thread, so I sew myself up. Eventually. I pass out in the middle of my leg, even with the small bottle of booze in the medical kit. But soon enough I get it closed. Doesn't matter much. I expect to be sitting for most of this trip.

My plan is pretty simple—arm the bombs in the hold, ram this thing into Valhalla, and make so big a hole in that fuckdamn city that they will be hurting for a while. I don't know enough to make it strategic. If I'm lucky, I'll take out the Cabal or some of the top Valhallan leaders. At the very least, I hope to hurt them. And with the stinging they'll take at the helium plant, it should take them a while to recover.

It's a brute-force play, but with enough strength behind it to do some damage.

It's the best I can hope for at this point. Maybe not a fitting end to a life like mine, but a satisfying one.

As I lie here, setting my mental course, I should get up, should stay alert for any other ships, for any weather disturbances, for anything. But the pull of gravity, of sleep, takes hold of me even here on the *White Wolf*, and I'm not strong enough to resist at the moment.

So I don't.

I wake up some time later, annoyed with myself but also realizing that I needed the sleep. I'm carved up like a fresh piece of meat, and I'm lucky if I'm not concussed. This plan won't work if I get feverish or fall into a coma.

I drink some water and eat some overripe fruit and seat myself at the controls.

No other ships in sight. Flat land beneath me.

Nothing to do but fly.

Out in the Blue.

It makes me think of Dad, of course. He would think this was all stupid. He would try to talk me out of this. But he's not here.

Was that really you back at the temple, Dad? I guess I have to get used to the idea that I'll never know. If that was him, then I will go to my death having failed him. But I've lived with that failure for so long that I can die with it. Still, I wonder what it would have felt like, to have that failure removed. To no longer feel the weight of it in my own personal ballast. Would that human beings were more like airships and we could just dump the extra weight we carry with us.

But nothing is ever that easy.

I think about what I would say to my father if he were here with me. Even if it were just the ghost of him. *Sorry, Dad. Sorry for letting you live on as a thing. Sorry for not watching your back better. Sorry for being an extra mouth to feed and an extra body to watch. And, of course, thank you. Thank you for teaching me what you did. Especially how to fly. Thank you for making me a good forager and a great pilot. Even if I was never a great man.*

Not that you were all great. You were hard, and distant, a lot of the time. I think you were doing it to protect me, to keep me hard, but it was lonely. I was with you for most of my life, most of the days and hours and minutes, and yet there were so many times that I felt alone.

Still, I don't know that I would have done any better. I almost certainly would have done worse. Taking care of something else. Someone else. I've never been very good at that. Not with you. Not with Miranda. Not with anyone. People who cross my path often end up dead. Or, if not dead, then grounded, like Diego.

So in the end, Dad, you were a better man than me. I think I like it best that way.

I don't believe that there's anything after this world, and I know you didn't either. It's not our way. Still, I sometimes think about it. A place where you are reunited with everyone who went before you. If so, would you be there with Mom now? I hope so. Wouldn't that be an amazing thing.

I think of her a lot, too. Or at least the fuzzy space in my head that stands for her. When I was younger, I remembered things about her, but that all got lost long ago, washed away by the torrent of danger and survival. Of all the things I've lost, that's one of the most painful. All I had were the stories you told of her. There was a time when I was jealous of you for having so much time with her. Those memories. But it was only later that I realized what it must have been like for you, to have lost the one person who meant everything to you, to be left with a young son, alone, to be reminded of her every time you looked at me.

There's something freeing about saying good-bye, unburdening myself of the feelings, of the guilt. And I have so much guilt, so much to answer for.

To Diego, for example. He was right, back at the plant. I have mired him in a long stream of shit. Everything that he laid at my feet was true. Ruining his chances for a council seat on Tamoanchan when I brought a live Feral to the island. Convincing him to go to Gastown, only to be captured and tortured. And while I wasn't the one who asked him to get me off of the island after Mal arrived, he did it for the reason that he does everything—he's a good man. *I always knew that, Diego. You have so much to give people. But I just saw that as more for me to take. I'm sorry. I haven't had many friends in my life. You were one of them, but I know you could have been much more of a friend if I had just been one back. I have never known anyone in the Sick more loyal, more steadfast, and more willing to do what's right. That I'm only realizing it now is a tragedy.*

And of course your sister, Rosie. She and I, we never really got along well. We push each other's buttons too much. And she's kicked my ass on more than one occasion.

But, Rosie, the truth is, if it came down to it, there are few other people that I'd want more on my side in a fight. You're sharp and one hell of a fighter, and one of the toughest people I know. I gave you a hard time for what happened with Maya, for getting played and letting her escape, but the truth is that the Cabal played all of us. What they did to you was cruel. I know how lonely life can be. You thought you'd found someone to make the loneliness go away. I'm sorry I didn't say that. I'm sorry for my part in all of that.

Thoughts of new friends get me thinking of old friends. Of old times. Claudia and Mal and the others who used to fly with us at times. And Tess.

Tess, I'm glad I killed you. I'm sorry, but I am. You thought you were doing your job, playing all sides, standing neutral in the center. I get it. You wanted to survive. That's what motivated me for most of my life. If staying alive meant not getting involved, well, that was just how it had to be. But Miranda helped me see how not picking a side was actually picking a side. I'm no hero, but I've tried to do something right with my life—most of that came from helping Miranda. You just sat in your library, on your throne, hoarding—information, supplies, secrets—a greedy queen of a bloodstained world. I'm sure you helped some people. But you certainly harmed some as well. You lived a long life, but it had to end. I'm glad I was the one to end it.

Mal . . . you're maybe the hardest person of all to untangle from this knot of history and feelings. You want me dead, and I get why. Maybe I deserve it. I left you behind, all those years ago, left you to die. The truth is, I'm sorry for it. I thought I was doing the right thing, making the right choice, sacrificing one life to save three others (one of them myself). But I can't help thinking that one of those lives was Tess, back in the beginning of her empire. That's the thing about choices—you never know where they are going to lead. But the thing I'm most sorry about is for not trying. I might have been able to figure out a way to try to save you. I might have been able to come back and try to track you down, or at least confirm, as I thought, that you were dead. But I didn't. The truth is, I was scared, and I ran. And now we're enemies.

Deep down, that eats at me. Because we once were friends. I once thought it was going to be you and me, Mal and Ben, gallivanting through the sky, foraging and bartering and trying to outdo one another. Fuck, I wanted to be you. As cool, as capable. I wanted to be the man you challenged me to be. But, again, I was scared. Scared to leave my father, scared, maybe, to step into that role. Thing is, I'm really proud of who you've become (minus the wanting to kill me). I knew you were great, but I didn't expect you to be such a good leader. You take care of your people. You liberated Tamoanchan. And you took the fight to the Valhallans at Gastown. If you have someone like Rosie willingly following you, then you must be doing something right. So I'm sorry. For failing you. And for failing our friendship.

That leaves only two more good-byes, to two of the most important people in my life.

Claudia . . .

I don't even know where to begin. Excepting my father, I've known you longer than anyone. I had a thing for you the moment I met you. I couldn't have asked for a better traveling companion or someone to have at my side in a sticky situation. When we got together, I thought to myself, this must be what love is. And it was . . . only not the kind of love I came to know later. But that's okay. I have never felt more comfortable with another person, not even my father. I could be myself around you, even with all the ugliness. And while you might have called me on it from time to time, you always accepted it, accepted me, and I will forever be grateful for that.

You always had my back. Always. I'd like to think that I always had yours. Until the end. I'm so sorry for the way that I treated you. For the way I shut you out and climbed down into that hole. It seems stupid now. Why didn't I just talk to you? If anyone, it could have been you.

I don't blame you for cutting me off. I don't blame you for not wanting to ever see me again. I just wish that I could say I'm sorry. In person. Look you in the eyes and thank you for all that you've done for me over the many years. The countless times you've gotten me out of scrapes, the endless number of arrows you've used to help save my ass, the patience and the care that you've shown since we first met.

There will never be another like you, Claudia Nero, and I'm just glad I got to spend as much time with you as I did. I know I caused you pain, and I know I left a broken trail behind me, but I hope you at least take some comfort from the good times.

❋ ❋ ❋

That leads me to the last good-bye. The one I've put off saying for all these months. The one that I've been trying to avoid.

Miranda.

What can I say, Miranda? What can I put into words to express how I feel about you, and about what happened to you? You literally changed my life. When you ran into me, chased by a pack of Ferals, I didn't want anything to do with you. Little did I know, that moment was a point around which my life would pivot. You won me over. With your intelligence and your determination, and the vision that you painted of the future. I didn't think very much beyond the next day or the next week back then. You were talking about the next year, the next ten years. And saving the world.

I thought you were crazy. I still think you were a little crazy. But that craziness infected me, more tenacious than even the Bug. You showed me that there was still something to believe in, not matter how difficult the path. You showed me that there was still hope in the world and that there were things worth fighting for.

So I tried to. I tried to stand by your side and be your support and help do the things that you couldn't do (not that there were many of those).

The simple truth is, you made me a better man, Miranda. In all kinds of ways. I was never fully reformed, not really. I still fucked up a lot of things. But without you, I would be dead, or hollow, and neither of those things appeal to me much.

I never got to say it to you, and I will always regret it, but I love you. I never would have imagined it. Not back then. But you came into my life like a wildfire and set everything alight. I didn't know how much I loved you until you were gone. And I wanted to be gone, too. Some part of me still does. But I didn't realize, until now, that that part of me that wanted to be gone as well was the old Ben. Wanting to escape the pain. Thinking about myself. That's not what you would have done. That's not what you did even while you were fighting off the Enigma virus. You fought up until the end. Against the enemy. And I should do the same if I want to honor you. If I want to honor the love I had for you.

So that's what I'm doing. I'm going to fight the enemy. If it means sacrifice, well, so be it.

And if that idea is true, that we see our loved ones on the other side, then I hope that you'll forgive me. For leaving you. For letting you die alone. But I promise you, if you let me, you will never be alone again. I will never leave you alone again.

Saying my good-byes, especially to Miranda, only hones my commitment to my current course. I am an arrow, already fired, and I must find my mark. So it's important that I keep the *White Wolf* on course, with no interruptions or mishaps.

Navigating on an airship in the Sick is not an exact science. You're lucky if you have a few maps, luckier if you have distinct landmarks to orient by That's why the west of the country always seemed easier. You have the mountains there, and the cities seem more clearly demarcated. Move east, however, and everything just kind of blends together. How to tell whether you're over the ashes of Kansas or Missouri or Illinois? But that's where I'm heading, east and up to the ruins of Old Chicago.

I can tell when I'm getting close. It's mostly a straight shot east and, at my speed, I should be close to my target. So I have to prepare.

I start by bathing. There's plenty of water on the ship, and though it's not warm, I find the touch of cold invigorating. I find some soap and wash myself. We had access to water and soap at the plant, but it was a pragmatic affair—get in, wash yourself, get out. Now I take my time, enjoying the feeling of my clean skin after I scrub it. Then I wash my clothes, too, such as they are. They took my coat at the plant, and the Star of David that was pinned to it, the second one I had (the first one, my father's, I had lost).

I put back on the worn shirt and pants, the boots that have seen better days. But they're mine. And they're clean. I'll face the day as myself.

A little over two days, mostly because a storm a day into the journey pushed me off course, and I'm finally coming up on my target. I've been checking the maps and my instruments, and I think I see it, a dark speck, off in the distance.

Things were probably much easier back in the Clean. Dad said they had devices that would give them their exact position no matter where they were on the planet. Of course, those went to shit after everything went down. No one was around to maintain whatever network they relied on, so everything died.

Like everyone else in the Sick, I use charts and landmarks and compasses and the sun. It's a large part of why most people tend to stick to areas they know well. I've known zeps, pilots, who head out in one direction or another, willing to deal with whatever they find. Hoping for new frontiers, new places to forage, anything. The more rational of those types head toward the eastern part of the continent. I've met others who headed south into what used to be Central and South America. There are fewer airships out that way—the US invested most heavily in that mode of transportation in the first place—but raiders and pirates hide out in that region a lot. It can be dangerous sky to thread. The crazy ones sail east hoping to make it to Europe. The really crazy ones fly west, heading for

Asia. I've only met a few of them, and I never saw them again. But that doesn't mean much. Maybe one of those guys is sitting pretty in a safe space in Old England. Or maybe some of them found some sanctuary in Japan or China or India somewhere. Me, I've heard horror stories of those places, enough to make me not want to try my luck.

My part of the sky is big enough. Does the Cabal have hands large enough to hold it?

I don't know.

The speck grows larger in the window. Not a ship. Something bigger. Something mostly stationary. Valhalla was the first city built in the sky. The concept was the same as Gastown—inflate enough ballonets and fill enough envelopes, and you can float almost anything. But whereas with Gastown they had a lot of people coming together to build it, people who were investing with their ships and their barter, ships that could help control the city's position (and which could help compensate for the weather), Valhalla didn't have that. Valhalla was constructed, the way I hear it, out of force of will. They didn't have the ships. Not at first. So they needed something to help keep the city stable.

They settled on mooring it to a building, the tallest building they could find. And that, in this area, was the Willis Tower. I heard at first they used metal cables some forager found that were long and strong. But soon they added to this, more and more cables woven into it. Rope, too. And cloth. Much of it colored. So it became known as Bifröst, the rainbow bridge that some ancient people believed led to heaven. Which suited the people running Valhalla.

I've heard about Bifröst for a long time. Always wondered what it looked like. I once asked Dad if we could go visit Valhalla, wanting to see the city in the sky. This was before Gastown existed. He said no. I didn't understand it at the time—I just thought he was being controlling. But after I met a few Valhallans, I understood why. Dad didn't trust them. I didn't trust them, either.

Now, through the optics mounted in the gondola, I see Valhalla. A long platform, suspended beneath a mass of balloons. On the edges, connected by their own cabling, are an assortment of ships. They look like hard ships, combat ships. No fluffy junkers here. These are raiding ships, pirate ships, warships. Some of them look like they've seen action.

Four ships break off from their positions around Valhalla and move toward me, growing ever larger in my view.

This is it, then. The moment of truth. I just need to get close enough. I've dumped all my extra ballast. I've rigged the engines. Now I jump the last obstacle.

My hand hovers over the radio switch. I hesitate. *This is for you, Miranda. For you, Dad.*

I flip the switch into the on position, and almost immediately a voice barks over the connection. "*White Wolf,*" it says, recognizing the ship. "Why are you returning so soon, Shiv?"

"This isn't Shiv," I say, hoping my voice sounds confident, and not as shaky as the rest of me feels.

"Where is she?" the voice asks.

Thank you. "She . . . didn't make it."

"Who is this?" the voice asks, full of alarm and menace. "Give the passcode."

"My name is Tran," I say, reaching for the name of a boffin I knew. I don't say, "one of the Cabal," because of course that's just a name that Miranda and I made up, but that's what I'm going for. "The plant is under attack. It might have fallen by now."

"We know," the voice says. I had wondered if they did. I'd heard they sometimes relayed messages between ships, using their radios. "Why are you here?"

"Cargo," I say. "Helium. And data. The results from the experiments. All they could salvage before the plant fell. I was told to bring it here."

"Hold," the voice says. So I do. But I check my windows. The ships are still moving toward me. They all carry weapons, trained on the *White Wolf*. If they were to hit the cargo hold, the whole ship would go up. *C'mon. Just one last bluff. Let this work.*

Another minute or so passes. Then another. The enemy ships move forward. But so do I. I'm edging nearer to the city, but not close enough. At this speed, if they start shooting, I *might* be able to crash the ship into the far edge of the city, but it would be close. And if they rip apart the envelope, there's no chance of that.

The radio crackles to life. "Bring her in slowly," the voice says. "We want a look at what you have. Those escorts will guide you."

"Copy that," I say, as a smile breaks out on my face. I reach for the controls, ostensibly to do as they say, but I push the engines harder than I should. It will take a few moments for me to overcome inertia, but my acceleration is enough that I'll soon jump ahead—and then I'll be within range of the city and they won't be able to stop me unless they manage to incinerate the whole ship.

The plan is to put myself between them and the city. Shooting at me would put the balloons of the city in the direct line of fire, not to mention the people on the city itself.

The real trick is going to be avoiding the guns below. Too many guns on Valhalla would mean too much weight, so they put them down on the skyscrapers beneath us.

I'm out of ballast, and I've already vented some of my gas, so this will be tricky.

I take the few minutes before the engines kick in to run down to the cargo hold. Three Firestorm bombs stand in a row, webbed together with a cargo net. Three tapered cylinders with glossy orange hulls and guts of liquid fire. I arm them each in turn, aided by the instructions in each of the boxes, and my earlier review of them.

When I get back to the gondola, the *White Wolf* is just pulling ahead, and immediately the bullets start to hit the air. But I'm on a course with the city and the *Wolf*'s belly is full of hot death.

The chatter of gunfire is loud, even in the gondola, and I can feel several bullets find their target. The dash lights up—some of the ballonets have taken a hit, and two of my engines are gone, but I still have speed.

Choke on this, you bastards!

This is it, then. The moment before the sky falls. Hopefully on all of us. I close my eyes and think of Miranda, and—

The radio crackles to life. "Ben." A voice I recognize.

"Rosie?" I grab for it. *How in the hell?* "Get clear! You don't—"

"Miranda's alive."

I pause for a moment. It doesn't make sense. "What?"

"Miranda's alive. She got word to Malik."

"No," I say. "That can't be." *Can it?* "How? Where?"

"She's on Valhalla!"

It's a trick. It has to be. Mal found out I was at the plant, and he's using Rosie to turn me back around. Using the one thing they both know will make me.

And yet . . .

"Ben," Rosie says. "She sent one of her journals."

Damn it.

Every second we're moving closer to collision. Every moment, pieces of the *White Wolf* are splintering off into the sky.

"Ben," Rosie's voice calls across the void. "I know it sounds ridiculous, but it's true. She survived the attack. She's on Valhalla."

I shouldn't believe her. But I want to. If there's a chance, no matter how small, that what she's saying is true, then I have to make sure. If it turns out to be a manipulation, then someone is going to pay.

I'm on a collision course with the city, I've armed all the bombs, and this ship is blown to hell. There's no way I'm pulling out of this in time.

There's no time to spare. None. But things slow down and part of me, the pilot I've been trained to be all of my life, takes over.

I reach for the ballast controls and vent gas from the forward part of the envelope. The panels on the dash protest, but I ignore them. I jam the controls to tilt us downward, making sure I line the nose up just right. Then I run for the cargo hold.

The *White Wolf* plummets at an angle, and I'm suddenly climbing up toward its rear. The stitches in my leg pull at the effort, and it's all I can do pull myself into the cargo bay. The Firestorms are sliding toward the front of the bay, one already butting up against the wall there, the others sliding into it. I tense as I climb past, hoping that they don't explode and burn me to a cinder.

I hit the door release and then grab for the parachute. I strap it on. I have no way of knowing whether it's intact, whether it will work, but I'm close enough and high enough that I should be able to coast to the city.

Should be.

If I miss the city, there are the buildings below.

Unless the chute doesn't work and I splatter against the ground.

Fucking ground.

No time to think. To plan.

I snap the harness closed around my chest, pull myself up to the door, and then out.

The wind grabs me and pulls, like Claudia pulling back her bowstring, and the cold shocks me senseless. Then the bowstring is released, and the stinging cold becomes clarity, and for an instant I'm flying. Beautiful, glorious flight.

Then gravity gets hold of me and yanks.

I fall.

A feeling of terror so deep and so keen grips me, and for a second I forget. Everything.

Then sense returns, and I reach for the chute release and pull.

Nothing happens.

I'm going to die. I'm going to splatter. I'm going to—

Once more I'm grabbed and pulled, only this time I'm jerked upward. Above me the chute unfurls, and I thank gods I don't even believe in. Ganesh jumps into my mind, his outstretched hand waving.

Then I'm gliding. I pull on the ropes holding me to the chute, try to angle them toward Valhalla. I'm above the city, but still far from its edge. I'm moving toward it, but I can't tell if I have the right angle.

I try to shift myself.

Gunfire cuts through the roar of the sky.

Bullets whiz past, close enough that I can hear them.

Then I see the tracer fire, burning bright lines all around me. One glowing trail tears though my chute, leaving the edges flaming. Then another joins it. I start to spin, descending faster than I need to.

As I plummet, I know that I'm going to miss the edge of the city.

I'm not going to make it to Miranda.

Fuck.

Fuck.

Fuck.

Fuck.

Fuck.

I start spinning, and falling, and there's the city, its balloons, then its edge, and they're close enough that I can see buildings, see some of the people, and then I'm falling below the level of the city. As I spin, I see the *White Wolf* descending, headed straight for Bifröst, bullets tearing into it as it flies.

What will get me first? I wonder. The ground? The bullets? The explosion?

I slam into something. Hard, but not hard enough to crush myself. The air goes out of me and I roll instinctively, one of my legs screaming in pain.

What the fuck?

I don't see anything beneath me, but I'm on top of something. Something that's rising. I put my hand down, look at it.

It's the envelope of an airship. The material is strange, partly reflective.

I lay flat against it, stretching out to keep myself from rolling or blowing off, and I shrug myself free of the chute. It's too tattered anyway. No point in getting torn off into the Blue.

We rise, the ship and me, and soon we're above the side of the city. I see the railing of metal and rope and wood that hems it. Then we're above Valhalla, and I'm still wondering where we're headed.

We move forward to the edge of the city.

Then blinding light blots everything out and the sound of the world ending sends everything tumbling through the air.

CHAPTER TWENTY-SIX

MIRANDA

The ground shudders.

One moment I'm thinking about using heat to denature proteins, and the next I'm steadying myself against the table. A shock wave ripples through me. All around me, bottles fall over, some crashing to the ground, shattering pieces of glass everywhere.

I look at the others. Dimitri. Maya. The rest.

An attack? Here? On Valhalla?

I steady myself against the desk. Something feels different. The floor feels different.

"What's happening?" I ask Maya.

"I don't know," she says, in a tone that sounds honest. Maya is a consummate liar, but I believe she's in the dark. "Stay here," she says, before ducking out the door.

I move to Dimitri. "What do you think it is?" he asks.

There's the slightest bit of alarm in his usually impassive face. "Nothing good."

Maya reappears a few minutes later. "Some kind of explosion," she says. "People seem to think that something happened to Bifröst."

"The tether? How?" I ask.

"I don't know." She sounds frantic, worried.

Bifröst. Without the tether to the ground below, the city will be unstable. But what could sever that connection? What kind of firepower would it take? And how? The city is protected with guns, ships.

"We need to evacuate," I say. "The city is unstable."

"It's too early for that," she says. "We don't know exactly what's happening."

"When will we find out?" I ask. "It might be too late by then. We should leave. And take the data with us. Just in case. If it's nothing, we can just come back."

"Really?" She sighs. "There's no way out for you, Miranda. Not on a ship. Not even in an evacuation." She smiles. "And don't worry about the data. We have that well in hand."

Another shudder runs through the building and some creaking as something pulls at the city. Rudimentary physics diagrams run through my head. Without the tether, the city will be moving. If there was an explosion, there will be structural damage to the city's architecture. It's only a matter of time before pieces of it start breaking off.

"We need to go." I repeat. "Now."

Maya opens her mouth, about to fight me again, but before she can, Blaze walks in. "She's right." Her voice cuts through the room. "Evacuation is the prudent thing to do."

"But the labs," Maya says. "The equipment."

"Are not worth anything if we all go down with the city. We knew the day was going to come when we would have to abandon this place. Set up our own base of operations. This just accelerates things. We can take the data. We have it all backed up. We can rebuild everything else."

"It will take years," Maya says.

"Yes," Blaze says. "But we have time."

"Do you know who did this?" Maya asks.

"No," Blaze says. But she looks at me as she says it. Gears turn behind her eyes. "Gather up everything valuable, and get them to a ship. You." She points to Dimitri. "Come with me."

Then she takes Dimitri with her, heading deeper into the building.

"You heard Blaze," Maya says. "Grab your data and follow me."

I reach for my notebook and the portable drives on which we store our compiled data. But as we're moving for the front doors, Valhallans enter, led by Surtr. Suddenly, I wish I had a weapon, something to make him hurt. But I don't, and he's flanked by his guards.

"We need to leave," Maya says.

Surtr shakes his head slowly at Maya. "No. You both need to stay right here."

"But the city's falling apart."

He turns those cold eyes on me. "This is because of her," he says. "Your friend, he said he sent a message."

Clay? He was trying to get a message out. But I didn't think he had been able to before . . .

"They're here for her," he says to Maya. "And I intend to be here when they come."

CHAPTER TWENTY-SEVEN

I cling as tightly as I can to the envelope of the ship as we're tossed forward into the city. At the same time, the city seems to rise toward us, the ground accelerating to meet us. I slide forward, rolling over the envelope and down to the ground. I try to halt my skid, my descent, hands grasping for any hold, but there's nothing and I fall, spinning out into space. Again.

I hit the ground hard. And I think for a moment that at least I hit something solid, but it's not. It's moving, tilting, shuddering and writhing beneath me.

Get up, Ben.

Miranda.

I push myself to my knees, then my feet, my whole body screaming out, my bones feeling brittle and close to breaking. The wound in my leg burns, and it's a miracle if the stitches haven't ripped open. I'm not even sure I can put my weight on it.

Now that I'm no longer astride it, I have a better view of the airship I had landed on. In front of me is a ship I recognize. I called it the *Dumah*. Mal called it the *Argus*. Fast. Quiet. Really hard to see. A beautiful ship no matter what the name. Or at least it used to be. Right now its front end is crumpled, smashed into Valhalla's edge.

All around me, Valhalla is shifting. The clouds in the distance are speeding past faster than they should be. The city is moving. The *White Wolf* and its bombs must have burned through Bifröst, and now the whole city is careening in the sky. Who knows how long it can handle the stresses.

I turn my attention back to the *Dumah*, pushing the pain away. Rosie must have taken it. If so, she's still in there. Miranda is waiting, but I won't leave Rosie to die here. Not after she came all this way. I run to the gondola.

Someone smashes through one of the gondola windows as I get there. Rosie climbs out. "Are you okay?" I ask, moving toward her.

"Yes." She nods. She turns back to the window and reaches in to pull another person out, struggling to squeeze them through the opening. It's Diego. Of course.

Diego gives me the slightest of nods, then reaches back in the window. Who else did they bring?

Diego brings out two rifles, then a third. Then he reaches in and helps someone else out. I go cold when I see who it is. Mal exits the window as if he does it all the time. He shakes some glass off of his clothes and looks at me.

My hand instinctively reaches down for the revolver, but of course it's gone.

Mal casually slings one of the rifles around his chest.

Neither of us says anything for a moment.

"I'm not here for you, Benjamin," Mal says.

"Miranda?"

He nods.

"We need to get out of here," Rosie says. "Now."

I look back to see Valhallans exiting from buildings, collecting in the streets. Rosie, Diego, and Mal move to take shelter behind one of the nearest buildings. I follow. Not knowing if it's the right thing to do, but knowing that I'm in a hostile territory and these people don't seem to want to kill me at the moment.

I duck behind the wall and turn to Mal. "Miranda drugged you and stole your ship."

He smiles. "I know. I like her."

I keep staring at him.

He meets my eyes and sighs. "I spent time on the island, Benjamin. I saw her work. I saw her virus detection test. It's obvious that she's our best chance for a real future."

The city shudders beneath us.

"We have to move quickly," Mal says.

"Where?" I ask.

He pulls out a piece of paper from his pocket and unfolds it. It has a simple sketch on it. A rough shape that I take to be Valhalla, a few buildings marked in its interior, and an X on one area that I take is where Miranda is being held. The good news is that it's not on the other side of the city. The bad news is that it's pretty close to the center.

"Where did you get this?"

"We don't have much time," Mal says. "But if you must know, I interrogated one of the prisoners back at the helium plant."

"Then you took the plant."

He meets my eyes with a cold, hard stare. "Of course I did."

"How are we going to get to there?" I ask, pointing at the X.

In response, he starts unbuttoning his coat, and Diego and Rosie do the same. I'm about to ask them what the hell they're doing when I catch sight of what Mal is wearing underneath his coat. It's a leather and fur-coated shirt. Diego is wearing something similar, a vest decorated with bones, sleeveless to reveal his massive arms. Rosie's wearing a leather outfit with a stag's head over the chest.

She catches me looking at her. "We took these off of some people at the plant."

"Smart," I say. Only I don't have camouflage like they do. As if reading my mind, Mal shrugs himself out of what he's wearing and holds it out to me. Mal's chest is marked up with scars, many of them thick and dark. They climb up his arms, too. So many of them. That I think I know where they came from makes the whole sight more terrible.

"No," I say. "I'll make do on my own."

His arm remains outstretched. "Benjamin," he says. "I am here for one reason, and I do not intend to let you interfere with that. Take it. Time is wasting."

He's right about that, so I wriggle out of my own coat, letting it fall to the ground, then strip off my shirt. As I do, the bandages pull from the gash in my chest and I gasp. After a moment, though, I press them back and tug the shirt over my head. Mal's eyes flick to my wound, but he doesn't say anything.

Mal stands there, shirtless. "Aren't you cold?" I ask. I'm cold, despite the leather and fur on me right now.

"Yes, Benjamin. I'm cold. I choose not to let it bother me."

He stalks off through the city. I follow behind him, noting the scars all over his back as well. More accounts never come due.

I follow Mal, and Diego and Rosie come with me.

"What happened?" I ask Rosie. "How did you find out?"

"Miranda managed to get a message out of here to Tamoanchan. It arrived after we left to assault the plant, but the island relayed the message to us. Miranda's people even verified her handwriting. I told Malik you had flown off, so he took the *Argus* and flew us straight here."

"But how is she alive?" I ask. "I saw her house on the island. It was completely destroyed. And she was dying—Enigma."

"The message said that they smuggled her out before they blew it," Diego says. "They sent a team in for her."

"So they wanted her?" I almost ask why, but it's obvious. Miranda is smart. She's spent her life working on the Bug. Either she was a threat or she was a resource that they could use. They had spies on the island for weeks. Enough to know where she'd be.

Yet I still can't believe it. I've been living with her death for so long. Feeling it, every day. How can I just accept this?

"C'mon," Rosie says. "Chew on it as we move."

The streets around us, such as they are, are filled with Valhallans and some that I take for Cabal. Without Bifröst, the city is shifting and the wind from the west is pushing the whole bulk of Valhalla to the east. I can't imagine it was constructed to take such forces.

The city's skeleton groans around us, the structure of it flexing and warping as the wind shifts it, untethered for the first time since its construction. People emerge from buildings, running this way and that. Everything is chaos as they try to determine what to do. It doesn't take long for people to start running for their ships, abandoning the city to save themselves. It's what I would do if I were them, but stripping away the tethered airships will make the city even more unstable.

Mal, Diego, Rosie, and I continue on our path, though. We're here for Miranda, and we're not leaving until we get her out.

"How far?" I ask.

"It's difficult to tell with all these people and this chaos," Mal says.

"Let me see."

"Patience, Benjamin." There's a sharp edge to his voice that prevents me from grabbing the map from his hands. It's true he's probably doing a better job than I would. He takes a moment, his keen eyes almost piercing the map. Then he says, "This way," and sets off at a fast walk.

"We need to go faster," I say.

"We don't want to alert the Valhallans," Diego says. "If they see us running, it might attract their attention."

"And if we don't, this place might tear itself apart." I feel this pressure, all over me. This need to get to Miranda in time.

"Diego is right," Mal says. "But . . ." He looks around. Valhallans are moving at speed now. "We can certainly increase our pace."

I stare at Mal, amazed at how he, too, has come around to Miranda's vision for the future. Her message of hope. Together we're two of the most cynical people you'll find and yet now, with her, we're like moths to the flame.

We move. I follow Mal and try not to look around at the world falling apart on us, or the heavily armed and violent men and women who live on this city.

Until one of them slams into me. His hands grip my shoulders. He has bright-red hair and pale skin and faint blue tattoos in swirls over his skin. He looks into my eyes, then at Diego and Rosie and Mal. "Good," he says. "I need your help," he says. "Come with me." He has two other people with them, a tall bald woman and a short squat man.

"No."

I'm thinking it's Mal who should be talking, but it's me who says the word.

Red Hair looks at me questioningly.

"We have orders," I say, keeping my face grim.

Red Hair frowns. "From who?"

I don't know what to say here. Who to use as my bluff.

Mal steps forward. "From Surtr," he says.

Red Hair continues to frown. I can see it on his face, that he wants to ask what we're doing and why. But Mal meets his eyes, cool and confident, and Red Hair doesn't have the nerve to press him on it.

"Fine," he says at last, and moves off, his people trailing him.

"Thanks," I say to Mal.

Mal just shakes his head and moves on.

Diego and Rosie move with determination. Even if I killed the friendship with both of them, they still care for Miranda. They've known her since we first arrived at Tamoanchan, and she never failed them, not in the way that I did. And the truth is that I'm glad to have them here, with me. Because even if I don't make it out of there, I know that they'll find a way to get Miranda out, and there are very few people I would trust to make that happen. With the exception of Claudia, they're all here.

The city shudders again, and this one sends us all to the ground.

"We have to hurry," I say.

Even with our measured pace, my leg, where the Valhallan knifed me, is staring to ache. My ankle, where I hit the top of the *Argus* (or rather the *Dumah*), feels weak and watery. Even worse, I don't have a weapon—not a good one. All I have is the knife I took from the Valhallan, and my last nail. *Great, Ben. You're in wonderful shape for a rescue mission in the heart of Valhalla.*

"There," Mal says, suddenly. He points to a tall building with windows on its upper floors. "That should be it."

Stairs lead up to the entrance, a set of double doors set squarely in the side.

"We all go together," Mal says. He pulls his rifle forward, within easy reach. Diego and Rosie do the same. I pull out the knife.

We mount the stairs and move to the double doors. Mal reaches for the handles and hauls them open.

Then the air fills with thunder and Mal falls backward in a spray of blood.

Diego and Rosie retreat behind the stairs and start firing into the building.

I catch Mal as he falls, drag him out of the line of fire, down into the street.

He's covered in blood, swimming in it, and it's all over me, too. This should scare me, but I can't let go of him. I get him to the ground and cradle him like a baby. "Just hang on," I say. "We'll get you help. We'll get you out of here."

I know that it's nonsense. There's no help. Not here. Not now.

"Benjamin," Mal says. It's a breathy gasp. He shudders as the pain of his injuries ripples through him. He looks up at me. "It's too much."

"No," I say. I hold him tighter. "No. We'll find someone."

"Benjamin . . ."

Tears fill my eyes, and through them I can see how pale his face is. Still feel the wetness all over him. He grunts. "I'd hoped . . ." He sucks in air. "There's still so much I wanted to do."

"I know," I say, smoothing back the hair from his face.

He nods, then winces. "It's okay," he says. "I found . . . I found a home for my people. . . . I-I struck back against our enemies. I can go, knowing I . . . I fulfilled my promises."

He doesn't mean it to sting, but it does. When I think of all the promises I've left unfinished.

He coughs, and bloody froth coats his lips.

"Benjamin . . ."

He looks up at me, unguarded. Strangely childlike.

"Benjamin."

"What?"

He smiles, weakly. "You know the reason I liked you so much? Why I considered you a friend?" He coughs again. "Because I saw greatness in you. Buried, yes, but there. Almost . . . almost to match my own." One arm, slick with blood, reaches up to grab my own. "But you've always been too afraid to embrace it. You've spent your life in the sky, but you've always been pulled down. By your doubt. Your fear. . . . Afraid to let go and fly."

A groan erupts from him, and he flexes against the pain. He grimaces.

It passes and he meets my eyes. His hand reaches up from my arm, grabs my cheek. "Embrace your greatness," he says.

I stare at him, wide-eyed.

A smile creases his face. His smile is a red gash in his face. "This time," he says. "This time, I definitely got there first." Then his eyes glaze over, leaving a lifeless face looking up at me.

My vision blurs and I hold him close, for a moment, until gunfire breaks me out of the stillness.

✳   ✳   ✳

I don't want to leave Mal, but Diego and Rosie are pinned down by gunfire. So I untangle Mal's rifle from his bloody body and get to my feet. I wait until there's a pause in the shooting, then, signaling to Diego and Rosie to cover me, I bound up the steps from the opposite side, firing at two Valhallans there. My eyes are still filled with tears, and there's a cold rage inside of me. I feel joy as I gun the two men down.

High on my victory, I swivel around the doors, panning the rifle to the other side. But before I can find a target, the rifle barrel is batted up toward the ceiling, then out of my hands. A large man, with large hands, grabs me and throws me into the wall.

My head slams up against the plaster, and tiny white stars explode across my vision. His arm hits me in the midsection, and I feel a rib crack, then his hand closes on my neck, choking me.

The face seems to be made of steel, the bald head hard and shining. A tattoo, a fiery sword, stabs down one eye. The eyes fixed on me are cold and dead, like ashes. I reach for the knife, but my hands are weak, ineffectual. I think *this is it*, so close to the end. So close to seeing Miranda again.

Then a large, dark shape slams into the bald man. I recognize Diego as he tries to wrestle the Valhallan. Diego's big, but this man is bigger. He joins his hands together and hammers them into Diego's head, then his body.

I'm on the floor, having slid down the wall, sucking in breath. I manage to pull the knife from its sheath.

Then Rosie walks in and fires her gun at the ceiling. All eyes turn to her.

The big man stops trying to pound Diego's skull into the floor. And two people step forward into the hallway. The first is Maya, the traitorous scientist we brought back into Tamoanchan. One of the people who introduced the Enigma virus to the island and who later escaped.

The other is Miranda.

I gasp. My eyes aren't completely dry from Mal's death, but they fill up again when I see her. Standing there. Looking much like when I left her. Her hair is shorter. But she looks good. She's alive.

Maya moves forward to Rosie, who is frozen. Back on Tamoanchan they had something going. Not just a fling, either. Maya meant something to Rosie.

"Rosie," Maya calls out. They both are still, staring at each other across the space. "You're here."

Rosie doesn't say anything.

"I know," Maya says. "I know that I have a lot to answer for. That there's a lot of . . . complications between us. But . . ."

"But what?" Rosie asks. Her voice is hard, but her face looks hopeful somehow.

"I've missed you." Maya steps forward. I don't trust a word that comes out of her mouth, but she seems sincere. "I was sent to Tamoanchan on a mission, yes. But . . . What we had was real."

"Why should I believe you?" Rosie asks.

"You probably shouldn't," Maya says. "I probably wouldn't. Believe me. But you were there. Those nights. Together." Another step forward. "I think you felt what I felt." Another step. "I think you know it. Here." She reaches out and presses Rosie on her chest.

Rosie's eye fill with tears, and Maya's cheeks glisten. "Please," Maya says. "This place is falling apart. Let's go somewhere and talk." Her hand goes to Rosie's cheek. Rosie lowers the rifle.

Maya leans forward and kisses Rosie, and for a moment, the whole of Valhalla seems to center on this place, on this kiss. It goes on for a long time, and Maya's arms encircle Rosie, even as Rosie's are down at her side, slack, as if reluctant but unwilling to protest. They kiss, and it's one of the most intense kisses I've ever seen (as few as I've actually seen).

When Maya eventually pulls away, their faces are both covered with tears. Maya smiles.

Rosie smiles.

Then Rosie raises her rifle and fires five shots into Maya's body.

The whole room freezes, and Maya arcs backward, blood in the air, before she falls onto the floor.

Rosie bends down to look at Maya, mouthing something inaudible, and the big Valhallan takes advantage of her distraction to attack. He throws his huge arms around her neck, trying to lock her into a hold.

I scramble to my feet, the spell broken. I run toward them.

Rosie breaks the hold and spins into a kick.

The Valhallan catches her foot and with a quick drop of his elbow slams down into Rosie's leg. The crack is loud enough for all of us to hear. Rosie shrieks in pain. Then the Valhallan kicks her and steps forward, backhanding her, causing her to spin away.

"Surtr!" Miranda cries, as she runs to Rosie. Surtr turns to Miranda even as I stalk up to the him, the knife still in my hand. He's facing away, and I pull back for a strike, but as I lash out, he pivots and bats my arm away with the flat of one hand. I keep hold of the knife, but my arm goes numb.

The Valhallan falls into a fighting stance.

I'm in trouble. He's better trained, he's stronger, and he has a longer reach. But all I need to do is buy some time.

"Miranda," I call. "Take Rosie and Diego and get out of here."

"I can't," she says.

"What?" I say.

Surtr moves in. I lash out with the knife again. This time he pulls back, lets it sail past, then kicks me in the ribs, and follows up with a punch to my face.

I stumble back, but he doesn't press the advantage. I still have hold of the knife. It's my only edge in this fight.

The pain from my ribs radiates up into my chest and all across my torso. Every breath sends a jolt through me.

Run, Miranda.

I can't see where she is and I don't want to risk looking. Instead I strike again. I imagine myself like a snake, whipping out my right arm in a quick attack.

Surtr moves, and then everything gets crazy. One hand grips my left arm. The other grabs my right hand, the one with the knife, and he bends it toward me. I gasp as the knife scrapes against the shirt Mal gave me.

He pulls the right arm toward him, then, and I can't pull it away. He twists my wrist, and suddenly he has the knife.

He plunges it into my chest.

I cry out as the blade slips in, as it scrapes against my ribs. Suddenly it's a lot harder to breathe. I look down. My hand is on his, preventing the knife from going all the way in, but the tip is inside of me.

I push back against the Valhallan, but he slams a fist into my face and I fall. I gasp on the floor.

CHAPTER TWENTY-EIGHT

MIRANDA

I bend over Rosie, trying to stabilize her. She has a clear fracture in her leg where Surtr struck her, and I'm pretty sure she's in shock. Ben wants me to go, but I can't go without Dimitri. Or the data.

That Ben is alive and Rosie and Diego are alive, after all that happened . . . it was too much to hope for. But Rosie's injury is serious and I can't even get to Diego at the moment.

Surtr sinks a knife into Ben's chest. Ben's eyes roll up for a moment, and he falls to the ground.

I get to my feet without thinking, and run at Surtr.

I don't have any weapons, but I have to stop him.

Surtr is bending down over Ben. He sees me at the last second and tries to turn to me, but I barrel into him and send both of us sprawling to the ground.

He quickly throws me off, but I scramble to my feet.

"I've been looking forward to this for a long time," he says, his voice a deep, cracking sound.

I hesitate for a moment. I'm not a fighter. I never have been. Surtr has spent his life training for this and only this.

But he killed Clay and he's going to kill Ben, so I move. Not to Surtr, but to the gun lying on the ground, the one that one of the guards dropped in the firefight. Kneeling on the ground, braced, I raise it at Surtr, my finger reaching for the trigger.

Then I stop, my finger shaking and rigid. Because Surtr is holding Ben, hauling him up with one arm. "Go on," he says. "Shoot me."

"Put him down, Surtr."

He sneers, then spits. There is something so crude and masculine about him that I feel like pulling the trigger, just to stop him from being. But I hold myself back.

Surtr smiles broadly. He moves toward me, holding Ben up like a shield. Ben's head lolls on his chest. His eyelids flicker, but he doesn't seem fully conscious.

Then Surtr cocks his head to the side, lowers Ben down, and gets a good grip on his head with one massive hand. "Put the gun down."

I hesitate.

"Now. Or I snap his neck."

I lower the gun to the ground.

Surtr's grin grows wider. "Slide it to me," he says.

I slide it across the floor to him, almost to his feet. With his hand still on Ben's head, Surtr bends down, placing the knife on the floor and raising the rifle up.

"I'm going to enjoy this," he says.

CHAPTER TWENTY-NINE

mages, shapes, shadows flicker. Pain is the one constant, the endless scratch of the needle against the record. Every now and then the needle skips or jumps and the pain jumps with it.

Then words come in over the song of pain, and they're ugly words in an ugly voice. I rise and fall again, and something grips my head. I smell oil. Metal. And blood. It's difficult to breathe, but I can smell.

As I come back to where I am, I see Miranda straight ahead of me, her face full of worry and concern. The huge Valhallan, Surtr, the one who stabbed me, the one who turned up the music, the song, grips my head with his left hand. He leans down and with his right hand he puts the knife on the ground, picking up a rifle.

I took the knife from a Valhallan. I think I should give it back.

I break free from his grip as he's rising up again, and reach for the knife. I grab it up in my hands and sink it to the hilt into Surtr's crotch.

Surtr roars, and the rifle shoots out in response. I look to Miranda, but she's already scurrying for cover.

Surtr slams one fist into my head, and I fall away. It's hard to stay conscious and everything here is filled with pain, but that's what I use to hold onto, to keep me here, and when I can, I start moving away, putting ground between me and the him.

When I look up, Surtr has removed the knife from his groin and has let it fall to the ground from bloodstained fingers. His face is the angriest thing I've ever seen, red and rigid, lips skinned back from his teeth, his canines two sharp points in his mouth. He raises the gun and sprays the room with bullets.

I scramble away, looking for cover, not finding anything.

Diego runs up behind Surtr and wraps his enormous arms around the man, pinning the gun arm to his side.

Surtr slams his head back, and Diego's nose breaks with a loud crunch. He wavers for a second but retains his hold on the man. They're both struggling now. Surtr is taller, but Diego is broader. It's a toss-up as to who's stronger.

Surtr throws his head back again, into the bloody ruin of Diego's face. Diego stays upright but starts to sway. Surtr tries to break free.

I leap to my feet and run forward. I kick at Surtr's crotch, where the knife went in. It's a solid hit. Surtr's mouth drops open and he sucks in air.

"Ben!" Miranda yells, and I turn to see her handing me the bloody knife, the handle out toward me.

I grab the handle, feel the sticky blood all over it.

I look up at Surtr. "You dropped this," I croak. Then I jam it up under his chin and into his head.

There's a look of surprise and astonishment on the man's face. Then his eyes freeze, the painted flames on his skin still hot, the pupils growing large and cold. Diego lets go, and Surtr falls to the ground. Diego teeters on his feet, his face a mess of blood, the nose crushed, but he's alive. Grateful, I grab his arm and give him a nod. He nods back.

Then I turn and Miranda is there. Miranda is in my arms and I'm in hers, and through all the pain, and the spinning, and the labored breathing, I have a moment of peace. A profound sense of things being right. Of things being joined correctly, seated together, connecting the way they are supposed to.

"I thought you were dead," she says.

I laugh and taste blood in my mouth. "That's my line."

"Your chest!" she says. She starts stripping cloth from her shirt and from mine and wrapping it around me. Stopping the bleeding. There's pain, but all that I can take in is her face. I've missed that face.

The ground shakes beneath us, and I remember where we are. "We need to get out of here," I say. "The city won't last much longer."

"I can't," she says. "Not yet."

"Why?"

"Ben, they have more data here than anywhere I've ever seen. I've been working on a vaccine. We've made strides. This is too important to lose."

"But, Miranda . . ."

"I'm not leaving without it," she says.

I should be mad. I'm surprised I'm not. But this is Miranda. I know her. If she says it's important, then it is. She's always been our best hope at a better future.

I turn to Diego. "Take Rosie," I say. "Find us a ship."

"You want me to leave?" His voice is distorted by the broken nose.

"I'm going with Miranda," I say. "I won't leave her alone. Not this time. But we're going to need a way off of this place before it completely falls apart. Can you do it?"

He looks at me, then at Miranda. "I think so, yeah. It won't be easy with Rosie, but we'll find something. But how will you find us?"

Miranda nods. "We have to go up," she says. "When you have the ship, go to the top of this building. We'll meet you there."

"Okay," he says. "Good luck."

"Same to you."

Then I turn to Miranda. "Come on. Let's go get your data."

She grabs my hand and pulls me through the hallways. She knows this place, it seems, so I let her lead the way. "You don't look so good," she says.

"I'll survive," I say. "Though it's hard to breathe."

She looks at me gravely. "Probably pneumothorax from the stab wound. Air is pressing on one of your lungs."

"Great," I say. "Good thing I have two of them."

"I can fix it. Try to, at least."

"We don't have time."

We pass some people making for the exits, but they leave us well enough alone. Aside from the fanatics, like Surtr, everyone is looking to save themselves. Otherwise, it's a mad dash behind Miranda. I have the rifle I took from Surtr, and the knife is secured through a loop in my shirt.

Finally, we reach one of the upper levels. It looks like some kind of lab. More high-tech and, well, Clean-looking than Miranda's setups in the past. This must be the center of the Cabal's power.

We rush in. Miranda moves around the tables, rifling through papers, and grabbing small portable data drives.

I see the armed woman in there before Miranda does. The stranger stands over a table, stuffing papers and electronics into a bag.

I lift the rifle. "Miranda."

She looks up in time to see the woman advance.

She's tall and dark-skinned, her hair pulled back in a bun. A dark-blue jumpsuit. "I already have the data," she says.

"It's over, Blaze," Miranda says. "Your city is falling apart."

Blaze shrugs. "Cities are replaceable." She smiles at Miranda. "People are replaceable."

Miranda shakes her head. "That's what you don't get, Blaze. They're not."

Blaze looks amused. A man walks up behind her, older, with gray hair and a beard. He holds a pistol in his hand and pens in his shirt pocket. I make sure to cover them both.

"Dimitri?" Miranda says.

It's his turn to shrug and smile.

"He's been one of ours all along," Blaze says. "It was, I have to say, the best of my ways to deal with you. I figured you couldn't resist another prisoner, a confidant. Maya said that you had a friend. Or more of a father figure. A Russian?" Blaze tilts her head to the side. "Seemed like an easy thing to give you a surrogate."

"You bitch," Miranda says. I can hear the hurt and betrayal, the disbelief in her mind. And, I'm sure, self-recrimination that she was so easily duped.

A look of disgust comes over Blaze's face. "You are, like so many of the weak, easily led by your emotions," she says. "You care too much, Miranda. It leads you astray."

"You are a monster," Miranda says.

Blaze's smile grows wide. "The only monsters here are the ones we breed. Speaking of . . ." She whistles, and Miranda starts to look around in alarm.

The way she's looking is getting me worried now, and I try to keep the two Cabal members covered while also scanning the room.

Then I catch sight of it. Coming up behind us.

The unrestrained Feral stalking calmly into the room.

✳   ✳   ✳

It's one of their creations, not a stringy, wiry Feral, but one bulked up with muscle, larger than it should be. This one, strangely, wears clothes, a set of tight shorts over its genitals, and a tight t-shirt over its torso. But it's just walking toward us. Not bounding or crouching, not gibbering or howling. It's not even eyeing us greedily. But there's something there. Something held back.

I swivel the rifle toward it, aware that there are two armed enemies behind me now, but even more aware that a mutated Feral is in the room, full of the Bug and built to kill. Right now it's not close, but it soon will be.

As I turn, I hear another whistle, and the thing goes from calm to violent in an instant. My bullets tear through where it was, and then it's on me, arms outstretched, long nails filed down to claws. I do the only thing I can and block it with the rifle. The impact pushes me backward, and I fall over a desk and onto the floor, pain hissing and crackling from me like a wet log in a fire.

Dimitri appears to my left, gun raised, and I'm forced to dive for the gap between two desks as he starts shooting. The Feral is still coming for me, and two enemies with guns are just waiting for a decent shot.

Not to mention I'm beat to shit.

Blaze yells, "Leave him!" Dimitri moves away. He and Blaze walk to the door and hurry out of the room.

I pop up and fire a long burst at the Feral, who scurries for cover.

Miranda beckons to me. "We have to go after them," she says. "Quick!"

She rushes out the door, and I get to my feet and run.

The whole room shakes. Plaster and stone and whatever else is holding this place up fall into the room. I reach the door at a run, but the ceiling has fallen in, and as I try to pull the door open again, it doesn't budge. The solar lights flicker.

"Ben!" I can hear Miranda yelling my name over and over on the other side of the door.

"Go!" I scream back, even as I run for cover.

The yelling stops.

Leaving me alone, in a closed room, with a Feral.

✳   ✳   ✳

A loud thump behind me. A grunt, then a roar.

I turn to see the Feral vault over one of the desks. It lands in front of me.

I fire the rifle at it, but it's already moving to one side and I miss. It darts forward and sweeps up a long-nailed hand, pulling the rifle from my grasp.

Its other hand rakes my chest. My injuries cry out in protest, but the leather and fur holds and blunts the worst of the nails.

Bracing myself against a table, I kick out with both feet and connect, sending the Feral backward, but also sending a streak of pain through my injured leg that makes me cry out.

I roll over the table and onto the floor, my clumsy landing sending waves of nausea through me. I scuttle forward, looking for some kind of weapon now that I've been disarmed.

I grab for anything I can reach off of the tops of the tables—boxes, glass, machines that are small enough to heft—and I hurl them at the Feral. Several of them connect, but the beast just shakes them off, still advancing.

The knife I used on Surtr bangs against my chest with the movement, just about where my collapsed lung is. It's a weapon, but I can't use it on the Feral. Too much blood. Too much risk.

But I can throw it.

I pull the knife loose, then stand up, already swaying with the effort. Gripping the blade between sticky fingers, I let it fly. The blade arcs and the Feral doesn't even try to move away. Then it hits, at least the side of the knife does. It clatters to the floor. The Feral hisses.

Then he pounces.

It closes the space before I can move, one of its hands gripping my arm, the other going for my throat. I pull back, and its momentum pushes us both over another table and to the ground in a crash of falling machines and broken glass.

Too close! The voice screams. *Its blood. Its saliva.*

One of my arms is pinned. Its weight presses down on my chest, and it's all I can do to suck in a thin trickle of air.

Then it opens its mouth, a look of hunger in its eyes, and I know it's going to bite me.

In desperation, I reach for my pocket with my free hand, find the last nail there, and toss it into the Feral's mouth.

This throw works better than the knife. It flies past the teeth into the back of the throat. The Feral coughs, then pulls back and shakes his head. The pressure eases off of my chest and my arm. I reach for a rack of slender tubes and smash it into the side of the Feral's head. Again. Again.

Then I scramble away as it's reeling. If I can get to the—

It grabs my trailing foot and pulls. I slide backward. I grab for anything I can reach. My fingers come down on a shard of glass.

Damn you, Dad, for making sure I always laced my boots all the way up.

I twist around, taking the shard, and bury it in the Feral's leg, behind the knee. Then I hit it in the groin, trying to use whatever strength I have left in me.

It drops me, reaching for the glass still in its leg.

I don't know if I can get to my feet, but I crawl, as quickly as I can, to where the rifle was.

The Feral yells again. From the corner of my eye, I can see a massive arm smash the contents of another table. Broken glass and papers fall on top of me as I crawl.

There, ahead of me, I see it in the flickering light. The rifle. I stretch out to it.

The Feral's foot comes down hard on my back.

For a moment I can't see, can't hear, can't think. Whatever damage Sarah had done to me comes back, worse this time.

My hand flails for the rifle, fingers brushing against the grip, not sure if any of the rest of me can move, only knowing that my fingers can. I spin it around toward me, slide it backward, even as the Feral pulls on my foot again, reeling me in like a flopping fish caught on a fishing line.

The Feral roars, feeling its triumph, the impending kill. Blood drips into one of my eyes, and I only hope that it's mine, or else none of this will matter.

And I still need to get Miranda out of here.

I manage to get the barrel of the rifle pointed behind me, where the Feral is. I can't get the rifle off to the ground, so I swivel the muzzle toward the thing's foot, and I jab for the trigger.

The rifle spits out a burst of bullets that deafens me, but the Feral drops my leg. I turn to see it bracing itself on one of the tables, a red, dripping ruin where one of its feet used to be.

I pull myself forward with my hands and arms, hauling the rifle with me, hoping that there are still bullets left.

The Feral comes after me, actually lifting its bloody stump as if it still were a foot.

I continue crawling forward.

The stump comes down, and the thing doesn't even seem to notice.

Then the stump slides out from under it, slipping on the blood, and it falls to the ground.

It braces itself on its arms, then lifts its head and snarls.

Calling on what little strength I have left, I jerk the rifle forward and jam the barrel into that cocksucker's mouth. Then I pull the trigger until the body falls limp to the ground and all I hear are clicks.

I drop the rifle and try to sit up. My legs feel numb, my back feels like a swollen knot of pain. Just pulling my knees in almost makes me pass out. But the legs move. I get up to my hands and knees and crawl to the door. There's no time to lose, and I don't have much gas left in the tank.

Time to get Miranda out of here.

CHAPTER THIRTY

MIRANDA

The building trembles, and parts of the ceiling rain down into the hallway. I turn back to the door and try to pull it open but it won't budge. *Ben. He's all alone in there with the Feral.*

I pull again, but the door is stuck in the frame and I can't get enough leverage or bring enough force to bear.

Ben!

"Go!" he yells. Only I don't want to leave him.

Then a voice in my head says, *You can wait and do nothing or you can go after Blaze and Dimitri.*

It's not really a choice.

"I'll come back for you, Ben."

I run up the stairs, taking two at a time. The whole building is falling apart. Walls collapsing inward, ceilings falling down, but I focus on reaching the roof. Climb. Climb. Climb. Then . . .

The door to the roof is open, and I bound out of it into open air. Blaze and Dimitri are there, looking out over the city. Blaze holds a lit torch in her hand, the fire bright in the oncoming darkness. All of Valhalla is tilted, the part of the city to our right angled toward the ground. If I'm not mistaken, the city is rotating. Whatever forces set it in motion must have imparted spin to it, and so things on the city will be pushed toward the edges.

Airships fly in the distance, most of them departing the city. That, too, might have set it spinning as they decouple from the edges. A few hover over it, though, trying to pick up people or supplies, or maybe just looting now that everything's turning to shit.

Blaze and Dimitri turn toward me, a look of surprise, maybe even admiration on Blaze's face.

"You are persistent," Blaze yells. "I considered taking you with us, but I know that you will never stop being disruptive. It's too ingrained in your nature.

Normally that's a good thing. We prize those who don't accept the natural way of things, who seek to change it. You are one of the best I've seen." She shrugs. "It's like you were made for this."

She moves forward, points the torch at me with her right hand. "But you have no guiding principle except insipid old-world morality. Help everyone. Cure everyone. What then? How will this world we've inherited sustain so many people? How will everyone eat? How will they live? Without order, you are left with chaos. Violence. Crime. Injustice."

"You want to talk to me about violence?" I ask.

She inclines her head. "We use it. Yes. You prune back the leaves and the flowers so that the fruit you get has more flavor. We use it like a scalpel, to cut out what isn't wanted, what threatens the whole organism. Not the optimal solution, maybe, but your way would be an indeterminate cutting, all over the body, with no goal or reason."

"Your way is wrong," I say.

She smiles and shakes her head. "I'd ask you to show me the evidence, but I'm afraid we don't have any time left. It's time you go, Miranda." She steps forward, almost as if to embrace me, and thrusts her hand forward, the blade snapping free from its arm sheath.

Only I'm ready for it. I never forgot her showing it to me. I grab that wrist and twist it to one side. Then I punch her in the throat.

She falls back, choking, her hands going up to her throat. The torch drops from her hand.

I smile.

Blaze leaps at me, her face covered in shadows thrown off by the nearby torch. "You little bitch," she says, her voice a harsh rasp.

I grab her arms, but she sweeps my leg, and I fall with her landing on top of me. The back of my head slams into the roof.

My senses take a moment to come back. Blaze straddles me, the knife still extended from her wrist. I hold it off with both of my arms. The torch is next to us, casting her face in red. Something dangerous and wild lights her eyes. Something that maybe was always lurking behind the cool exterior and the rational front. Something hot. The source of her ambition and her command.

"You could have had so much," she says. "Power. Influence. Whatever tools and instruments you wanted for whatever you wanted to study." She leans her face close to mine. "You could have had a place."

"I already have a place," I say. I let go of her wrist with one hand and she presses down, preparing to stab me.

With my free hand, I grab for the torch and slam it into her face.

The heat of the fire scorches my face as it passes in front of me. I hear her skin and hair sizzle a moment before I smell it. Her scream is more of a growl, and she falls back, batting at her face.

I roll toward her and swing the torch at her a few more times, the hits sending embers flying.

"Stop!"

I freeze, my arm pulled back, still holding the torch. Dimitri has the pistol aimed at me. "Drop it," he says.

I let the torch fall to the roof.

"All this time," I say. "All those nights, you were playing me."

"All of them."

I hold my hands out, palms up. "Was any of it true?"

A sour smile creases his face, and he shakes his head. "No."

"You weren't press-ganged."

His smile becomes prideful. "I sought them out," he spits at me. He waves the gun around. "You are so blind. So caught up in your fairy tales. You've seen the world. You've seen what it's become. It needs order. It needs us."

He lowers the gun.

"It needs her," he says, looking at Blaze.

He raises the gun again. "It doesn't need you."

CHAPTER THIRTY-ONE

By the time I reach the door, the crumbling of the building has done much of my work for me. I wriggle my way out through the new opening, feeling one or more of my ribs wobble as I press through. I crawl up the stairs, using my hands, feet, knees, and elbows. It takes all of my energy to push myself up, pull myself ever higher, running on half my wind. One eye is crusted with blood, despite my efforts to wipe it clean. I can still feel the bite of the glass embedded in my cheek.

I think there's only one more floor, but it feels like the stairs are endless. I scrabble like an animal. Get the next arm over the next stair. Then a foot or a knee. Then another. Repeat that. All the while, I'm thinking of Miranda. At the top. Waiting for me.

I wish I had a gun.

I wish I had a working body.

I'll just have to improvise.

Eventually I reach the top. The door is ajar, and I see two shapes out in the open next to a burning torch. One of the shapes starts to raise a gun, and I'm suddenly aware that the target is Miranda.

Something happens inside of me. Something white-hot and blinding. Something that burns through my whole body, and suddenly there's no pain, I'm not tired, and everything is clear and precise. The phoenix, bursting from the ashes of my destroyed body.

Dimitri's arm lifts as if underwater. I know I can't reach him in time.

So I run for Miranda instead.

The gunshot cracks the air, somehow loud despite all the noise around us and the buzzing in my ears.

I collide with Miranda, sending her sprawling across the roof.

Then I'm falling, and I don't know why.

A moment later, the pain hits me and all that fire fizzles out, leaving me, trapping me once again in the wreck of my body. I clutch for something, some thread of strength, some sense of where I am, but the pain blots everything out. I can't breathe. And Miranda still needs me.

RAINING FIRE

I hear gunfire in the distance. Big guns. Either down in the city below, or from the ships. I smell fire. It's not safe. We have to go.

But my body won't obey me.

CHAPTER THIRTY-TWO

MIRANDA

Dimitri pulls the trigger, then suddenly Ben is there and he sends me flying. By the time I can turn around, he's falling to the ground, a sudden dark splash spreading across his chest.

I start to run to him and then change course. Dimitri still has the gun. He turns it toward me, but I'm moving quickly. I collide with him, on hand on the gun, pushing it away. He's stronger, but my momentum sends him staggering.

My eyes fall on the pens in his pocket. Even as he's pushing his gun hand against mine, trying to angle the barrel toward me, I reach for a pen, pull it out, and jab it into his neck, into his carotid.

I pull back as his hand goes up to his neck. Blood gushes from the wound, into his hand, between his fingers. He drops the gun, using that hand, too, to hold his neck. He gasps and then turns to try to crawl away. The gun lies next to him, forgotten.

I reach for the gun, then stand up and away from him. He'll bleed out soon enough.

I run back to Ben. He's on the ground, writhing. He's covered in blood. It takes me a moment to see the bullet wound, through his side. No telling if it hit any major organs.

"Stay with me, Ben," I say. *You can't die. Not now.*

I need to get him off of this roof before it falls to the city below.

I run for the torch and grab it, waving it in the air, hoping that Diego will see me.

In the light of the torch I can see Blaze, crawling off. I raise the pistol, then lower it. The city breaking apart will likely kill her.

But as I wait for Diego to come get us, I realize that a Valhallan ship or a Helix ship could come and get her after we leave. I think of the knowledge she has, and her intentions. Then I walk over to where she crawls, aim down, and empty the pistol into her until she stops moving. I drop the pistol next to her body, then move back to Ben.

A moment later, airship lights bathe the roof in light. It pulls up, lowering the cargo doors to the roof. Diego. I know it. I grab Ben by the armpits and use all of my strength to pull him onto the ship. It's slow going, but I get him on board. Then I reach for the radio in the cargo bay. "I have him," I say.

Then I turn back to Ben as we sail off into the sky.

CHAPTER THIRTY-THREE

come to as Miranda is dragging me into the cargo bay of whatever ship Diego must have stolen from Valhalla. There's a funny smell inside, and it's dark so I can't see much, but Miranda lowers me to the floor and I lie there as the ship moves away.

She disappears for a moment, and I start to panic, but then she returns. Sitting next to me. Examining my wounds. My whole body aches, but I can't really feel it anymore. Even when she prods a wound or peels back my shirt or removes a piece of glass from my face, I'm just happy to be there. We got her out. And she's alive.

I reach up and grab her hand. "Miranda," I say.

"Ben," she says. She smiles, though I can see the worry in her face. "You should rest. Save your strength."

"No," I say. "No more interruptions. I . . ."

She looks at me.

"I love you," I say. As if released, tears well up in my eyes and spill down over my cheeks. "I love you, Miranda. I should have told you that before."

She smiles at me. "I know." She squeezes my hand. "I love you, too."

"You are . . . you are the best thing that ever came into my life. You're the best thing that ever came out of the Sick, Miranda."

"Ben—"

"No," I say. "Let me say this. Miranda, I . . . I believe in you. I've never believed in anything in my life. Except getting through to the next day. But I believe in you. I believe you can do what you say you will. And I would love to be able to see it."

I know that's not going to happen. Saying all of this is like letting go of weights that have been holding me down for so long. Mal told me to let go. Mal told me to fly. This is probably not what he meant, but I can feel it. It's time. Miranda is safe. She's alive. She can save the world. I had some part in making that happen. I can let go now. I can relax.

I can rest.

I smile up at her. And let the world drift away as I float up into the sky for the first time in my life. I feel so light. Gravity can't touch me. I'm free, I'm—

No. I can't leave her again. Not again. I try to reach back, to the pain, to the now, try to call out to her, touch her.

But I'm falling free into the void.

CHAPTER THIRTY-THREE AND A THIRD

I suck in air. Suddenly the world grabs hold of me. Gravity comes back, gets its hands around me, and pulls me down. Pain gets its fingers in, too—everywhere—and I want to be anywhere but here.

Then I open my eyes and look into Miranda's. She's straddling me, her hands joined together over my chest. Diego is next to her, pulling out bandages and sterilizing a knife.

"You don't get off that easy," she says, listening to my chest. She meets my eyes. "There's still work to do." Her fingers lace with mine, a bright harmony in the discordance.

As they get to the gory work of putting me back together again, I realize she's right.

ACKNOWLEDGMENTS

This being the last book in the series, I owe thanks to all of the usual suspects: to my Clarion West Class of 2008, and to Mary Rosenblum, Paul Park, and Cory Doctorow, the instructors who helped shape the initial idea. Thanks to the entire Pyr team for once again dealing with a perpetually late and difficult author. Thanks as well to my agent, Barry Goldblatt, and Patricia Ready, his tireless assistant.

Special thanks to Chris McGrath for his stunning cover art. Having his artwork on my books has been one of the highlights of this journey.

Thanks as well to Maggie Schnider, whose contributions surpass mere words. Mags, you are the best.

This book would not be possible without the enthusiasm, support, and iron will of my partner, Elisabeth Jamison. She worked on this with me from the initial synopsis through to the final version and never let me cheat or reach for the easy solution. In fact, the odds are good that if you have a favorite part in this book, it was her idea. What can I say, except that she makes me better in every way.

Finally, this book is largely about finding your will to fight, and about trying to defeat the bad guys. It's fiction, of course, but there are people out there right now who are doing the same for some very real problems. People and organizations who help those in need, and who fight when there's a threat to justice or to unity. So I'd like to thank these real heroes—Planned Parenthood, the ACLU, the Southern Poverty Law Center, the Human Rights Campaign, the Trevor Project, the National Immigration Law Center, and the Center for Reproductive Rights. They fight the good fight, they stand up for and defend those who are in the crosshairs, and I appreciate and thank them for all of the good work that they do.

Last, but certainly not least, I'd like to thank you, especially if you have been with me (and Ben and Miranda) on this whole journey. Thank you so much for taking this ride with me, thanks for sticking it out to the end. I've had a lot of fun writing this series. I hope you had fun reading it.

Until next time,

Rajan Khanna
New York, NY
February 2017

ABOUT THE AUTHOR

Rajan Khanna is a writer, narrator, and blogger who fell in love with airships at an early age. He is the author of *Falling Sky* and *Rising Tide*. His short stories, narrations, and articles have appeared in various markets, both in print and online. He currently lives in New York City. Visit him at his website, www.rajankhanna.com; or on Facebook, www.facebook.com/rajankhanna; or on Twitter, @rajanyk.

Photo by Ellen B. Wright